W9-BRC-561

THE LITTLE FRENCH BRIDAL SHOP

THE Little
FRENCH
BRIDAL SHOP

JENNIFER DUPEE

ST. MARTIN'S PRESS
NEW YORK

First published in the United States by St. Martin's Press, an imprint of St. Martin's Publishing Group

THE LITTLE FRENCH BRIDAL SHOP. Copyright © 2021 by Jennifer Dupee. All rights reserved. Printed in the United States of America. For information, address St. Martin's Publishing Group, 120 Broadway, New York, NY 10271.

www.stmartins.com

Library of Congress Cataloging-in-Publication Data

Names: Dupee, Jennifer, author.
Title: The little French bridal shop / Jennifer Dupee.
Description: First edition. | New York : St. Martin's Press, 2021.
Identifiers: LCCN 2020042049 | ISBN 9781250271525 (hardcover) |
    ISBN 9781250621870 (ebook)
Subjects: GSAFD: Love stories.
Classification: LCC PS3604.U653 L58 2021 | DDC 813/.6—dc23
LC record available at https://lccn.loc.gov/2020042049

Our books may be purchased in bulk for promotional, educational, or business use. Please contact your local bookseller or the Macmillan Corporate and Premium Sales Department at 1-800-221-7945, extension 5442, or by email at MacmillanSpecialMarkets@macmillan.com.

First Edition: 2021

10 9 8 7 6 5 4 3 2 1

In memory of my mother, Kathe Hill Dupee

Part I

FALL

CHAPTER ONE

The house, a stately brick Colonial, stood at the peak of a grassy hill, the slope of its great rolling lawn dotted with graceful elms and sycamores, on the easterly side of the tiny seaside town of Kent Crossing, on the North Shore of Massachusetts. Perched on high as it was, overlooking the beach on one side and the quiet and compact Main Street on the other, it gave the impression of omniscience, as though it were guarding something. *No wonder,* Larisa thought. She hadn't told anyone yet, but she'd come to prepare the house for sale. She'd taken the train up from Boston that day, Saturday, arriving early afternoon and walking with purpose through the center of town—Main Street being the only street that really constituted "downtown"—past Duffy's Hardware, Antonio's Italian Bakery, and Sunshine Cleaners on the left; St. John's Episcopal, Shea's Tavern, and the Little French Bridal Shop on the right, leading on to the two-pump service station, just before the rise in the road that led to Elmhurst. Clutching the key the estate lawyer had sent her by FedEx, she had lingered for a moment in front of the trussed-up window of the bridal shop, taking in the puffed-up skirt and ivory satin corset of the showpiece dress, a mannequin's hand splayed out to the side, her head tilted slightly up and back in a pose of effortless elegance.

"I'm never getting married," Larisa had declared before continuing on her way, suitcase in hand. She said this frankly, without bitterness. Despite the looming pressure of turning forty the following summer, marriage was not on her mind. She hadn't had the burning desire, as some women had, she knew, to walk triumphantly down that aisle, tie that proverbial knot, fuse herself to another until death did her part. But given the fallout from her recent fight with Brent—the things she had said, those unforgivable things—her status as single *did* suddenly feel much more final. And now, as she approached the house, the rise and fall of its great lawn mimicking the undulating ocean beyond, she felt a tinge of sadness, a longing for things to be in alignment. But then, she reasoned, she always felt an attack of nostalgia when she came home—not to the actual childhood home she had shared with her parents—but to this, her hometown, and to the house owned, until now, by Aunt Ursula.

She gripped the key more tightly as she stepped slowly up the sweeping drive, aware of the house peering down. The great elm for which the house was named arched up around her, its boughs gray brown and sleek, like the curve of a woman's neck turning to look. Larisa could hear the roar and hiss of the ocean, which lay beyond the lawn to the back and left side of the house. She smelled the salty air and was re-minded of her father walking the craggy bluff overlooking the sea, its edges bordered with beach roses, their round buds and splayed leaves like royal crowns, the air around them in spring and summer always infused with that strong, sweet smell.

"Rosa Rugosa," he'd sing, referring to the Latin name of the shrubs, "there's no Rosa Rugosa here. Who's she?"

Larisa, as a small child, would giggle and skip ahead, pluck-ing a flower, sucking in its delicious fragrance. But it wasn't spring now, and though she could smell the ocean and could feel its mist on her cheeks, she couldn't smell the beach roses; they weren't in bloom. Instead the air smelled musty, of wet leaves tinged with the smoky ash of chimney fires. Sniffing and surveying the landscape, Larisa felt vaguely pleased, as she often did in the fall, that her auburn hair blended so nicely with the autumn leaves, their burnt orange and golden hues contrasting sharply with the clear crisp blue of the sky. Still, the air was just a little too cool, cooler than was comfortable, causing her to hunch her shoulders beneath her camel-colored wool coat.

She paused on the stoop. It felt so odd to be arriving for the first time without her great-aunt to greet her. Larisa had been back for the gathering after the funeral, of course, but the atmosphere had been different then. At age ninety-six, Aunt Ursula had lived a very full life. She'd gone quietly in her sleep, hadn't endured months of pain and suffering, hadn't broken her hip or contracted pneumonia. And so the mood had been respectful but not quite as somber as it might have been. There was a full turnout—the butcher, the baker, and yes, the candlestick maker—and everyone had stories to tell, either about Aunt Ursula or about not much at all. Larisa, perched on the arm of the couch, next to her parents, had found it hard not to laugh at how predictably provincial it all seemed. *This town is full of people making shit chat,* Aunt Ursula would say. You mean chitchat, the family would correct her. No, she meant idle *shit* chat. The funeral reception had been nothing but: commentary on the weather, the newly paved roads, the traffic light that had finally been put in at Four Corners. And even some actual shit chat about the new septic system going in under the library, the original pipes from 1910 having been infiltrated by a full system of tree roots from the neighboring maple. So much shit chat, they didn't know how not to be full of it anymore. It went on for hours—the new cement subfloor being poured at the police station, the skylights cut into the roof of city hall, the new fire hydrants installed up and down Main Street, the family of squirrels that had to be ousted from the barn attached to the historical society, what a ruckus they had made, squirrels being so family-oriented.

It went on like this all afternoon and into early evening until it became almost Zen-like for Larisa. Closing her eyes and leaning into the couch, she felt herself falling into a shit chat trance, settling into the hum around her, absorbing the buzz without really hearing the words. Then, finally, the clock in the front hall struck five and people collected their casserole dishes and apple pie plates and took the cue to head home to dinner. And after the crowd had thinned out, after the leftovers—cookies, cut vegetables, tea sandwiches—had been sealed up under plastic wrap, that was when she had gotten the ring: a square-cut sapphire encircled by diamonds, handed to her unceremoniously by her father, knowing Aunt Ursula, his father's younger sister, had been anything but sentimental about the family jewels.

"She would have wanted you to have it," he said.

"Would she?" Larisa gave him a half grin, eyebrows raised.

He had shrugged. "Well, who else would we give it to?" Then he padded back down the hallway to the study, where he continued sorting through Ursula's papers.

Now, as she slotted the key into the lock, pushed open the heavy oak door, and passed over the threshold into the foyer, the place seemed very still. Too still, even for Aunt Ursula's liking. Larisa would know, for she had visited almost every week from the time she had turned ten, when she was old enough not to be a nuisance, and until she turned seventeen and headed off to college. This house, once so familiar to her and now mostly just nostalgic, had a feeling about it that she couldn't find anywhere else, reminding her a bit of the industrial age, a bit of the board game Clue. Not quite as ornate, not quite as British, but with the same formal lay-out: a grand winding staircase leading to the second floor, a large living room to the left with a camel-back sofa and an upright piano, a stately dining room to the right. There were skylarks in the front-hall wallpaper, a bathroom under the stairs, an old-fashioned ice grinder mounted on the wall of the prep kitchen, a stack of metal blueberry buckets Larisa had once used on berry-gathering trips as a child with her babysitter and the other neighborhood kids. A butler's pantry, a laundry chute, a formal library with a rolling ladder on a metal track. There was even a conservatory, like in the game, a great glassed-in greenhouse sort of thing where, usually, sat Aunt Ursula herself—her hair pinned up, her eyes the color of French lentils—eating quiche or lemon yogurt, blanched asparagus or deviled eggs, the things that nobody ever ate anymore. There were bells wired into the walls for the maids, and even though Larisa knew those bells didn't work anymore, she liked to push them just to see if anyone would come running. Nobody ever did.

She moved up the stairs now, her eyes meeting those of her ancestors displayed in framed photos hung on the wall that followed the staircase up. A young man in a frilled shirt and knickers, a pert smile teasing the corners of his lips. A group of three girls, sisters, mounted on tall horses, arranged by height. There were some newer photos mixed with the old—an overhead shot taken from the rooftop at a family reunion; a shot of Larisa herself, her arms around Aunt Ursula. Then came one of Larisa's favorites: a sepia photograph in an oval frame, featuring a small girl in a white dress with long puffed sleeves, her hands folded neatly on her lap, a quiet expression on her tiny face, an enormous bow in her cascading hair. Larisa imagined it—the hair—to be red, like her own. Her eyes flitted back to the three girls on horses, their adult faces already beginning to emerge. She paused, thinking. Hers had been a family of strong women. Women who spoke in formal niceties and euphemisms but still always managed to get what they wanted. When Aunt Ursula called to say it was a shame she hadn't seen Larisa in several weeks, that meant Larisa was to come over immediately to pay her respects. When Grandmother Lydia, who had died much younger than her older sister-in-law, commented that Cousin Edward certainly had a healthy appetite at dinner, that meant he was overindulging. Was she a strong woman as well? Larisa didn't know. But exploring the house, running her finger along the brass bedposts, flicking the curtain tassels, palming the glass paperweights, she knew one thing: she could pretend to be strong even if she wasn't.

Working her way back downstairs, scanning the wall again, she paused for a moment to take in a photo of her parents, fingers entwined, emerging from the church on their wedding day, gazing deeply, lovingly, at each other as they still often did. Her father was dressed in a full morning suit with a top hat, her mother in a classic long-sleeved gown, clutching a modest bouquet in her free hand.

Larisa swallowed. *I want my mother,* she thought, and then inwardly chastised herself for the childish yearning. Her parents felt so distant, and not just in proximity, her mother having battled dementia now for several years, her father the sole caretaker with limited support from their retirement community in New Hampshire. Larisa knew she was partly to blame for the distance. She didn't visit as much as she ought; she didn't offer the support she should. But she didn't want to admit it was happening. She couldn't stand to see her mother deteriorate and fumble for words. Her mother, who had always been so caring, so capable. Larisa felt a surge of anger that she—Larisa—had no one left to care for her but herself. Then she felt immediate guilt. Thank goodness her father was so patient, so kind. Larisa could never live up to the level of care he provided. She didn't have to, did she? She was the child, not the spouse.

She left the photos behind and headed down the stairs to the dining room. She smiled, as she always did, at the wallpaper: a heavy navy blue imprinted with a repeating pattern of tan and white pheasants glancing over their shoulders, apprehensive. The pheasants looked so silly, startled out of their forward momentum, that she couldn't help but laugh. But her smile shrunk when she turned the corner and spotted a large strip of the paper peeling away from the wall above the fireplace, dangling like the tongue on a cartoon dog. "Crap," she whispered to herself. If her mother had been more with it, it was the sort of project they might have tackled together, a mother-daughter do-it-yourself special. Fixing up the house and taking occupancy. But no, it was too big to manage. Best to just make the repairs and sell the place. So, after balancing on a chair and trying, to no avail, to press the paper back into place, she gathered her things, headed outside, and tramped back down the hill toward Duffy's Hardware, where she hoped to find some wallpaper glue.

She'd almost made it there when, partway through Main Street, her gaze alighted once again on the mannequin in the window of the bridal shop. She stopped and peered in. The model's hand, she noticed now, had been painted with a pale pink French manicure and she had a faux diamond adorning her delicately raised ring finger. Larisa snickered, yet something took hold of her, a mischievous and imposturous side of herself that had recently been surfacing, to her surprise and delight. Wouldn't it be fun, just for a laugh, she thought, to take a peek at those dresses? To pretend for a moment that she was that mannequin or even her own mother, pre-illness, skipping down the steps of the church? How did one feel, she wondered, wearing such a dress? She suspected she'd feel ridiculous, pompous, and over-plumed, like a peacock. But no one would have to know she wasn't serious. Would she dare? She sucked in a breath and smiled to herself. Yes, she would.

And so this was how Larisa found herself with her hand on the doorknob deciding, to her own amusement, that perhaps she *would* go in and try on some dresses, just for the heck of it, why not, what else did she have to do? The wallpaper could wait. And so she stepped in, a little bell tinkling as she pushed open the door, and before she knew it, she stood directly in front of Mrs. Muldoon, her eighth-grade English teacher, who, with clipboard and pen in hand, seemed to be taking inventory. Larisa stood frozen, acutely aware that *now* was the time for escape. But then Mrs. Muldoon took down her glasses, letting them drop on a chain against her bosom. Looking a little perturbed or maybe just befuddled, she lifted her gaze to her customer.

"I'm sorry," stammered Larisa. "You weren't expecting me. I guess I'm supposed to have an appointment for this kind of thing." Though it was dim in her mind, Larisa must have heard at some point that Mrs. Muldoon had retired from teaching to open up a bridal shop, and so she wasn't quite as surprised as she might have been when Mrs. Muldoon's eyes lit up in recognition and she jettisoned the clipboard to smother Larisa in an all-encompassing hug.

"Not for a local like Larisa Pearl!" she crooned. "Honey, how *are* you? I'd heard you might be back, but my word, look at you. Larisa Pearl on *my* front stoop. Don't just stand there—come in!"

Larisa took a step forward so that she stood in the center of the room. The shop was small and square with a display case toward the back and dresses hanging all around the perimeter, some long and sleek, others puffed and gauzy, most of them some tone of creamy off-white. One corner featured a small collection of mother-of-the-bride and bridesmaid dresses—maroons, salmons, teals—while the other displayed an assortment of veils—lacy, piped, patterned.

"Well, I'm not really *back*." Larisa struggled to release herself from Mrs. Muldoon's hug.

"Timmy O'Leary saw you coming off the train this afternoon—he and I both get coffee after lunch at Antonio's—and somehow, don't ask me how, I knew you'd be by. I had a full-on premonition." Mrs. Muldoon stepped back and stood grinning at Larisa, hands on hips. "I just *knew* you'd come visit me at the shop."

Larisa nodded, trying to look noncommittal, not sure whether to blow her cover so soon.

"The gowns, are they actually French?" she asked, glancing around.

Mrs. Muldoon waved her hand in the air as if swatting a fly. "Oh, no, no, that's just a gimmick to get people in the front door."

They stood there for a moment, facing each other, while Larisa took it all in, her gaze starting at one corner of the shop and working around to the other.

"So many," said Larisa, not knowing what else to say.

Mrs. Muldoon flattened her palms in front of her and pumped them up and down as though halting a moving vehicle. "Now don't panic. It can be overwhelming. But don't worry, I can *absolutely* find something perfect for your special day. I have a knack for finding the right dress."

"No, no—" Larisa started again, but Mrs. Muldoon cut her off.

"Larisa Pearl is getting married!" she chanted, hopping in place on her medium-heeled pumps. "*Larisa Pearl* is getting married."

"Well, no, actually, I'm really just taking a peek at the dresses," Larisa tried to correct her, but Mrs. Muldoon wasn't listening.

"Did you bring a slip? A strapless bra?" Larisa stared, contemplating how to get herself out of the situation, as Mrs. Muldoon waved her hand around in the air again. "No worries, I have extra." And before Larisa could protest, Mrs. Muldoon had ushered her around the display case, down a small hallway, and into an oversize dressing room, pressing the loaned lingerie and a terry-cloth robe into her arms.

"Just put these on and I'll bring in some dresses. Do you have any clippings of what you might like?"

Larisa shook her head.

"That's OK. I'll bring an assortment."

And before she knew it, she was going through with this charade, stepping out of her boots and wool skirt and into the lacy undergarments. There was something, thought Larisa as she stood there nearly naked, about being in your underwear—or someone else's underwear, really—in front of a relative stranger, that gave one a false sense of intimacy. So she stood there in the borrowed bra and slip and let herself be carried away by Mrs. Muldoon's enthusiasm. What harm, she thought, could really come of it?

"I've always imagined planning my perfect wedding," Larisa said, "but I didn't think I'd find a dress shop so close to home." This wasn't true, of course. Larisa had never dreamed about planning any wedding, and certainly not a fairy-tale one; she'd barely given it much thought at all. Why was she doing this? She couldn't explain and yet she couldn't stop. She felt vaguely aware that she was avoiding the conflict, as she often did, but that wasn't her only hesitation. She liked the release she got, the escape. It felt incredibly liberating, really, to play this impersonation of herself.

"Well, you were so smart to wait, honey." Mrs. Muldoon's voice carried over the wall to the dressing room. Larisa could hear her sliding hangers and gathering the dresses from the racks. "My Sally, God love her, she's happy with her five kids—two of them teenagers!—but she's forty pounds overweight and working part-time as a travel agent. That's what happens when you get married too young."

Larisa nodded. She remembered Sally, who had been in her year at school. They'd been friends, of sorts, sharing some of the same classes and occasionally sitting together at lunch.

Mrs. Muldoon poked her head into the dressing room and deposited some dresses onto a tufted ottoman that was pushed against the wall. She prodded Larisa into standing on a small footstool that faced the mirror. "But you, look at *your* figure. Just like when you were homecoming queen."

Larisa felt more than a little unsettled that Mrs. Muldoon remembered her days as homecoming queen at KC High. She had forgotten how insular things could be in a small town, everything stuck in time. She had been embarrassed about the homecoming queen thing, hadn't seen it coming at all. She had been popular, she supposed, but not the type to attend sporting events or run for class office, organize dances and car washes and field day. More academic than most kids and quieter, too.

But before she could react, Mrs. Muldoon presented her with the first dress and gestured for her to step in. It had a textured top and faux feather skirt that fluffed out around her ankles, all of it tinted a light peach. Looking at herself, Larisa was reminded of an ostrich puppet she'd seen years ago at an amusement park, a man with a leather cap manipulating the strings so that the ostrich bounced along the sidewalk, its head bobbling from side to side, a ridiculous pink grin sewed across its felted face.

Mrs. Muldoon weighed in quickly. "Don't think so, do you? A little too much Zsa Zsa and not enough Gabor, if you know what I mean."

Larisa didn't quite know what she meant, but she agreed the dress was not right.

The next one was revealed—a sparkly Cinderella skirt with sweetheart neckline and spaghetti straps. Mrs. Muldoon helped Larisa step into it and zipped up the back. She tugged on the straps and pulled at the bodice until it was adjusted the way that she liked. When Larisa turned to face herself in the mirror, she didn't think it was too bad—perhaps a bit young and certainly too prima ballerina, but then that was the look. Mrs. Muldoon had her own assessment.

"Oh, hello—Glinda the Good Witch, anyone? I wouldn't let you do *that* to yourself. Speaking of which . . . honey, it's been so long. What *have* you been doing with yourself? Something wildly successful, I'm sure." She deposited herself on the ottoman, among the dresses, chin on fist, elbow on knee, and waited for Larisa to undress.

"Sotheby's," Larisa answered tentatively. She had actually recently been fired from Sotheby's, but it hadn't quite sunk in yet. "House Sales and Private Collections."

Mrs. Muldoon nodded and gathered the discarded dress in her arms. "Such a jet-setter."

Larisa's five years at Sotheby's had *not* involved much jet-setting. She'd been to London once for the annual meeting, but that was about it. Still, she wasn't against giving the impression of a thriving and dynamic career.

Mrs. Muldoon sprung up from the ottoman and started to sing again. "Larisa Pearl is getting married, married, married. Oh, honey, I'm just so happy for you."

Larisa smiled stiffly from her pedestaled position and once again considered setting things straight. But how, now that she'd gone this far? And anyway, Mrs. Muldoon seemed to be enjoying herself. Why ruin the woman's fun? She descended from her perch and allowed herself to be unzipped.

The next set of gowns were stiff and creamy, like meringue— an off-white number with sculpted curves in the skirt, reminding Larisa of an almond macaroon, and another with folds like ribbon candy, a third with a fishtail skirt. Mrs. Muldoon fussed with each one before dismissing them, all the while asking questions and often providing her own answers about Larisa's big day.

"And where will you have it? Oh, of course! At the house." Mrs. Muldoon clasped her hands in front of her chin, her eyes sparkling. "Elmhurst. I heard she'd left it to you, the poor dear."

"Well, no, to my parents, actually, but—"

Mrs. Muldoon gasped. "Oh, how *are* your parents? June and Ward Cleaver. That's how I always thought of Clark and Kittie. So happily married."

An image flashed through Larisa's mind from the last time she'd visited her parents—a dirty sponge floating in a half-cleaned toilet because her mother's mind had wandered mid-task. Her father, as usual, had stepped in to deal with it when Larisa had hesitated. God, she'd been a terrible daughter. How hard was it to remove a dirty sponge from the toilet?

"They're fine," answered Larisa, bluffing. "Busy as ever. Hiking in the Himalayas." She hoped Mrs. Muldoon didn't notice her hesitation, the telltale to her lie. She'd talked with very few people about her mother's illness, and she didn't feel like letting the whole town in on it just yet.

Luckily, Mrs. Muldoon went on without pause. "Always so active, those two, it's amazing!"

Until relatively recently, Clark and Kittie had still lived nearby in the modest center-entrance Colonial in which Larisa had grown up. Larisa's father, a public interest lawyer specializing in nonprofits, was well-known among the community. Larisa had memories of him sitting with local families, seeing them at church. A pat on the knee, a shake of the hand. *How're you holding up now, Charlie? Come by for a cup of coffee. You know Kittie—she always has a loaf of banana bread or some such thing coming out of the oven.* Several years earlier, they'd sold their house and moved to a retirement community in southern New Hampshire. The move had been planned for years, the community chosen long ago for its golf course and indoor pool and proximity to the lake house where they had sometimes summered. But not long after the move, Kittie, who had always been so organized, had begun to falter, her short-term memory failing first. She left the house to water the plants and forgot the meat loaf in the oven. She paid some bills twice and didn't pay others at all. She couldn't remember the place she'd left off on her knitting and so they would find her wringing the yarn over and over in her hands, trying to locate an entry point. No, Kittie couldn't manage in a house the way she once had. With her condition ever worsening, there had been talk of relocating them to Elmhurst. Larisa hadn't told her father yet, but she was against this. The house was huge, much too much for them to manage. No. Elmhurst needed a little fixing up and then they could sell it. People would be shocked, she knew, but really, they had no other choice.

Mrs. Muldoon had taken a break from the dresses and had entered into full-on inquisition mode.

"When will it be? Have you set the date?" Her eyes had grown wide, almost manic in anticipation. And Larisa, seeing Mrs. Muldoon so caught up in the moment, had been compelled to answer tentatively, "June?" which caused Mrs. Muldoon to clap her hands together and nod vigorously. "Nothing more perfect than a June wedding. Next June, of course? That only gives you"—she counted on her fingers—"October, November, December . . . eight months or so to plan." She rested her hand on Larisa's arm. "But don't worry, it's enough."

Then she suddenly clutched Larisa's hand—she must have spotted Aunt Ursula's ring—and began pulling on her finger to get a better look.

"Oh," she gushed, her eyes gleaming, "oh, he has *fabulous* taste."

Larisa felt like she really ought to explain that this was Aunt Ursula's ring, not something Brent had picked out, but Mrs. Muldoon, her focus unwavering, had begun to home in.

"Tell me about him. No, wait, let me guess. Tall, dark, easy on the eyes?"

Larisa nodded.

"Well, he'd have to be to land someone like you."

Brent hadn't exactly landed Larisa. She'd met him by chance two years earlier when she'd come up one day for a visit to Elmhurst. Aunt Ursula had just settled down for her late-afternoon nap when Larisa, standing by the upper hallway window, spotted Brent swinging on ropes through the old elm. Larisa knew Aunt Ursula hired an arborist every year to tend to the trees, but she had never seen one at work before. She watched, undetected, for over an hour as he hoisted himself into the treetops and positioned himself to delicately remove dead limbs and decaying bark. She'd been so fascinated by his work, both the idea of it—the removal of lifeless branches to make room for new growth—and the precision and care it involved. She stood transfixed as he maneuvered around in his harness, pulling saws and drills up on a rope, wiring some branches together and allowing others to fall to the ground. He wasn't tall or dark. Instead he was much stockier than most of the men she had dated, but he did have a rugged handsomeness about him, his shaggy blond hair curling boyishly at the ends. She watched him pack up at the end of the day and just when he was headed toward his truck to leave, she noticed a forgotten tool lying hidden in the grass. She hurried down the stairs and out the front door to retrieve it.

"Wait," she called after him. "You forgot this . . . this . . . What *is* this?" She held up the tool, which looked something like a ripsaw, only smaller and curved. The initials B. U. D. had been branded into the wooden handle.

The tree man swiveled and came back up the driveway. "Oh, thanks. It's a pruning saw." He took it from her and slid it into a sheath on his tool belt.

"I'm Larisa," she told him. "Are you Bud?"

The man laughed and fingered the letters on the saw. "No, Brent, actually. Brent Dempsey. Those are just my initials. My father stamped them there for me. He was the only one who did call me Bud, ever since I was a little kid."

He began to tear up and he wiped a sleeve across his eyes.

"Forgive me," he said, taking a deep inhale and letting it go. "My father is no longer with us, but he taught me everything I know about trees. Some days it still hits me."

"Of course," said Larisa. She hadn't seen many men express their emotions so openly, and it touched her. "I'm so sorry. How did you lose him?"

"Heart attack, when I was nineteen. It's been over fifteen years already, but sometimes I still cry like a baby."

"Oh, that's tough," answered Larisa. She thought of her mother, the disease beginning to take hold. "You must miss him."

Brent nodded. "People say a sudden death like a heart attack is better than watching a loved one suffer, but I wish I had gotten the chance to say goodbye."

Here Larisa swallowed. She'd have the chance to say goodbye, but she'd also have to witness some suffering. She wasn't sure how well she'd handle it.

"Hey," she said. "You wouldn't want to grab a cup of coffee, would you?"

Brent shot her a shy smile and glanced at his watch. "How about dinner instead? I'll go clean myself up and come back in about an hour?"

They went to dinner, where he talked more about losing his father. He had hoped to go to college—the first in his family—but his father's death forced him to get a job to support his mother and two younger brothers. With his mother so distraught, he'd practically raised his brothers, he'd said. He'd wept openly when he talked about it—the void his father had left, the strain it put on him to grow up quickly. Great heaving sobs shook his entire body as he spoke, and it struck Larisa that Brent was the first man who had let himself be truly vulnerable in front of her. He understood, she felt, something about what she was going through, and it all grew from there.

Before she knew it, they'd been together for almost two years, living in a two-bedroom apartment in Somerville.

At first it was great. Brent was attentive and caring; he liked to surprise her with breakfast in bed or a fistful of flowers when she arrived home from work. She loved how down-to-earth he was. He almost never wore anything dressier than a pair of jeans and a plaid shirt, and he wasn't obsessed with achievement the way many of her grad school friends were. He smoked a little weed, which she didn't love, but it wasn't the worst vice as far as vices went. And he adored her at a time when she felt a yearning for affection.

"It was fate," he'd say, "meeting you that day. Like my father was watching from above. If I hadn't left that saw behind, I never would have met you. Somehow we were just meant to be together."

At times it had seemed liked fate, just what Larisa needed to help her navigate her mother's burgeoning illness. But after a while she felt trapped by his words. What if they *weren't* meant to be together? And what did that even mean? *Were* some people actually meant to be together? Brent was sweet, sensitive, and she'd grown fond of him, sure, but if pressed, she'd have admitted that her heart wasn't fully in it. He was almost too fawning, giving his affection so freely that she felt she hadn't earned it. She felt stifled, unseen. She wasn't sure he really knew her at all; he'd just fallen in love with some idea of her. And his continual insistence on fate began to grate on her. He began talking about buying a ring, settling down; she hedged and asked for time to think about it. After that, just his general presence caused her to feel guilty and then resentful so that she found herself perpetually agitated—unsettled—around him, the way one might feel when wearing a piece of clothing that fit a little too snugly. And so, their recent fight and subsequent breakup had been a culmination of an entire year of discord. Small bouts of bickering had slowly grown more frequent until it seemed like every encounter ended with a quarrel. They'd both been working long hours and they hadn't slept together in months, though she couldn't be sure which had started happening first. Were they working so hard that they had no energy left for intimacy or were they working too hard on purpose, to avoid getting close, afraid of confronting the gulf between them? Larisa suspected the latter. She knew she should end it, and yet she wasn't sure how. She couldn't bear to break his heart.

Then one day, after a particularly difficult visit with her parents—*I hate you,* her mother had declared for seemingly no reason at all—Larisa had arrived home to find the kitchen a mess, Brent's work boots and jacket strewn across the floor, spaghetti sauce dripping down the side of the stove. This wasn't typical of Brent, she knew, but it struck a nerve and somehow unleashed all the emotion and irritation she'd been holding in. She'd gone ballistic. Larisa herself wasn't prepared for the level of rage that had surged through her. Before she could stop herself, she was screaming obscenities and be-rating him at the top of her lungs. She grabbed the closest thing in reach—one of the white porcelain dishes from the sideboard—and threw it hard against the floor so that the little pieces scattered everywhere. Then she threw another and another and another while Brent just stood there gaping, bewildered. And despite the mess she had created—yes, she saw the irony there—Larisa felt an absolutely incredible release.

This fight was symptomatic of the whole mismatch of their relationship. And it felt so good to break something, so satisfying to see the clean white porcelain strewn all over the muddied linoleum. God, she was just so sick of holding it all together. She would have kept on throwing, too, had she not gathered herself for a moment and counted the remaining dishes to make sure she had enough left for a dinner party of eight. Anyway, suffice to say, it was over with Brent.

But thankfully, Mrs. Muldoon wasn't asking about him anymore. She had produced another set of dresses, which Larisa dutifully slipped on, each rejected in turn by Mrs. Muldoon. Dress after dress, a dozen more at least, until Larisa began feeling like she would probably be there all afternoon. The act of undressing and redressing became a comforting ritual, a way to perpetually reinvent herself. Larisa began to imagine someone new in every dress. Was this the Larisa Pearl she knew and loved? Or this one? Or how about her?

And then, just as Larisa was settling into the rhythm of it, just as she had started to depend on it, they arrived at the last dress.

"Just one dress left," Mrs. Muldoon whispered, shifting her weight from side to side.

Larisa felt a very brief feeling of panic flicker through her. What if it wasn't right? What if she had gone through all the dresses and not one of them was a match? Of course, she hadn't forgotten that she didn't actually need a dress. But still, didn't everyone talk about finding *the* dress? She'd never been the sort of person to care about finding *the* dress. And yet, after all this, how would she feel if she couldn't find one?

Mrs. Muldoon seemed entirely unconcerned. She had

dragged the ottoman over behind Larisa and now stood on it, her mouth full of bobby pins. She began securing Larisa's hair into an elegant twist.

"Sometimes it just helps to have the hair up. It completes the look."

Larisa turned her back to the mirror as Mrs. Muldoon removed the last dress from the protective garment bag and helped Larisa step into it.

"This designer is known for his beading." Mrs. Muldoon pulled the top this way and that, smoothed out the skirt. She assessed the last dress silently with a self-satisfied smile as she gently swiveled Larisa to face herself.

Larisa gasped. The dress had a simple scoop neck constructed of cream-colored lace bordered with tiny gray pearls. This top connected seamlessly to a fitted bodice ornamented with dainty silver-cut beads arranged in small florets in a delicate vining pattern that worked its way down through the waist. The dress hugged her hips and then flared out to a full tulle skirt that swept the floor as she walked, which she had begun to do, Mrs. Muldoon having extended a hand to help her off the footstool. She swiveled and shimmied and spun in front of the mirror, peering over at her smiling reflection. She felt elegant, regal, dignified. Something about it brought things into focus for her. She began to see herself, really see herself in a way she hadn't in a long time. Yes, *this* was the Larisa Pearl she knew and loved. And yet, simultaneously, the Larisa Pearl she dreamed of becoming. No, she hadn't expected it at all, but the dress was perfect.

Mrs. Muldoon came and fastened a light veil to the top of her head and together they exited the dressing room, Mrs. Muldoon holding the train of the dress as Larisa began to step solemnly around the shop. Mrs. Muldoon started to softly hum and then sing the "Wedding March."

"'Here comes the bride, all dressed in white . . .' Da da da da-da, dum deedley dee do do . . ." She fussed with the veil, fanning it out so that it fluttered gently behind as Larisa circled the store. They made their way around like this several times before stepping back into the dressing room and onto the footstool, where Larisa faced herself once again. Her feelings of recognition had only intensified. Standing there, stunned, her eyes met those of Mrs. Muldoon full on for what seemed like the first time all afternoon. She held the gaze, Mrs. Muldoon aglow, Larisa herself buzzing with excitement.

When they could hold the silence no longer, it was Larisa who finally spoke.

"Larisa Pearl is getting married," she whispered, a soft smile spreading slowly across her face.

CHAPTER TWO

Jack Merrill had been the caretaker at Elmhurst since he was seventeen, before he had any idea what he'd gotten himself into. He was in his late thirties now and had grown used to it. Heck, he thrived on it. But back then, he'd started almost without meaning to, responding one day to an ad in the *Kent Crossing Chronicle* asking for lawn-care help. A quiet boy with a penchant for doing things with his hands, he'd mowed the grass at his own house since he was ten years old, and so even though the Elmhurst plot was five times larger than the meager one for which his parents had scrimped and saved, he'd known he was up to the challenge. Starting at 7:00 A.M. and trying not to lose himself in the constant surging of the surrounding sea—he'd grown up on the ocean, it called to him—it had taken him until almost ten. Afterward, as he'd stood wiping the sweat from his forehead with the flap of his bangs, Ursula had approached him almost ceremoniously with a glass of iced tea and told him to come back the following week. Before long, he came every Saturday.

He trimmed the hedges, mulched the gardens, staked the tomatoes. He pruned the holly, cleaned the gutters, stacked the wood. He collected stray sticks for the compost heap and repaired things for Ursula—a transistor radio, a faulty sprinkler, a flat tire. Jack had been enrolled in the vocational tract since his freshman year at the public high school, but he'd also always been the type of boy who could study a book and apply what he'd learned. And so, eventually, as he grew older and less apprehensive and then graduated to trade school, he took on bigger challenges, checking out how-to books from the local library and then using Elmhurst as his test subject: he shingled the roof of the carriage house on a sweltering summer afternoon, his shirt off and back to the sun; he took several weeks to rework the electrical in the main house as the spring rain battered the windows; he re-tarred the massive driveway that curved up like a snake from the bottom of the hill.

But that was a long time ago, a lifetime. He'd gotten married at age twenty-five to Holly Weaver from the grade below him. Then four years later, after saving up some money, they'd had three boys—triplets!—and before he knew it, eleven years had passed and yes, his fortieth birthday loomed. He'd flourished during his time at Ursula's, even building himself up over the years into a proper tradesman and launching his own business with the name, Jack-of-All-Trades, airbrushed onto the side of his retrofitted truck. And they'd gotten by like this—him doing odd jobs, electrical and carpentry and landscaping projects around town, while Holly ran a home day care out of their living room. And always, throughout it all, he continued his visits to Elmhurst, coming around every day except Sunday, when he had a stint driving the launch at the Westgate Yacht Club, which was where he was one fall morning, pondering the new twist his life had taken.

That morning, he'd started earlier than usual. Launch service—the transport of sailors to and from moored boats—didn't start until 8:30 A.M., but Jack pulled in just after 7:00, shaking the sleep from his eyes as he eased the truck over the gravel parking lot and into the first spot next to the clubhouse. He stepped out of the car, yanked a small duffel from the front seat, and slung it across his back, cradling his metal coffee thermos in the crook of one arm. He pushed the car door closed with his hip and lifted his free hand to wave to two lobstermen at work on Shaw's Wharf across the way. They nodded back, their gloved hands busied with stringing their traps and stacking them into the hold of the classic Beal lobster boat.

"Off to a late start today, Jordy?" Jack called, tapping his left wrist though he wore no watch.

The captain shrugged and thumbed the suspenders of his bright orange foul-weather pants. He gestured toward the sea. "No worries, mate. A rising tide lifts all boats."

Jack smiled, jutting his chin back in acknowledgment. He swiveled to face the water. Sure enough, the current was moving swiftly through "the gullet," as they called it, the narrow channel that connected the inner harbor with the outer one. Ah yes, a rising tide. It was a shimmering fall day, the kind he liked best, when the ocean seemed to wink and glitter like a jewel in its case and the salt on the air sunk deep into his lungs as he breathed. The sun still hung low in the sky, but the air hummed with the distant drone of lobster boats motoring out to sea, a tangle of seagulls swirling after them, their plaintive cries echoing in to the shore.

Jack strode across the lawn, past the flagpole and the row of whitewashed storage lockers, and made his way down to the boat, bracing himself against the wooden footings on the ramp that led to the dock. He heaved his duffel over the high topsides of the launch and into the cabin, and then jumped in himself. The duffel held his fleece, some rain gear, and a brown-bag lunch. Just like Holly, he thought as he shoved the duffel into one of the storage holds under the benches that lined the sides of the launch. Just like Holly to still pack him lunch despite their big fight. But he didn't want to think about that now.

He fished in his pocket for the key and fitted it into the boat's ignition. The boat chortled to a start, a gush of bubbles churning out the back, a rainbow film of gasoline pooling with it. He pushed her into gear and maneuvered away from the dock, heading down the gullet, past seaweed swaying against jagged shore and bits of driftwood wedged in rock. He breathed and took it all in, gliding into the outer harbor and slowly past groups of boats tugging at their moorings: a fleet of Rhodes 19s, their hulls painted bright greens and reds and blues, their metal stays clanging against the masts; some larger pleasure boats with bigger keels and thus anchored in deeper water, their wooden cabins lacquered to an impenetrable sheen; some smaller sloops rocking on the outer edges of the harbor, one in particular, its sail furled neatly against the long, graceful boom, and its name, *Misery*, hand-painted on the back, a reference, Jack knew, to the many hours the owner had sunk into building the boat by hand.

Leaving the boats behind, Jack edged up the throttle and motored out beyond the limits of the harbor, past a few small swimming coves. He cruised by the metal bell buoy that clanged its warning on stormy nights, and chugged steadily toward the craggy promontory where the great house stood. Elmhurst. He felt her pull even from afar.

Back when Jack had started working at Elmhurst, Ursula Pearl had been a spry old woman in her early seventies, unlike anyone else in town. That was the late eighties. Big hair and bold patterns were *in,* and even Jack's own grandmother, a stalwart Irish immigrant, had taken to frosting her hair and wearing neon leggings to her Sweatin' to the Oldies exercise class. But not Ursula. Sure, she had a no-nonsense Yankee down-to-earthness about her, but also the poise and grace of a bygone era. She wore ankle-length skirts with boots, fitted jackets with Italian silk scarves. She braided her long gray hair and pinned it up into an elegant bun. She listened to records on her Victrola, did jigsaw puzzles on the card table, corresponded on Crane stationery. She read *The New York Times* at breakfast, peering through her spectacles, fingering the stem of the silver pedestal out of which she spooned her soft-boiled egg. She took her late-afternoon tea in a china cup in the drawing room, and she never allowed side dishes to be served in their store-bought containers. Rather, the milk for the tea came in a miniature pitcher accompanied with matching sugar bowl. Stone-ground mustard or fresh-made mayonnaise had to be spooned into gold-leaf condiment dishes. Smoked salmon was served on a silver charger and the accoutrements—the capers, the toast points, the chopped red onion—came on porcelain plates. One was expected to carefully scoop the capers out with a silver spoon, grip the rye toast with the tiny silver tongs. She had a glass candy dish, a covered cake stand, a china tray with convex wells for her two dozen deviled eggs. And after dinner she sipped decanted port from a tiny crystal goblet.

And how did Jack know all this—how did he even know the names of these delicate things—when he was supposed to be working on the house, on the grounds? Because he came at all hours—before school, after school, weekends, afternoons—and because, over time, she insisted he join her for tea. Timidly he came, kicking off the dirt from his work boots and stepping softly into the conservatory. At first he had no idea what he was supposed to do—should he stand? Should he sit? Should he take his cup and leave? But then she instructed him with a swift pat of her hand on the cushion of the wicker armchair next to hers. She motioned for him to help himself to tea and jam and scones, which he did with trembling hands, feeling her eyes on him. Then, when he had settled quietly into his chair, holding his breath and trying not to rattle the teacup against its saucer, she held one hand to her lips, turned to the Victrola, and lifted the arm onto the first record.

Music blared forth, turbulent and dramatic, terrifying in parts. A symphony that he later learned to be Mahler's Second. Jack glanced at Ursula, but she had set down her cup of Earl Grey and leaned back in the chair, her eyes clenched at times, her body seeming to convulse with the music. So he relaxed into his chair as well, letting himself be drawn in. They sat like that for well over an hour, letting the music pour over them. The opening made way to a playful lilting section followed by a darker bit with horrific outcries from the instruments, like the sounds of a thousand someones shrieking. Eventually a build to a big finale with a chorale section and the great thrum and blare of percussion and brass. Jack entered a kind of trance, staring up through the glass panes of the ceiling, sucking in the wet earthy smell of the plants surrounding them, their leaves quivering in response to the music, it seemed. Ursula opened her eyes and looked at one point as though she might cry. Then finally, ninety minutes later, it all ended on one lingering chord that seemed to reverberate from all corners of the conservatory.

At which point she turned to him. "Isn't it marvelous?"

He nodded, tentative, his mouth forced into a frozen smile, wondering vaguely whether he would be paid for his time.

He was. After that, the teatimes happened more regularly—not every week, but several each month. They listened to Mahler and Beethoven and Schubert. Sibelius, Prokofiev, Mozart. Rachmaninoff. Mendelssohn. Brahms. And soon Ursula began to expose him to other things, too. She taught him how to set a formal table. How to make a dry martini. How to carve a turkey. How to cultivate orchids. Ursula introduced him to Dickens and Shakespeare and Milton. Often one of Ursula's great-nieces, Larisa, stopped in and she and Jack would embark on their lessons, as he came to think of them, together. Though he and Larisa were high school classmates, they'd shared only a gym class. They didn't really know each other. But at Ursula's, they were thrown together to act out a scene from *King Lear* or to take turns reading Whitman or Tennyson or Dylan Thomas's *A Child's Christmas in Wales*. He felt silly at first, but both Ursula and Larisa embarked on these exercises with such earnestness that he couldn't help but get caught up in it. With Larisa by his side, he threw himself into his performance, the tips of her auburn hair grazing his bare elbow as she leaned into him during their rendition of Moliere's *The Imaginary Cuckold*, each of them playing multiple parts. Afterward, Ursula would pass judgment, clapping vigorously or dismissing the performance with a wave of her hand or shaking of her head slowly. Over time, Jack found himself surprisingly eager to please her. Engaging in lessons like these, he couldn't help but notice that he and Larisa were a little like Pip and Estella under Miss Havisham's instruction. Having read *Great Expectations* in full by this time, he sometimes felt a little wary of where it all might lead. But Ursula didn't seem wasted or bitter. She seemed merely to want the companionship and to impart the knowledge associated with a certain manner of life that was slowly slipping away. Moreover, Jack didn't feel any particularly romantic leanings toward Larisa. He wasn't captivated by her the way Pip was captivated by Estella. Sure, he found Larisa attractive, but in the same way he found his two sisters attractive: with some distance, without yearning, no drama.

Month after month, year after year, these lessons with Ursula continued, even into his early twenties, before his relationship with Holly had blossomed and after Larisa went off to college and could no longer participate. But despite their frequency, he told no one about the sessions. Who would he tell? His carpenter dad? His seamstress mom? No. And yet he treasured them in a way he had treasured nothing before. He treasured them in a way that made him feel almost ashamed.

Back on the launch, Jack took a slog of coffee and shuddered against the cold. In open seas, more exposed to the elements, he felt the brisk sting of the salt air against his cheeks. He pulled his windproof fleece from the duffel and slipped it on. He was moving faster now, tapping the side of the wheel in anticipation and bracing himself for each slap of the bow against the water as he edged ever closer to Elmhurst.

"You're married to that house, that's who you're married to," Holly would say, and she was right. He didn't even try to deny it anymore, knowing he'd spent more time there in recent years than with either Holly or the kids, creeping out at all hours of the night, using the weather and Ursula's age and almost anything else as his excuse. The fact was, he had tired of her. Holly. Her dirty underwear, crotch up, in the laundry hamper; her unwashed hair; the purple eyeshadow she'd been streaking across her lids since before they were married. As newlyweds, they had been crazy about each other, chasing each other around the apartment, dropping everything to make love on the counter, the kitchen floor, the double futon. And she had dressed up for him—sparkly low-cut tops with miniskirts, feathered hair, and dangly earrings. Now she kept her sandy-blond hair unstyled and only ever wore jeans, which more often than not he found bunched up in the corner at the end of the day after she'd gone to bed early without saying good night. If he was married to the house, then she was married to her job. Jesus, he thought, they couldn't even be adults around each other anymore because she didn't talk about anything other than that day care. Coloring books and developmental blocks and PBS programming. He came home, mid-afternoon, to

Dixie cups of apple juice lined up on the toddler-height table, stacks of graham crackers, bundles of carrot sticks.

And the boys—their three boys, now nearing eleven—sprawled on the rug in front of the TV while the toddlers tripped over their legs as Holly corralled them back to the snack area. The weekends had become an endless bustle of soccer games and swimming lessons and trips to the shoe store. How could it be possible? They constantly needed new shoes. So yes, he had found excuses to leave, creeping over to Ursula's to fix one more broken pipe, shim one more section of the sagging floor. And yes, afterward, he often slunk off to the bar, sipping one Guinness after another, flirting with the waitstaff a little more than he should. He knew she knew. And she knew he knew she knew. And they'd both tacitly agreed not to talk about it. But this past Friday night he'd gone too far. He hadn't returned home until Saturday morning, slinking in well after the boys had woken and settled into their pancake breakfast, their syrupy mouths pausing mid-chew as he entered. They looked to him, to their mother, and then back to him again. Holly had just stood facing the stove, her shoulders slumped, the spatula sticking out to one side. They'd spent the day not talking. And then Saturday night, last night, she'd told him. That it was all over, that she didn't love him anymore, that she wanted him to move out. She wanted a divorce.

"A *divorce*?" he said aloud to the squawking gulls who called their sympathy back.

My God, he thought, had they really gotten to this point?

But before he could think about it more, he had rounded the corner and the house came into view, easy to see now with only the thinning fall foliage to shield her. Ah, Elmhurst. The mistress of whom Holly was most afraid. He killed the engine, the air around him momentarily quiet as his ears adjusted, and then alive again with the lap and gurgle of the water against the hull, the hiss and crash of the waves on the shore. From the water, the house—with its broad eight-over-eight windows and paneled shutters—looked regal, pristine. He'd repaired those windows himself, reglazing and weatherstripping them, replacing the torn sash cords. He'd painted the shutters and oiled the hinges. Beneath those back windows lay the slate patio whose slabs of stones Jack had fitted together, edged in by the neat row of boxwoods he trimmed every year. Beyond that—the great lawn and the line of Rosa rugosa bushes huddled against the seawall; he could imagine them rustling against the summer wind as he edged the grass that bordered them.

Of course, he wasn't the only one who toiled on the property and he wasn't the only one who enjoyed it. There had been a cook, two maids, a driver. And on holidays, Ursula often held parties, inviting the general public to stop by. They came to watch the fireworks on the Fourth of July. They gathered for clambakes on Memorial Day, barbecues throughout Labor Day weekend. On Christmas, she greeted guests at the front door with cookies. On Halloween, she decorated the patio with pumpkins and dangling spiders and other macabre accents, including an actual human skull stolen by an ex-beau from Harvard Medical School, or so she claimed. And practically the whole town, it seemed, had shown up to celebrate Ursula's eighty-fifth birthday. He remembered standing in the back of the room with Holly. Larisa, home for the weekend and trussed up in a formfitting turquoise dress and two-inch heels, had come by to say hello. Cocking her head, she'd stood in front of him for several seconds before commenting, "You look different all cleaned up," and Holly, seven months pregnant with the boys, had dug her nails into his hand so hard, her teeth clenched in a crooked grin, that he had let out an audible squawk.

But the point was, sure, lots of folks had gathered at Elmhurst. Lots of people knew her from the outside looking in. But only Jack Merrill knew her from the inside out. Every screw, every board, every aging brick—he had laid his hands on them, or most of them anyway. He knew her complexities, her idiosyncrasies, her most secret and vulnerable parts. And Holly didn't know, she had *no idea*, what it really meant to care for a house like this. To feel her bones, her taut frame, her soft and pliant core.

Jack kicked at the base of the foredeck. He started up the boat again, coaxed her around, and headed back toward the harbor. He moved slowly on the way back, bringing the boat in closer to skirt the rocky shore with its pebbled beaches and intimate coves. Though the town still seemed to be sleeping, he caught the smell of wood fire on the air and the singsong of voices echoing in from the beach. A flock of Canada geese squawked by, their shadows riding the water. The bells from the Episcopalian church began to chime, calling the early birds to the 8:00 A.M. gathering. To the church where Ursula's service had been. He sighed. As she'd grown older, Ursula had become more feeble and more solitary. She'd required more rest, less activity. And though he still made it to Elmhurst several days per week, he kept to his chores and therefore saw less of her. He knew she'd been declining. Still, he'd been shocked by her death. Ursula Pearl. She seemed like the sort of woman who would live forever.

He glanced back at the house, his eyes landing on the glass dome of the great conservatory, where the music had started all those years ago. And then suddenly his mind flashed back to a memory. Larisa had just returned home for the summer after her first year of college and Ursula had ushered them into the conservatory, her eyes aglow. She pointed to a lead-gray plant with a thick stem and wide, flat leaves positioned in the corner beneath the riser of orchids. Its gangly limbs, three of them of various lengths but all close to one foot, seemed to point and waver uncertainly toward the early morning light, one of them displaying a six-inch pod sprouting from one of its leaves. A singular bud, held out for them to admire, the way one might admire a newly acquired engagement ring.

"It's from a cutting my mother gave me," Ursula told them. "But it hasn't ever done much. A plant like this can take years to mature."

Jack shuffled from side to side, impatient to move on to his list of chores. The plant didn't look like anything special. He hadn't ever even noticed it before. But Ursula knelt next to it and cupped its dormant bud gently in her palms.

"It's called"—she raised her eyebrows—"the night-blooming cereus."

"*Serious*ly?" Larisa grinned, emphasizing the homonym.

"Shh." Ursula scowled. "It only blooms once a year, at night, and only if you're lucky."

Larisa, a twinkle in her eye, had turned to Jack. "Are we lucky?" And Jack had smirked back.

Ursula nudged her in the ribs. "*Tonight* could be that night. Think about that. All year dormant, nothing but this drab little plant. And then one night of glory before the bloom drops away forever."

Jack did think about it. It seemed like a lot of effort for no big payoff. He shrugged and shuffled off to his work. But throughout the day, as he made his way around the house, he'd come upon Ursula peeking at the flower again, humming her Mozart and sipping her tea, and speaking softly to the plant. Larisa caught his arm at one point and made a circling motion with one finger around her temple.

"The old lady's finally lost it," she whispered.

But as evening fell and Ursula scurried back and forth from the dining room to the plant, leaving her poached salmon with dill untouched on her plate, even Larisa and Jack began to be drawn in. They followed her into the conservatory, the sky almost dark now. The three of them crouched together and leaned in toward the bloom. For yes, the bud had miraculously, over the course of hours, turned itself into a barely open bloom. Jack reached a finger toward it, but Ursula slapped it back.

"Don't touch!" she snapped. And the three of them sat silently, watching the flower emerge. They paused. They looked away. They met each other's eyes. And always, after looking away for several minutes, amazingly, the bloom had revealed a bit more of itself, its crinkled white petals slowly unfolding into a still-scrunched star. The transformation was slow, but steady; they could almost see it in real time. They took a break, finished dinner, made some tea. And when they returned, cups in hand, that was when Jack began to understand the magic of this plant. The fully bared bloom was enormous, a huge, multifaceted creamy-white star as big as a saucer around. And the smell was intoxicating, heady and potent and tropical, with hints of vanilla and rum, jasmine and musk, absolutely filling the room.

"Ah, *quelle beauté*." Ursula turned and clutched her hand to her chest. "So sad to think that by morning it will be gone forever."

And Jack had heard her, he had. But he didn't really believe it, that this vibrant blossom could be gone so soon. He and Larisa had stood, the two of them gawking, the smell so sweet and full and delicious that he'd actually come close to kissing her, not because he'd ever thought of her in that way, but because he was eighteen and alive and, by God, the night-blooming cereus was in bloom. But the next morning, when Jack returned to Elmhurst in the early hours just after dawn, the flower had withered and closed and fallen to the cool brick of the conservatory floor, just as Ursula had predicted it would.

Down the gullet and into the inner harbor now, the yacht club in sight, Jack could see his boys clambering on the shore, waving their arms, wheeling around, and kicking playfully at one another's shins. Alex and Ben and Charlie. He eased the boat into the dock, threw the stern and bowlines over, and waited for the boys to stumble down to tie him up at the cleats. They glanced at one another, seeming unsure which of them should speak, before Alex, the firstborn, piped up.

"Something's wrong with Mommy," he said. "She's still in bed."

Jack sniffed, bluffing, as he stepped onto the dock. "She sick?"

They shrugged. "We made her breakfast, but she didn't eat it."

Jack smirked, ruffling their hair. "Well, what did you make her? With you three jokers as cooks, I'm not sure I'd want to eat it either."

They giggled and nestled into his hold, a constant jostle for position between the three of them. Oh, how he loved these boys. Sure, it was a struggle sometimes, just to keep up. But he wouldn't give them up for the world. He thought of Holly, sniffling beneath the covers, her eyes red-rimmed, her lashes wet, and something softened within him. After they'd been married a few years, Holly had wanted kids so badly. They'd tried and tried for months before they finally went to a specialist. Then that took months as well. The day she found out she was pregnant and then the day those little fetuses had made it through the twelfth week, she was glowing, just beside herself with glee. He was ecstatic too, but he must have shown a touch of fear at the enormity of the future to come, for suddenly she grabbed his hand and squeezed.

"Don't worry," she'd comforted him. "We're all in this together. We're a family, Jack. A *family*."

The tears had started streaming down both of their cheeks and then he'd heard that refrain for years. *We're all in this together.* Jesus, he'd made a mess of things, hooking up with another woman for no good reason, no reason at all. He felt the shame surge within him and then the horror at what might lie ahead. Divorce. No, he couldn't do that to his family, he couldn't be the cause of it. But Holly had seemed resolute; she'd take some convincing. He clapped each of the boys one more time on their shoulders and then reached for the brown bag lunch. Then it struck him. *The lunch. There was hope.* She'd left him an opening, showed him she still cared. As with the night-blooming cereus, time was limited, he had to act now. He'd have to show her he cared as well, more than she knew. He'd have to earn back her trust—it wouldn't be easy—but he could do it. In another month, the harbor would be clear, all the boats brought in for the winter, and soon a gentle snow would settle. His work at the yacht club would be done for the season and he'd have an extra day to spend with Holly. Couples therapy, walks in the woods, trips to the mall. He would do what it took to re-electrify the marriage, fill it with magic and scent and romance. Yes, he'd been a bad husband, a mediocre father. But he was going to change all that. He was going to be good. Yes, he would win her back. A rising tide lifts all boats.

And there was something else. He had to give up Elmhurst as well. With Ursula gone a few months already, his time as caretaker of the grand old house had come to a close. He could get a "real" job, develop his own business into a full-blown contracting gig. He'd heard Larisa was in town. Sam Whittaker, the dockmaster, had seen her emerging from the bridal shop on Main Street—was Larisa getting married?—which meant she must be staying at Elmhurst. He would simply go and tell her that she needed to find a new caretaker, that he'd done his time, that he was just no longer up for the job.

And so with a new resolve, he made his way up to the office. Not many sailors went out on the water past Labor Day; Jack was sure he could beg off launch duty and get Sam to cover. As he neared the flagpole, Sam emerged from the clubhouse and raised his mug of coffee to Jack.

"Ahoy, sailor," he said, grinning, his great burly build sheathed by a dark blue fisherman's sweater.

"Listen," said Jack, slapping him on the back. "Think you can make do without me today? I've got some business to attend to."

Sam snorted. "I'm sure you do. I saw you moving in on that young 'un the other night at Shea's."

Jack frowned, remembering his foolishness, and then shook his head. "No, no. Business at Elmhurst." His eyes flared and flickered toward the boys, who were taking turns trying to stuff one another into one of the open lockers.

"Ah." Sam nodded. "A man's always a slave to his house."

Jack nodded. "Not for much longer. Thanks, Sam."

Jack motioned the boys over and told them to tell Holly he'd be home as soon as he could, that he had to take care of something first. Then he packed himself back into the truck and set off toward Elmhurst. He parked at the bottom of the hill, next to the carriage house, and began the long walk up the drive. Now that he'd made his decision, he felt energized. He quickened his step. Approaching the front door, he dug in his pocket for his key, but paused. If Larisa was home, he decided it would be better to knock. He lifted the door knocker and rapped it a few times. Then, more suddenly than he'd expected, the door swung open and there stood Larisa herself in Ursula's denim overalls, covered in white dust and debris.

"Jack," she exclaimed, pulling him into an embrace. "*Just* the person I need to see."

CHAPTER THREE

She'd bought the dress, of course. And she had no intention of regretting it. Mrs. Muldoon had carefully explained that all sales were final, the dress was nonreturnable. And Larisa, standing at the cash register, credit card in hand, had in fact experienced a brief flurry of doubt. When the time had come to change, she'd found herself almost unable to step out of the dress and leave it there for the future fittings that would take place, as Mrs. Muldoon had instructed, in the months to come. But now, dressed again in her wool skirt and winter coat, the borrowed lingerie hung neatly back on the padded hangers by the dressing room, the magic of the dress had worn off, if only a bit. She knew she should think twice about buying it. For starters, there was the not so small problem of the lack of a fiancé. She and Brent were definitely *not* together; they might never be together again. There were no prospects on the horizon, and anyway, she wasn't really in the mood to start dating. It felt good to be single again, independent. She didn't even actually miss Brent much. It had already been three weeks since their breakup and Brent's move to his brother's basement, and some days she hardly thought of him at all. She now had days on end where she didn't have to be accountable to anyone, didn't have to share her life, her kitchen, her bathroom, her pima cotton sheets. And so yes, she heard that distant voice in the back of her head insisting that this move was unwise. But she ignored it, pushed it as far out of her consciousness as she could, and allowed herself to purchase the dress, despite her better instincts.

And well, now that she'd bought the dress—yes, the charge had gone through, she'd signed the receipt—there was nothing to do but move forward.

As she tucked her credit card back into her wallet, waved her goodbye and thanks, and stepped out of the bridal shop and back out onto Main Street, she did feel a tinge of guilt for deceiving poor old Mrs. Muldoon, who had seemed so excited. But the truth was, this new deception was just the latest in a series of stunts she'd pulled, beginning over the summer before her split from Brent. It had started with small things, minuscule things. She'd shortened herself by three inches on her driver's license renewal. She'd listed her eye color as green instead of blue. Later that same week, she gave a false name (Priscilla) at the pickup counter for Chinese takeout. At the coffee shop where she ordered a skim latte every morning, she'd pretended she'd left her wallet at home and the barista had simply waved her away without payment, trusting that she'd make it up next time. But she hadn't. And now she'd done it two more times since, with different cashiers. She became bolder. One day, she'd reached out of habit for her phone with the intention of calling her mother, as she had every Sunday for years before the illness. But then she remembered how incoherent Kittie had become on the phone, no longer the maternal confidante she'd once been. Larisa couldn't say just what had gotten into her, but she'd driven to the mall and shoplifted a set of bra and panties from Macy's, walking right out the front door wearing the goods under her shorts and tank top. She was astounded at how easy it had been, yet how satisfying.

So really, in a way, she'd been steadily building to this new wedding dress delusion; she'd become somewhat comfortable with deceiving herself and others. And here was the thing: even though she'd bought the dress—yes, it was foolish—she hadn't actually *committed* to a wedding. It was just a dress; it didn't mean *for sure* that she was getting married. It just meant that she had bought a dress. Nothing more, nothing less. As she rationalized it this way, she knew she sounded crazy. She was deluding herself. But God, she was just so sick of being responsible. For Christ's sake, she was allowed to indulge herself for once, throw caution to the wind. Wouldn't it be interesting to just live impulsively and see what happened? And maybe if she didn't plot everything out for once, maybe she *would* eventually end up wearing it to a wedding—OK, *her* wedding. Or maybe not ever. And if Mrs. Muldoon felt cheated later when she found out there wouldn't actually be a wedding, well, she could just get over it. People canceled weddings all the time.

The light on Main Street had grown low, the chill in the air intensified in the way of fall afternoons that would soon make way to winter frosts. Clusters of dead leaves swirled in doorways, suddenly animated by the wind, before settling, dry and lifeless again, in the shadows. There were fewer people on the street, and those she encountered kept their heads down, eyes trained on the sidewalk, collars pulled high and tight. Larisa trudged on, past the drive that led to Elmhurst, toward the small public beach, where she watched a scarfed man throw a red Frisbee to a mangy black dog. Over and over the Frisbee soared and over and over the little dog scrambled across the wet sand, kicking it up in clumps as he catapulted his lean body into the air to clasp the plastic disk so briefly between his teeth. The dog never seemed to tire of it, returning his catch almost as soon as he obtained it and bracing himself in anticipation each time as he waited for the man to launch the Frisbee back into the sky. The ocean hissed and roiled behind him, reaching and then recoiling, a slither of froth. How long, she wondered, would he chase that Frisbee, hurl himself into the air, and clench his teeth around the toy? Would he ever grow weary of it, this repetitive action? Or would it sustain him perpetually, every day until he'd grown too old for puppy tricks? Until his dying days? *Rage, rage against the dying of the light,* Aunt Ursula would have recited. There was a level of trust in this interaction, an unspoken pact. The man would throw the Frisbee; the dog would retrieve it. And they would go on like this until it was time to go home.

"Maybe it's a dog I need, not a man," Larisa pondered aloud.

The black dog barked twice and pounced at the sand as the man faked the throw before casting the Frisbee aloft. A variation on the theme. Larisa thought of the dress once more, the way it shimmered around her hips, the boost of the bodice around her breasts. She could, if need be, convince Brent to take her back. Or else she could find someone else. The finite purchase of the dress—the certainty of it—would keep her focused. She'd find somewhere to wear it sooner or later. And with this vague resolve to stay the course without fully committing, she turned and walked back up the hill to Elmhurst, where she ate an early dinner—leftovers she'd brought with her on the train—and collapsed into bed before nine.

She woke to the flutter of sparrow wings in the bushes outside the windows. Neither drapes nor shades were pulled, and so the sunlight streamed in, framing her in Aunt Ursula's bed, where she sat, propped up on pillows, breathing in the view of the back lawn and the swells of ocean beyond. Groggy, she made her way in bathrobe and slippers down to the pantry, where she sniffed at the metal coffee percolator before choosing from a selection of teas instead. She clicked on the burner and waited, opening the fridge out of habit, knowing she'd not find much: a carton of sour milk from the funeral service, a wedge of wrapped Brie, a jar of orange marmalade in the door. She turned instead to the pantry and began nibbling at a handful of cereal from a box she knew to be recent. Before the kettle could boil, the phone in the front hall sounded, the distinctive ring from a phone of a different era—part rattle, part chime. She scurried to answer it even though she hadn't given the number to anyone.

"So," came the voice on the other end. "I hear you're getting married and didn't even bother to tell me."

It was a voice she'd know anywhere, that of Teddy Beauregard, the local florist with whom she'd worked weekends and summers throughout high school. She recognized it not only for its Southern lilt and nasal tone, but also for the blunt, no-

nonsense nature of the inquisition. Leave it to Teddy to cut right to the chase.

"Oh, Teddy," she lied, "it only just happened. Man, does word spread quickly in this town."

"Faster than green grass through a goose."

"What does that even mean?"

"Never mind, honey, it's Southern. Back to the matter at hand—what's this about a wedding?"

"No, it's nothing yet." She sighed, hedging again about the lie she now found herself further perpetuating. Teddy was not someone with whom she wanted to get into it. "I'm sorry, I should have called."

"Never mind, sugarplum. Just tell me the date and we'll get it on the calendar. Assuming you'll have me, that is?"

"Of course, of course." On impulse, she rummaged through the drawer of the front hall table and came up with a faux leather datebook with Ursula's initials embossed on the front. She quickly paged through and randomly picked a Saturday. "How does June sixteenth look?"

"No good." Teddy came back with his usual calendar-conscious intel, typical of a florist who depended on holidays for his living. "Day before Father's Day. Better go with something earlier, when the peonies will just be coming into bloom."

She scanned the datebook. "June second?"

"June second," Teddy echoed. She imagined him inking the date onto the wall calendar next to his desk. "Consider it done, love. And how are your parents?"

Again, Larisa felt the pang of guilt for keeping her distance. She really ought to visit soon. Or at least call.

"Oh, they're fine," she managed as the tea kettle began

to whistle from the next room. "Um . . . wintering in Palm Springs."

"Ooh la la, those two."

"Yes, right," said Larisa, the tea kettle insisting now. "Listen, Teddy, water's boiling, gotta go, talk soon, promise."

She slammed the receiver down, ran back to the kitchen, and poured the tea. Datebook in hand, she thumbed back through to June and drew a circle around the number 2.

June 2. Well. Now she had a date. She rolled her eyes at herself. First Mrs. Muldoon and now Teddy Beauregard. How far was she going to take this? And her parents *weren't* in Palm Springs. They *weren't* hiking the Himalayas, as she'd told Mrs. Muldoon. They'd moved, as planned, several years earlier into their own apartment on the bucolic campus of Lighthouse Retirement Homes.

"Light's on But No One's Home," Kittie had dubbed it the weekend they moved in. It was a remarkably suitable alias, actually, for a place that dealt with the absentminded elderly. And especially comic given that the community was landlocked, situated five miles inland, and therefore the lighthouse tower attached to the front office had no functional purpose. It didn't warn ships off rocks, it didn't send out clarifying beams on foggy days; it didn't even have a working light. Rather, the upper gallery was used primarily to display promotional signage and seasonal window boxes that were created in the many workshops offered to the otherwise idle residents. Clark and Larisa loved the pseudonym, shortening it to "No One's Home." At first Larisa came to visit every other weekend. She wanted to make sure her parents were getting on all right, and it was nice to get out of town. But then, not long after they moved in, the dementia had started. Suddenly the name didn't seem so funny anymore.

Larisa sipped her tea. She wandered toward the dining room and stopped in the doorway when her eyes landed once more on the peeling paper above the fireplace. Crap. What with the distractions and dress buying, she'd never made it to Duffy's Hardware the day before. Which was actually probably a good thing because now, in the brighter early morning light, as she stood on the chair again and took a closer look, she detected a slow but active leak behind the paper. In fact—how had she missed it before?—the entire floor in front of the hearth was covered in a pool of water. There had been wind and rainstorms earlier in the week and something must have come loose. With no one in the house, and Jack, the caretaker, only stopping by sporadically to check on things, who knew how long this had been happening? *Ugh*, she groaned inwardly, things were beginning to unravel.

She ought to call her father, really. But then she'd have to talk, if only briefly, to her mother. And it was too hard, really just too hard. Regardless, this leak—she needed to stop it. And so she set down the tea, went to the front hall closet, and rummaged around until she found Ursula's work overalls. She slipped out of her robe and into them. Tools? She thought for a minute before pressing the push-button light switch to the basement and heading down the narrow stairs that led to the workbench and tool rack. She selected a hammer, a small crowbar, and a handsaw, and hung them from the loops on her waist. Then, balancing a step stool over one shoulder, she came back to survey the wall.

She approached the task slowly at first, gingerly pinching

the edge of the wallpaper and giving a firm but gentle tug. The loose swath came away easily from the wall and she laid it carefully across the dining room table, thinking she'd perhaps be able to paste it back into place later. But when she inspected more closely, she saw that the paper above the loose bit was soaked through as well. She'd have to get behind it to get to the leak. Last time she'd phoned her parents, she recalled, she could barely talk to her father because he was so distracted trying to keep her mother from wandering out the door. From the guest bedroom, on her visits, Larisa sometimes woke at 2:00 A.M. to hear her mother rise and dress, rummaging through the closet trying to find her coat and shoes. At dinner, Kittie couldn't keep track of current events and so would interject with questions and confusion. Larisa sighed and headed back toward the phone anyway, hoping to get her father. Instead her mother's tentative voice warbled through the receiver.

"Hello?"

"Hi, Mom, it's Larisa." She did her best to sound cheerful.

"I know." The words were flat, monotone, unemotional.

Did she know? Larisa waited, but her mother offered nothing more. Only the low hiss over the phone line indicated they were still connected.

"Mom, are you there?" she asked. "Hello?"

Still nothing.

"Did you take your pills this morning?" she asked. "Where's Dad?"

More silence. Larisa searched her brain. It was so strange, so troubling, this disease that sometimes—but only sometimes—left her mother so unreachable. Larisa could never predict when the fog would set in, but when it did, nothing she said would matter. When her mother was in this state, the words just wouldn't land. Still, she wondered, couldn't she find something to goad her mother out of confusion and back to lucidity?

"Hey, Mom," she said on impulse. "I've decided to dye my hair purple. What do you think of that?"

"Oh."

"Hey, Mom," she tried next, "I'm going to get a tattoo."

No response.

She picked up Ursula's date book and shuffled through it to the June 2 date.

"Hey, Mom, I'm getting married."

Call my bluff, she silently urged, *I dare you.* But her mother said nothing. Larisa bit her lower lip. She imagined her mother staring at the phone with a perplexed expression, unable to determine its use.

"Are you scared?" she asked. Silence.

Larisa cringed, cupped her head in her hands, and hung up the phone. "I'm sorry."

She felt a wave of sadness shudder through her, but she steeled herself—*she would be strong*—before the emotion could take hold. Instead she marched back to the dining room, picked up the crowbar, and swung hard at the wall, her first strike landing with a wet thwack in the horsehair plaster. A small cloud of yellow-white dust crumbled down from the point of impact and spattered the slate hearth. The pheasants shuddered against the blow, their bewildered expressions amplified as they gaped in fearful symmetry at their poor comrade who had been speared through the middle. For yes, the crowbar remained in the wall even after Larisa released the handle. She yanked on it with two hands, but its metal teeth were caught behind the lath and so she began to pry and wiggle, until the wet wood snapped and shot out at her, the pheasant's ruptured innards exposed, the crowbar clattering to the floor. Larisa paused and assessed. Now that she'd started, she decided, she couldn't stop. So she repeated her steps. She heaved and pried at the wall, tore into it again and again, the plaster dust and pulpy debris coating her hair and eyelashes, lining her throat. And as she dismantled the wall, blow by blow, board by board, she began to think about her life and how on earth things had gotten to where they were now.

In the beginning, she had been so stoic; she had been proud of her ability to hold it all together. She'd taken over the bill paying and came often to help keep Kittie on target with basics tasks—cooking, cleaning, laundry. She'd been determined to remain practical, anchored by facts and plans and reason rather than emotion. But over time, it had gotten harder, excruciating. Larisa hadn't been prepared for her inability to deal with Kittie's deterioration. What did it mean about herself, Larisa wondered, that she couldn't face her mother's illness? Did it make her a bad person? And how did her father manage to keep on smiling despite it all?

In June, at Ursula's funeral, Larisa had reencountered all the locals who acted like they knew her, remembering her from her high school days, talking about a person she didn't know anymore. She felt a reaction to it, an aversion. Not because she disliked their version, but because she had begun to realize how far she had deviated from the person they described.

"So down-to-earth," said Mr. Wendall, recounting the conversations Larisa had struck up with shamefaced visitors at the food pantry where she volunteered during high school.

"So studious," chirped Mrs. McKenna, the head librarian, "poised to take over the world."

"So silly," said Molly Jenkins, who had only been a kindergartner when Larisa babysat her in the afternoons for most of her senior year.

Larisa's father had grown up in this town and so she had felt a certain quiet ownership of it, but she'd never felt the need to impress. In high school, despite her moderately privileged upbringing, Larisa had never cared much about popularity or appearance. She kept her hair long and straight, unstyled, and didn't think twice about running out the door in a T-shirt and pair of sweats. She didn't match her belt to her shoe color. She didn't buy a new dress for every new occasion. She didn't consult fashion magazines to mimic the latest fad. These were things that would never occur to her. But over her time at the auction house and since her appointment several years earlier as an associate specialist, reporting to the director of House Sales and Private Collections at Sotheby's, things had changed dramatically. She had her eyebrows waxed regularly, went for her mani-pedi every week. She kept her hair neat and styled, angular. And she took a chunk of time each evening to craft together her outfit for the morning, carefully selecting jewelry and scarves and other accessories that would help her make just the right impression, look the part.

Christ, Larisa chastised herself as she continued to pick at the wall, she'd become the wrong person. As a child and as a young adult, she'd had an idea of the person she wanted to be. She thought she'd end up in social services or working for some nonprofit, something to do with social justice. In high school she had written a play about homelessness and it had been put on by the community theater. All proceeds donated to the local shelter. And now, years later, she made her living auctioning fine porcelain and gilded candlesticks and marble busts. Sure, it was interesting, even glamorous at times, but was it meaningful?

And somewhere along the line, she'd become so angry. Her mind flashed to an encounter she'd had recently on the subway. It had been a long day, hours spent cataloging the inventory from a new estate, and she'd finally dragged herself out of the office, her head pounding at the temples. All she'd wanted was to relax on the subway with her book. But across the way was a small boy who could not sit still or keep quiet. He was old enough to know better—nine, ten?—but his mother did nothing to correct him as he jumped around and bellowed out the words and phrases he read from the ads overhead. So Larisa, hoping mostly just to silence the little brat but also to remind him of some manners—her own mother never would have allowed her to act his way—had fixed him with her most severe schoolmarm's scowl. But instead of taking the cue and sitting down in his seat like a good little boy, he had only paused, cocked his head at her, and let loose his rebuttal.

"Mommy, Mommy," he howled, "some lady's giving me the evil eye!"

Horrified, Larisa had hidden her face in her book before the mother could pick her out of the crowd. My God, when had she become that person?

After Ursula's funeral, when she returned to her apartment with Brent, she'd begun to think about just that—the person she had become. The town could define a version of her, an outdated one; but she needed to define herself. And then that was when the questioning had really started. Who was anyone, really? What did we ever really know? People trusted all the time that pilots wouldn't fly airplanes into mountains. That bellhops wouldn't make off with people's luggage. That mailmen wouldn't open W-2 envelopes and scribble down social security numbers. That a married father of four wouldn't swipe a FedEx envelope from a neighbor's front porch. There were a thousand moments every day when she was expected to accept the implied circumstances. That people would act as they said they would. And the whole world operated like this, on this incredible level of trust. It was terrifying, really.

And that was what had been troubling her lately. Her mother was supposed to mother *her*; Larisa had depended on this constant, predictable care. And yes, she knew she really ought to visit, that it was her turn to do the caregiving. This was how people expected her to act. But what if she just couldn't be the person they expected her to be?

Distracted with all these thoughts, Larisa had kept heaving and picking and chipping savagely at the wall. And now, before she knew it, she'd dismantled the entire damn thing. The floor was covered in splintered planks and piles of crumbled plaster and paper. She realized, too late, that she ought to have covered the rug and furniture, as they were coated in debris as well.

Lordy, Larisa thought, surveying the mess, what would Aunt Ursula say? She wondered now how on earth she was going to put it all back together again once she managed to stop the leak. But before she could fixate on the problem, she heard the terse rap of the door knocker against its metal strike. When she swung the front door open, there stood Jack Merrill, looking like he was working up the nerve to say something important. But she'd clearly stopped him in his tracks with her disheveled appearance, covered in dust and dressed in Aunt Ursula's denim overalls. Larisa ignored his stare and pulled him into a hug.

"Jack," she gushed, "just the person I need to see." She ushered him in and slammed the door. Amazingly, the thought hadn't hit her before, but Jack Merrill was exactly the person who could help her find the leak and put the wall back together. Of course. He'd spent years at Elmhurst, learning all kinds of trade skills. Years as a contractor as well. She should have sought him out in the first place.

"Uh-oh," he teased as he stepped over the threshold and into the house. "I've heard those words before and they always mean trouble."

Larisa took note now of him. He stood in the foyer waiting to be invited farther in, hands hung neatly in his jean pockets, an easy smile playing across his lips. He looked a bit tired. His hair—the rich, thick brown of dark rye—was tousled and untrimmed; a shadow of stubble darkened his chin. But despite looking worn, there was something still ruggedly appealing about him. Years of physical labor had sculpted his tall frame so that he remained as fit as she always remembered him, his buff physique somehow permeating through his several layers of clothes. Larisa felt her body relax. Something about Jack Merrill always put her at ease; she had a hard time looking away. But when she felt her stare lingering too long, she finally tugged at his elbow and motioned him wordlessly into the dining room to see for himself.

"We had a leak." She watched his expression move from placid calm to stormy seas and back to calm again. It pained him, she saw, to see the room torn apart like this, but he moved quickly to hide it from her.

"Yikes," he said, smoothing his hand tenderly across the intact wallpaper, "how many pheasants does it take to stop a leak?"

She sighed, shrugging. "More than it takes to screw in a light bulb? Somehow I started and just couldn't stop."

Jack bounded limberly up the ladder and poked his head into the wall. "Could be a burst pipe. Have you turned off the water main? Might as well do that until we rule it out."

Larisa spent the next hour trailing Jack around the house as he maneuvered up and down the stairs, peeking into closets and clambering up to the attic, where he finally located the leak—a faulty pipe joint, as he'd suspected. He'd retrieved his tool chest from his truck and was now rummaging through it to find what he needed. As he worked, the two of them chatted.

"How's the art world?" Jack beamed his flashlight into the work space. Larisa could see him calculating his plan of attack.

She cleared her throat. "Well, I was fired, actually."

Jack turned to gauge her expression and she nodded to show him she was serious. He handed her the flashlight, motioning for her to keep it focused on the pipe as he reached for the wrench. "Fired? What the hell happened to Miss Overachiever?"

"Well, exactly," quipped Larisa. "I'd been working my butt off, staying late and coming in on the weekends. I'd achieved all my goals for the year. And the boss still passed me by for a position that was rightfully mine. I earned that promotion and she passed me right by after leading me on like a little minx."

Jack shrugged as he yanked on the pipe joint with the

wrench. "So you didn't get the raise. But then why'd she actually fire you? You could have just stayed on as her underling, right? Until you'd figured out what was next."

Larisa chewed at her fingernail, not quite hiding her self-amused smirk. "Oh, that. Well, it might have had something to do with writing *FU BITCH* in silver polish on a mirror that went up on the auction block the next day, right across the front for everyone to see."

Jack dropped the wrench to his lap, eyebrows raised. "Wait a minute. Who *are* you? Have we met before?" He held a hand out for her to shake.

Larisa laughed. "I didn't mean for her to see it actually. I'd stayed late and the interns were the ones who were supposed to be doing the polishing, like they always do right before an auction. But one of them was home sick and the other one is Maud's daughter and had gone home with her for the night. So I got stuck with the job."

"Maud?"

"Maud Singleton, my boss. How would you like to work for someone named Maud?"

Jack considered. "I like the name Maud."

"No," protested Larisa. "It's like the headmistress from some awful British boarding school. *Maud.* And without the *e* on the end, it makes it worse. Anyway, there I am. It's past midnight and I'm surrounded by all these ridiculous pieces that still need to be polished—candlesticks and plates and baby cups—and the biggest piece is this dumb mirror. I haven't had any dinner and I'm so tired, I can barely keep my eyes open. So I just vented my anger across the front of the mirror. Forgot all about it until they held it up at auction under the lights and there was my special message loud and clear. Oops!"

"She does sound like a bit of a bitch, though." Jack shot her a mischievous smile and then turned back to the pipe. "I mean, she didn't have to fire you."

Larisa shrugged. "After that, she kind of did. But it didn't matter. By that point I was done anyway. Other than the embarrassment and the lack of a reference, I didn't actually care so much about being let go. Couches, armoires, four-poster beds—these things don't really matter. What are they? Wood, cloth, metal. People spend crazy money on all kinds of things in these collections. And they're just *things*." She gestured around as Jack packed up his toolbox and they made their way back downstairs. "Even this place."

Jack paused as he pulled the door to the attic shut. "This is your life, your history, your family."

Larisa shook her head. "It's just a house."

"Not just any house."

She lowered her eyes. "Isn't it? After everything is said and done?"

He didn't answer, but he avoided her gaze when she lifted her head to look at him again.

"And anyway," she continued, "I realized something that day. I grew up my whole life doing everything I was supposed to. It was kind of fun to be bad for once."

Jack snorted, heading for the grand staircase that led from the second to the ground floor. "Then how are you supporting yourself?"

"I've got some savings."

"Savings?" He shook his head. "You obviously don't have

a family to feed. You'll feel differently once you have kids. Speaking of which, how's that tree guy of yours? I could use his help with some of the branches of our oak; they're hanging a little too low over the house."

Larisa hesitated to respond. She thought about glossing things over, but she'd told so many lies recently, and Jack was someone who actually knew her, someone she could trust. So she decided to come clean. "Oh, well, it turns out that's over too."

Jack looked curious, concerned. "Then why did Sam see you coming out of that little French bridal shop?"

She froze, her eyes on the floor. Despite her stillness, he seemed to sense she was in turmoil. He stopped and waited, watching her with his quiet brown eyes.

"It's complicated," whispered Larisa.

Jack nodded. "Let's make some tea."

And so they did, carrying it into the conservatory on a tray. Larisa lay back on the chaise, feet splayed in front of her. "Tell me, doctor, how much do you charge?"

"Oh, you could never afford me," said Jack, grinning. "But we'll find some way to work it out."

Larisa ignored the undertone. She took a deep breath and released it. Sitting in the bright sunshine among Aunt Ursula's orchids, the air thick and earthy, she told him everything. The fights with Brent, the breakup, her flight to Elmhurst. Her deception at the bridal shop, her purchase of the wedding dress, her June 2 date.

"So now I'm signed up for this wedding and I don't even have a groom," she finished. She sat up, swung her legs over the side of the chaise, and leaned in toward Jack. "Let me ask you something. Would you want to marry me? I mean, if you were Brent?"

Jack hadn't said much as she'd blathered on. He'd listened quietly, leaning back in his chair, a sad expression deepening his features, nodding here and there as she'd filled in the details. Now he pulled away and shook his head. "I'm not the one to consult on marriages these days. Mine's not exactly going so well."

Larisa softened. "Sorry to hear."

"Long time coming." He gave her an exasperated look. "But let me ask—you've been with this guy how many years?"

Larisa calculated. "Almost two."

"Right. So why haven't you married him already? I mean, two years is long enough at our age. If you really wanted to marry him, wouldn't you have known it by now?"

"I don't know. I read this article recently. 'Twenty-Five Keys to a Successful Marriage.' Typed out like a to-do list. Want to know number twenty-five? Here it is: 'Everyone is hard to live with.'"

Jack shrugged as though this bit was obvious, but Larisa balked.

"I'm not hard to live with!" she asserted. "I make the bed every morning. I hang up my wet towels rather than leaving them in a heap on the floor. I do the laundry and change the sheets every Thursday night."

Jack shot her an amused smile.

Larisa sighed. "OK, OK. I'm hard to live with. But I don't know what it was about him. We just weren't in sync, not quite. Sure, he doted on me, but that just got kind of annoying."

"Annoying to have somebody do everything for you?"

"*Yes*. It felt like I was his only hobby. I wish he'd find something else to do with his time."

Jack pointed toward the dining room, conjuring the remaining pheasants and the heap of rubble. "And you've found that something?"

"Touché." Larisa stood and plucked up one of the large swaths of wallpaper that had been swept into the hallway during the teardown of the wall. She held it up in front of her and then attached it to a gilded mirror that hung in the hallway so that the ridiculous birds were framed there, any reflection obscured. "Maybe it's me, not him." She returned to the chaise and leaned back into it.

Jack smiled. "Well, for what it's worth, here's my lesson from however many years of marriage. People don't change. That much is for certain." He looked like he wanted to say more but stopped himself. Larisa suddenly wondered what he had meant when he said his marriage wasn't going so well, but she held back from asking. Men, she knew, didn't like to share until they were ready. Instead she stood and gestured for him to do the same.

"Come on," she said, "we may have stopped that leak, but we've got a lot more fixing up to do."

CHAPTER FOUR

So, great. Now he was in the shit house with Holly. Not only had Jack neglected to announce his resignation to Larisa that day at Elmhurst, as he'd been determined to do, but he'd also completely failed to make it home to his wife. After he'd dispatched the boys from the yacht club to tend to Holly and assure her he'd be there soon, he'd forgotten all about his intentions to make things good and instead spent from mid-morning through late Sunday afternoon with Larisa, chasing down the leak, then chatting in the conservatory, then hatching a plan to rebuild the dismantled dining room wall. By the time he did remember Holly, well after 3:00 P.M., Larisa had already corralled him into a thousand other renovation projects around the house. He had a hard time extracting himself.

"I really have to go," he had insisted more than once. He pictured Holly at home in tears, pacing their bedroom, her hands balled into fists. She'd probably already slapped their wedding photo in its faux-wood frame facedown on the front hall table, as she often did when she was upset at him. Of course, he knew he ought to call, but he'd left his cell phone in the truck, thinking he'd only stay long enough to give his notice, and he felt awkward asking Larisa to use the landline. He needed to get home, he kept saying. And Larisa had acknowledged his requests, she had. But somehow he never quite made it out that door.

Why? Maybe because though it really did slay him to imagine Holly in such distress, he was actually a little afraid of finally facing her, knowing her emotions had been building all day and she was likely to explode. But that wasn't the only reason. Sure, he liked being at Elmhurst, liked admiring his own handiwork after years of hard work. But he also stayed, he knew, because he liked being with Larisa. Yes, he'd felt something from the moment he walked in. A pull between them. It was something he hadn't felt when they were younger, as though they were just coming into each other's orbits after years of circling. He was sure she felt it too. And he was afraid of where that might lead. So in the end, this attraction to Larisa—the unspoken threat of it—was also the thing that finally compelled him to go home.

Holly was beyond pissed when he came shuffling through the front door of their modest Cape at half past five. At first she even refused to look up from her spot on the sofa, but when she finally did, her eyes bore right through him.

"I'm sorry, what? Was I supposed to wait around all afternoon with a rose in my teeth for Don Juan to finish with all his conquests?"

Jack tried to prevent any expression from fluttering across

his face. Best not to acknowledge the accusations when she was in a state. He hung his keys on the wall hook and peeled off his coat, wondering why the house was so quiet, where the boys were. "There was a leak at Elmhurst. Turns out Larisa's in town. I had to help—"

"Oh, of course," Holly cut in with mock compassion that quickly shifted to snide remarks. "That explains everything. Miss Priss sends out her SOS and you always go running. Tell me, is she still wearing those tighter-than-tight miniskirts?" She shot her eyebrows up at him, waiting for a response.

Jack's mind flashed back to the image of Larisa in Aunt Ursula's overalls, covered in dust, looking nothing like the temptress Holly imagined. He smirked despite himself but then quickly reeled it in. "Come on, Holl, she's like a sister to me."

The eyebrows lowered, but her sideways scowl showed him she wasn't convinced. "Heck of a lot better-looking than your sisters."

Jack lifted a conciliatory hand. "Hey, let's leave my sisters out of this." He spoke slowly and kept his eyes steady. "Nothing is happening with Larisa. I just lost track of time."

Her body relaxed a little and he could see that she believed him. Despite Jack's years of friendship with Larisa, he'd never given Holly any reason to be suspicious on the Larisa front. She only accused him now because she was so amped up.

"Fine, you lost track of time," she conceded. "But why is your time always more valuable than mine? I have to wait around all day with no idea what you're up to?"

"No," he protested. "I know your time is valuable."

She pounded a fist against the sofa pillow. "So valuable that first you don't come home last night and then you choose to spend all day at that house rather than fixing our fucking marriage?" She was ramping it up again, her face flush with anger.

"I'm sorry . . . ," he started. But what could he say? She was totally right. He'd failed at even this simplest of tasks—to get home to his neglected wife. And he couldn't even deliver the big news he'd been planning on, the thing that would pave the way for the rebirth of their marriage. That he'd quit Elmhurst, that he'd have more time to devote to her and the boys, that they were truly all in this together. Because not only had he utterly failed to quit, but with merely the urging of four simple words from Larisa—"I'll pay you well"—he'd actually signed himself on for more work than he'd had there all year. Yep, he was way up shit creek for sure and even two paddles wouldn't be anywhere near enough to get him out.

"Here I was thinking that the threat of divorce would jolt some goddamn sense into you," railed Holly. She stood, approached, and flung her arms to her sides in anger. "Stupidly, I thought you'd think about our fifteen years together—*fifteen years, Jack*—and you'd see that this marriage would be worth working on. And you'd come home."

"I *did*." He took a step toward her but stopped when she backed away, repelled.

"You *didn't*. All you had to do was show up for once and you couldn't even do that." She held up one hand like a stop signal, closed her eyes, and shook her head. "You know what? Just go. Pack a bag and get the hell out."

He stared, trying to read her expression and gauge her sincerity. She kept her eyes on the carpet, her head turned slightly away. Something about this stance told him she'd worked out this plan long before he got home.

"You don't mean that," he said, his voice as quiet as he could make it without whispering. He tried to connect his gaze with hers, convince her.

She took a long inhale and let it out slowly and lifted her eyes. Her immediate anger, he saw, had subsided, but she'd thrown up the wall, her face stony, expressionless. She'd be unreachable now. "Actually, I *do* mean that. Clearly, we need space. There's gotta be some room for you over at that stupid house, especially after Miss La-Di-Da breezes out again. Just go there for a while."

Jack thought. It was a natural suggestion, especially now that she didn't consider Larisa a threat. For all Holly knew, Larisa was just home for the weekend, tending to the estate; she had no idea about the renovation plans. And Jack had spent so much time at Elmhurst over the years that even Holly thought of the house as practically his. It would be the logical place to hole up, where no one would ask questions the way one might if he suddenly showed up at his parents' house across town. He could fly under the radar a bit, regather himself. And yes, even though he didn't like to admit it, he agreed that a little space might do them well. Still, he tried once more despite himself.

"Where are the boys?" He peeked around the corner into the dining room, though it was obvious they weren't home.

She folded her arms. "At my mother's. You can see them in a day or two."

Damn, she'd removed the boys to make it a cleaner break. He thought about leaving them a note, but what would it say? No, he'd have to call them instead, let them know he was thinking of them, he'd see them just as soon as he could. He went up to the bedroom, packed his toothbrush, a few shirts, a handful of underwear, and then made his way back down to the front door, glancing doubtfully over his shoulder to see whether she'd changed her mind. But she had already retreated to the kitchen, her back to him. There was nothing to do but leave. As he slipped his jacket back on, grabbed his keys, and turned toward the door, his gaze landed on the wedding photo—yes, flattened, as he'd suspected—on the front hall table. Beside it, a black frame displayed a picture of the boys taken from their last vacation. Before he went, he quietly slipped both into his bag. Holly was sure to notice them missing and he hoped it would at least show her he still cared.

And so he left and headed to Elmhurst, arriving with a drive-through hamburger in hand, letting himself in this time with his own key. Larisa padded down the stairs in sweats and a zippered hoodie, patting her wet hair with a towel.

"You're back?" She sat on the steps and took him in.

He nodded and glanced around the foyer. The scrap of pheasant wallpaper remained affixed to the mirror, where Larisa had placed it earlier, the birds still frozen there. Jack paused for their assessment, feeling their backward glance on him.

"I know, I know," he told them. "I'm not proud of myself either."

"Oh," said Larisa. "Your marriage again."

"Right." Jack gestured toward the stairs with his duffel. "You mind if I take one of the back bedrooms for a while? I'll stay out of your way."

She moved to let him by, pulling her sweatshirt tighter

around her waist as he passed. "Sure, plenty of room. Stay as long as you like."

"Thanks." He heaved himself up a few steps and then paused, his gaze landing on the photo of Larisa's parents on their wedding day. He whistled. "Boy, it's been a long time since my wife looked at me that way."

Larisa nodded knowingly. "They *still* look at each other that way. But not everyone can have what they have. Brent kept saying we were meant to be together, but when I look at them in comparison, I'm not so sure."

Jack shook his head. "No one's just meant to be together. You have to work at it."

"You don't believe in destiny?" She raised her eyebrows in question and then let them fall again. "No. I guess I really don't either."

"Nope, I believe in commitment. Though I'll admit, I haven't been so good about showing it lately. Which is why I'm going to bed. See you in the morning."

He continued up to the landing and settled himself into the small butler's room in the back hallway, placing the photos of Holly and the boys carefully on the bedside table beside him, a reminder.

The next morning, he found Larisa at the dining room table, staring into her coffee.

"Hey, you OK?" he asked.

Larisa shrugged. "I guess. I'm more conflicted than I thought I'd be."

"About Brent?"

She nodded. "When he started talking about getting

married, I just panicked. But I think buying that dress made me consider it a little more. He's a good guy, with a big heart. Am I just being stupid?"

Jack didn't answer. He looked past her toward the torn-up wall. "First things first. We've got to take down the rest of these walls, pick up this mess, so we can see what we're up against."

Larisa recoiled. "Didn't I take down enough walls yesterday? I'm not sure I'm ready for more."

Jack clapped his hand on her shoulder. "No way but forward now. You don't want the mold to take over, and anyway, sometimes you've got to let things get messy before you can build them back up again." He fingered the wedding band on his finger.

"Huh," said Larisa. "Seems like you've done this before."

Jack went out to his truck and came back with his tools, two pairs of gloves, and a couple of face masks. They worked together for the rest of the day, until the room was down to the studs and the front walk was a pile of debris. Jack picked up some heat fans from the hardware store and faced them toward the open walls to dry them out.

"See," said Jack. "That wasn't so hard. We make a good team."

Larisa glanced sideways at him.

"You know," she said, "since Brent moved out, I've gotten so used to being alone. It's feels kind of strange to have company again."

Jack hooked his thumb toward the front door. "Oh, well, I could give you some time alone if you want."

"No, no," answered Larisa. "That's not what I meant. You're not Brent and you don't want to marry me, so it's different."

"Very different," agreed Jack.

"Anyway, I'm going to wash up and then grab some groceries for dinner. Do you care to join? For dinner, I mean? I'm not the best cook, but it's probably better than drive-through."

Jack smiled. "If you're sure."

"Of course. Anything you don't like?"

Jack let his gaze fall on her. "I like it all."

He hadn't meant it to sound as flirtatious as it did—the last thing he needed was a fling with Larisa when he ought to be showing every bit of contrition he could toward Holly. But things had been so easy with Larisa from the minute he'd walked in. The comfortable banter between them, the facility with which they worked on the house together, the capacity for companionship that he hadn't felt from Holly in a long time. They had the freedom to coexist without all the tension that came with a fraught relationship. Of course it was easy, he reminded himself. It would be easy with almost anyone other than Holly right now. Still, he'd be fooling himself if he didn't admit he was attracted to Larisa.

She either didn't notice or pretended she didn't.

"Great," she said as she mounted the stairs. "Dinner at seven then."

The next day, they took down the kitchen cabinets, dismantled the counters, and disposed of the old dishwasher. Over the course of the week, they chose tile together and beadboard and lighting fixtures. They measured walls and cleaned out closets and consulted *This Old House*. Before long, they were deep into a full-on renovation project in multiple rooms throughout the house. Jack brought in his work crew to help, but the guys arrived early and always packed up by 3:00 P.M., while he and Larisa kept at it for hours more and continued to eat dinner together. Sitting in the dining room every night, with the walls still down around them, they talked.

"Have you heard from Holly?" Larisa asked at the end of the first week.

Jack leveled his gaze at her. The day after he'd moved into Elmhurst, he'd told her about the trouble he'd been having with Holly, his transgression, and the real possibility of divorce. "I'm not gonna stay forever, if that's what you're worried about."

"Do I look worried?" answered Larisa. "And who said anything about forever?"

Jack's smile vanished quickly. "I did, I guess, when I said my vows."

Larisa gave him a sympathetic moue. "People make mistakes. You and Holly have a lot of history together. She can't see past this?"

Jack shook his head. He'd gone over to take the boys out for pizza a few nights earlier, and Holly had barely even acknowledged him. "She won't talk to me. The only thing she will say is that she's not ready for me to come home yet."

"That's tough. What have you told the boys?"

Jack shrugged. "Nothing really. Only that we're taking a little space. At least she's not keeping them from me. That would really kill me."

"Of course not. She knows you're a good father."

"Better father than husband, I guess."

He winced as he rose from his chair and then headed up to bed.

Days went by and then weeks. He and Holly had been separated before, but never for very long. Jack had fully expected to crawl back after a few days. But somehow "a while" had turned into three weeks, something they'd gotten used to. Holly didn't invite him back and he didn't push for it. He was too tired or too confused or maybe just unable to face it. He didn't want to fight anymore. Then, before he knew it, they'd reached mid-October. Not at all sure where things stood, he clung to the things he knew. For years he had reserved Columbus Day weekend to take his small boat out on the water, and so he'd recruited the boys away from their video games for one last sail.

It was a crisp fall morning, a tad chilly, but full of the whitecaps and bluster any seasoned sailor would love. By the time the boys showed up on bikes around midmorning, Jack had already gotten a ride out to the mooring and brought the boat, a seventeen-foot daysailer named *Hat Trick* after the triplets, around to the dock. They left the bikes in a heap by the clubhouse and came clamoring down the ramp, trailing their bright orange life jackets behind, tugging at the sleeves of the foul-weather gear their mother had made them wear.

He watched as they climbed aboard and moved to their places, long trained in the tasks that would get them underway. His crew. Alex and Ben and Charlie. The boys shared a lot of common features—shaggy brown hair, eyes varying shades of blue—but they weren't actually identical, as many assumed when they heard the word *triplet*. Alex was the most athletic of the bunch, moving limberly from the cockpit up to the foredeck to ready the jib for rollout once they had reached the outer harbor. This same simple series of steps up to the bow would have tripped Ben up several times. He was taller than Alex and much less coordinated, with a tendency to get tangled up in his own limbs. He was the reader and writer of the group, the quietest, often taken to studying the detailed charts when Jack took them on longer sails. But now he first stowed the cooler with their lunch in the hold and then checked their gasoline supply and the outboard motor attached to the stern. Next he busied himself with dropping the centerboard and uncleating the mainsail so that Charlie would be ready to raise it when the time came. Charlie, for his part, had already untied the sail from the boom. He attached the head of it to the halyard, the line they'd use to hoist the sail, and guided the edge of the sail through the groove in the mast. He was the loudest of the three—the actor and impressionist. Now, for instance, he instructed himself and the other two at their tasks, all the while answering his own commands.

"Ready to hoist that main? Aye, aye, skipper. OK then, matey, hoist away. Hand over fist now, steady as she goes, all hands on deck, don't forget to batten down those hatches, ye salty dogs!"

Alex and Ben watched with amused eyes, but said nothing, permitting Charlie to go on with his prattle uninterrupted. Jack took it all in proudly from his place by the tiller. Yes, the three were distinct for sure. Still, there was a connectedness to their existence, a fluency to their interactions that was extraordinary to watch. They moved together like a line of finely trained hockey players, anticipating one another, responding to the same rhythm, keeping one another in check. And all the while communicating with their own language of gestures and grunts and facial expressions. Each was distinct yet each had a bit of the other in him, making Jack wonder how they might evolve once they were apart for any length of time. At college, for instance—he was determined, they would go—would they explore other sides of themselves? Would Alex become more Ben? Would Ben exhibit more Charlie? Or might they all resemble Jack? Perhaps entirely new entities would emerge. It was mind-boggling, Jack thought, as they all settled into their places on the cockpit lockers that served as seating, and headed under power down the gullet to the outer harbor.

Before long they were under sail. The sky had grayed a bit, but with gusts coming out of the north, the day was perfect for heading upwind toward the cove at Lighthouse Island. The boys, he knew, liked to go fast. So once they got going, Jack kept the boat close-hauled, pointing her upwind and reining in the mainsheet so that the sail stayed taut and full and the centerboard began to hum. The boys hopped up on the rails and hooked themselves over the side, hiking out to keep the boat from heeling, letting the swells spray up at them. Jack hadn't seen the boys as much as he would have liked and he relished it now. Though Holly had never quite gotten her sea legs under her, the boys were as comfortable as he was on a boat and it was a joy to see, their hair tousled with seawater, their cheeks ruddied by the wind. Holly had tried, he knew, and that meant a lot to him. But even with the Dramamine, she got sick every time and eventually stopped going. Thus, it had become a thing he only did with the boys.

If truthful to himself, Jack had to admit he liked the separation from Holly, both out on the water and over the past three weeks since she'd kicked him out. He felt more relaxed than he had in years, enjoying the freedom to move about as he liked. At home, Holly cataloged his every move, as though he were one of the toddlers from her day care. Jesus, he couldn't scratch his nose without her wondering why. But though he welcomed his freedom, he hated being away from the boys, who he'd only seen on Wednesday nights—Holly's bowling night—and sporadically over the weekends for a few restaurant meals. Though they knew where he was living, they hadn't come to Elmhurst yet and they didn't ask about Larisa. Boys, Jack knew, didn't talk about things, especially if you went right out and asked them. A generalization, though one he'd found to be true. But if you engaged them in an activity, they might get around to expressing something. And this was what he was hoping for as he coached them calmly out on the vast ocean.

"Trim the jib, Charlie; let's get rid of the luff. Alex, secure that line." Charlie yanked on the jib line and the sail stopped flapping. Alex deftly coiled the loose rope around his elbow then hung it from the hook above the hold. Charlie smiled broadly from where he sat and shimmied over toward Jack on the bench. Jack clapped an arm over his shoulder and signaled for Ben to take the tiller. "There you go, Benbo; now hold your mark."

Ben fixed his course and before long the others took a turn at the helm too, tacking their way toward the lighthouse, calling out the familiar "Ready about, hard-a-lee." They sailed for the better part of an hour and then when Charlie let out a loud, chest-thumping, Tarzan-like "I'm hungry" crow, they anchored in the shelter of the island to eat some lunch. Ben pulled out the cooler and distributed the sandwiches, presenting each boy with his preference. Alex liked mayonnaise; Ben preferred mustard; Charlie almost always went with PB&J. Watching them chow down, Jack felt his own stomach growl.

"Hey," he said, "don't suppose your mother packed something nice for me?"

They froze mid-chew, consulted one another with glances,

and then came back at him with apologetic smirks. Alex tried to hand over a half, but Jack brushed it away. "Never mind, sailor, the old man can starve. Keeps the belly from getting too big."

They giggled as he patted his stomach, and then returned to their lunches. Jack lay back on the bench, legs stretched out in front of him. He took in the scene, the beauty of it, the wonder. Before him, the beautiful gray-green ocean endlessly sifted the rocks on the pebbled shore; the trees shook the russet leaves from their tops; above him, the iron-bellied clouds began to part. He relaxed into the heat of the emerging sun and the gentle roll of the anchored boat, settling in so nicely that he might have drifted off to sleep had one of the boys not spoken.

It was Ben, uncharacteristically, who broke the silence, head cocked curiously to the side. "What are you doing with that lady?" he asked.

Jack followed his son's gaze to the house in the distance, on the edge of the sea. He had forgotten for once about Elmhurst, but there she was, more visible now that the leaves on the trees had thinned, the few remaining ones weaving themselves ferociously against the wind.

"What do you mean?" said Jack.

"That lady," said Ben again, pointing at Elmhurst.

"Mommy says you're married to that house," Alex mumbled.

"That lady?" Jack repeated. "Come on, Benny, you've known Larisa your whole entire life. You can't say her name?"

Charlie chimed in now as well. "Are you gonna marry her?"

Jack felt the question land in his gut. God, he thought, kids were like that. You could spend all day beating around the bush trying to protect their emotions and then they just came out and said it. Sure, they overstated things, but their instincts were right on target, getting to the crux of the matter in no time at all. He scuttled into a sitting position to face them. "What? Of course I'm not gonna marry her. I'm married to your mother. Nobody's getting married."

In truth, the friendship between him and Larisa had deepened. There was no denying it. That pull he'd first felt when she'd opened the door had only intensified over the past weeks as they'd worked on the house together. True, he'd overheard her multiple times on the phone trying to patch things up with Brent. But the guy had yet to show up and Jack wasn't holding his breath. Just this past week, Jack had taught her how to use the electric drill. He showed her how to fit the drill bit into the chuck and then tighten it. And then he'd leaned over her, smelling the perfume of her hair and feeling her breath on his neck as he demonstrated how to keep the drill still and push firmly, but steadily, against it. But no, he couldn't think about that now. The boys were watching him, looking like they wanted to say more. He raised his eyebrows, encouraging them. Finally Charlie asked what the others had been silently urging him to ask. "Are you and Mommy getting a divorce?"

He'd sensed it coming and still Jack felt his muscles tense. He turned to them, unsure of how to respond. Honesty, he decided, was the best approach. "I don't know. I hope not. Your mother and I just need a little time. To figure things out. But I can tell you one thing for sure. Nobody's getting married. And certainly not me and Larisa."

But even as he said it, something in him balked. It struck him that he'd known Holly for as long as he'd known Larisa, but the relationships felt poles apart. There was a certain familiarity with Larisa, a recognition and ease to their interactions. Why, he wondered, couldn't he have that same symbiosis with Holly? Was it possible, Jack wondered, to be somebody with one person and somebody completely different with another? There was a side of himself he just didn't know how to share with Holly, try as he might. When he told her about the symphonies he'd listened to with Ursula and the classic novels he'd read, an interesting article in *The Atlantic*, she only stared at him, her eyes glassed over. She didn't tune into that frequency. She preferred him to be rugged, unaffected. But what if that other side—the side that enjoyed music and literature and fine wine—what if that side was the core of him, *the essence*, and he'd only been pretending with Holly all this time? He shuddered. It was too much to think about.

"Alex," he called, "weigh the anchor and let's get underway again."

He watched his son haul up the anchor and fasten the line in a figure eight around the cleat. The crew settled back into their positions and Jack brought the boat around and surveyed the scene. The boys were quieter now, more fragile, and he couldn't help but flash back to the time at which they were first born. They'd come seven weeks early, in the middle of April, weighing a meager three pounds apiece and each with premature lungs. They were so tiny—one hand could fit within the diameter of a quarter—that he couldn't believe they would ever make it out of the NICU. At the same time, he couldn't allow himself to imagine they wouldn't. A month later they came home and Holly, she had been amazing, tending to all three babies like it was nothing, coaxing them slowly forward. He marveled at the things she could do that he couldn't, the tenderness she shared, cradling them softly in her arms, quieting them with just her touch as she palmed their precious heads and kissed their vulnerable brows. And oh—Holly had been so beautiful then, her blond hair feathered to her shoulders, her blue eyes bright, a radiant light that just emanated from her pores. She'd been so sweet and earnest and excited, wife and mother and lover all in one.

He and Holly had become a team. They were exhausted but they were exhausted together, falling asleep in a heap on the living room floor. There had been a camaraderie to it, an alliance. And that was the thing he got hung up on when he dared to think about the end of the marriage. Holly wasn't just anybody; she was the mother of his children. He couldn't have survived that first year without her. This was no small thing. *We're all in this together,* she had said, and he had repeated it like an oath. He had a responsibility to this family, a moral obligation. Fifteen years. He couldn't just walk away. And yet he was so damn tired of trying to make it work.

Jack sighed. As he mulled it all around in his head, he thought of something that had been bugging him. Something he'd learned from Larisa during their conversation together over the past few weeks. They'd been sitting at the breakfast table, trading pages of the morning paper, sipping from matching coffee mugs. Remarkably, he remembered doing the same thing years earlier with Ursula. It was strange, he knew, sharing a meal like that with an elderly woman. He and Holly rarely had breakfast together, each of them eating on the go. They never shared the newspaper. Holly would've looked at him cross-eyed if he'd tried. Thinking about it, he posed a question to Larisa. "Why didn't your great-aunt ever marry?"

Larisa looked up, surprised. "She never told you?"

"Told me what?" he asked.

"That she was jilted. Not quite at the altar. But still. She'd been keen on this one local guy, but the family felt he wasn't worthy. So they shipped her off on a summer cruise to Europe. Soon after she returned, she became engaged to one of the neighbors—a proper match from a prominent family. But it was never meant to be. He broke it off months before the wedding. By then, she was almost past the marrying age, practically a spinster. She was single for the rest of her life."

Jack took a minute to digest the new information, facets of it dawning slowly on him—had he been a kind of stand-in groom for Aunt Ursula? God, that was weird. No, no, he reassured himself: he'd been more like a stand-in son. At least, that was how it had felt to him. He loved his dear parents, but the two of them had both worked so hard trying to support the family, raise the kids, that they'd had little energy at the end of the day to do much beyond getting a meal on the table. So when Ursula began to introduce him to all of her interests, he reveled in it—the novels, the teatimes, *The Threepenny Opera*. They hadn't talked much about the other parts of their lives. He couldn't imagine during which conversation she would have brought up her failed engagement and yet he felt excluded. But no matter. Everyone had secrets and it was none of his business, really.

Back on the boat, on the long downwind reach now back to the channel, he and the boys decided to fly the spinnaker, letting the great sail balloon out in front, tugging them in. Many people, Jack knew, liked a showy spinnaker, but he had chosen a simple one. It had a thick solid blue stripe down the middle with red borders at each side, looking like a family crest as it billowed with the wind. He loved the look of a boat under a spinnaker. Now they were really sailing. It was glorious.

Charlie pulled the mouth of the spinnaker bag over his head like a bridal veil and then released it, his arms spread to the sides.

"Nobody's getting married!" he called in falsetto from the prow, and they all laughed at his antics. But before long, they passed South Buoy and came into the harbor and it was time to de-rig.

"OK, boys, let's furl the main," Jack called. They worked together to bundle the sail and tie it neatly against the boom. They punched the spinnaker back into its bag and rolled the jib. Later, after he'd pulled the boat from the water, Jack would take all the sails, spray them down, and lay them on the lawn to dry before packing them away for the winter. They pulled up the centerboard, secured the loose lines, and went back under power. But instead of heading down the gullet and into the inner harbor, they motored to the public boat launch where Jack had already parked his truck with the trailer.

As they approached, Jack called out the same joke he always did when they packed it in for the day and returned to port.

"Hey, boys, what did the skipper say to his crew when they ran aground?" Without a beat, he answered the joke for them. "Don't worry, mates, we're all in the same boat!"

He turned to see the mock exasperation and laughter in their eyes. But something had changed in the mood, he could tell by the glances between them; they had seen something he hadn't. He swiveled toward the shore and then spotted Holly at the end of the road that led to the landing, headed their way. The expression on her face told him that she was not pleased. Oh Christ.

As the boat softly beached herself on the sand, they all jumped out and into the water. The boys held her steady as Jack jogged over to his truck and then slowly backed the trailer into the water next to the boat. By the time the boys had tugged *Hat Trick* around and positioned her to be pulled ashore, Holly had reached them, her hands beckoning for Alex and Ben and Charlie to hurry it up.

"You're late," she said to Jack. "I had to put the bikes on the rack by myself."

Jack lifted his arms, exasperated. "Come on, honey. It's only a few extra minutes."

She glared. "I'm not your honey."

"Jesus, Holly, what's with you? It's like you don't want anyone else to have any fun if you're not having some yourself."

"Who's not having fun?" she snapped as the boys bustled away up the street toward her car. "I'm having fun. I love doing all the laundry. And solving math problems and cooking dinner and cleaning up and making breakfast and packing the lunches for *three preteen kids*."

Jack waited for the boys to be out of earshot. "OK, OK. I get it. You do everything. So let me come home."

She paused a beat and then shook her head. "Nothing's changed." She turned and then headed up the road after the boys.

Jack thought back to his conversation with Larisa. *People don't change,* he had told her. Over the past few weeks, in between drywall and plumbing and trips to the lumberyard, Jack had listened to Larisa's conciliatory calls with Brent. She seemed genuine in her desire to patch things up. And still he had to resist the urge to seduce her. Nothing intimate had happened between him and Larisa and yet it lingered there, the tension between them. He could sense it about to happen. He resisted. He wanted to be good. A committed father, a faithful husband . . . and yet. He sighed. It was true: people didn't change. He still believed that. But circumstances could. They had been happy once, he and Holly, a team. They could be happy once again. Damn it, he just wished he could figure out how.

CHAPTER FIVE

Larisa hadn't intended to move into Elmhurst when she'd arrived in late fall, but then she hadn't expected to find so many projects around the house. Sure, Jack had kept things in good working order over the years, but Aunt Ursula had forbidden him, she knew, from making more modern improvements. Though frivolous in some matters, Ursula had been excruciatingly frugal in others—a Yankee through and through—and so the house was grand, but also fussy, old-fashioned. No dishwasher, no microwave, no cable hookup—decidedly lacking in basic amenities. The tall glass-front kitchen cabinets displayed sagging shelves and a cracked veneer. The original wood counter had been replaced in the late eighties with a cheap geometric-patterned laminate rather than granite, and the bronze bin pulls were scratched and missing screws. Though the electric had been converted to circuit breakers, none of the rooms had enough outlets and few of them were grounded. The wood floors had been sanded too many times, the tongue and groove showing in spots. The window seat on the second-floor landing required a new cushion, the current one being moth-eaten and marred with water stains. The laundry was still in the basement, the chandelier was missing crystals, the chimneys were coated in soot. The list went on and on. Of course, Larisa had known all this, having been in the house many times; but she'd never had to look at it with a seller's eye before. At first she thought she'd only tackle a few projects, fix up the dining room and the kitchen, just enough to convince modern buyers they weren't in over their heads. But once she'd started, she found it hard to stop. She'd spent so much time in this house over the years but knew almost nothing about how it worked. She had the interest and the means—a trust fund and some savings as well—and she had Jack on board to help her see it through.

Jack. Larisa knew Jack hadn't intended to move in either, at least not for any length of time. But now he'd stayed two months already and didn't seem to be going anywhere anytime soon. Thanksgiving had come and gone. Jack had gone to his parents' house; she had gone into the city to visit friends and then on to her Somerville apartment, one of several such missions to replenish her supply of clothes and toiletries. Jack had made a few trips home as well, though he seemed to keep a leaner stock. Did he think he'd be back in his own house soon? Larisa somehow doubted it. He'd told her that he planned to quit his job as caretaker once the renovations were complete, but she didn't buy that, either. He seemed to love Elmhurst too much to quit.

"Why are you so into this house?" Larisa had asked him

one night as they were finishing dinner, the walls around them newly exposed. "It's like an obsession with you."

Jack smiled. "I don't know. Not every guy can work on an old house. It takes patience, care. You have to pry things open, take it slowly." He stood and ran his palm gently down one of the hardwood studs that framed the walls, and then turned to look at her. "You have to find out what's hiding behind the walls."

Larisa felt the intensity of his gaze. She held it for a moment and then looked away. Her eyes fluttered from one end of the open wall to the other. She hugged her arms protectively around her torso. "But aren't you afraid you'll do something wrong? What if you pry too hard? Couldn't you mess everything up?"

"Sure, but that's part of the challenge. You have to use your brain, trust your instincts. I take things slowly, carefully. Notice how she responds. The house will tell you what's going on if you look and listen carefully enough." He returned to his seat and sat back, watching her.

Larisa bit her lower lip. "Do you ever get tired of it?"

Jack shook his head. "My house, yes. This house, no. How about you?"

"What about me?"

"Don't you love this house as much as I do?"

Larisa smiled. She felt, suddenly, the desire to reach out and grab his hand, that same strong hand that had touched the wall stud, but she resisted. She rested her chin on one hand instead. "I guess so, but in a different way. There's a comfort here for me. Even with all this work we're doing, the house will largely stay the same. It's formal, but predictable, steady." She pointed toward the living room. "That picture will always be there. The couch fabric will always be Wedgwood blue. The library ladder will always squeak a little in its track. And there are so many memories here. Memories from my relatives—my mother, my father, my great-aunt—everyone who's been here before me. I like to think about them here celebrating birthdays and weddings and anniversaries. But now that they're all gone, it feels sort of sad. Like the memories will fade away into the walls to be forgotten."

"You'll remember," Jack assured her. "And you'll get married someday, maybe have some kids. And then you'll fill the house with the new memories."

Larisa lowered her head and peeked up at him. "Will I?"

She still hadn't come clean about the wedding ruse. Jack knew the truth, but no one else. A few days earlier Mrs. Muldoon had dropped by with a few bridal magazines. Larisa knew the wedding wasn't real, would never be real. But now that she'd bought a dress and thought about flowers—ah, those peonies in early June—she found herself captivated by what a wedding—*her* wedding—could be like. She hadn't expected to feel that way. The magazines showcased all facets of the Big Day and on a whim, she began to flag her favorite pages with orange Post-its—flower arrangements and bridesmaid dresses and handheld bouquets. She'd picked her signature colors (green and gold), and she'd even occasionally involved Jack in a few of her musings—this tie or that one, colored linens or plain?—so that the pretend wedding had become a bit of a running joke between them. He teased her about it and she knew he found it all a bit absurd. But here was the thing. Even if it was all a joke, even if she didn't get married in June—no, she knew she wouldn't—she'd have a starting place for when she did get married someday.

"Sure, you will," said Jack in response to her question. "And then the legacy will go on."

He stood and strode into the foyer, opened the drawer to the front hall table, and came back with a pencil—the same pencil Larisa had used to circle her June 2 date. Jack pulled her up from her chair and over to the wall.

"Here," he told her. "Sign your name and then I'll sign mine. And then we'll both live on behind the walls of Elmhurst forever."

Larisa felt a flicker of guilt that she hadn't told him about the potential sale of the house. She paused but then took the pencil and signed and watched as he did the same.

Now December had come and the first snows with it. They'd hung the Christmas lights on the front yard boxwoods, sat together in the evenings, stirring cinnamon sticks into apple cider and paging through the bridal magazines. As Larisa walked from Main Street back toward Elmhurst, she could imagine her life going on like this with Jack forever. But, no. Over the months of working on the house together, she'd recognized something in his eyes. A longing so strong that she could feel him tracking her from room to room. She knew where this could lead. And she had decided that she would *not* engage. She'd seen the photos of his wife and kids on his bedside table, and besides, the last thing she needed was a rebound. She needed to get her own life together and not go about wrecking his. So even though over the past few months she had felt a strong desire to touch him—just to hold his hand and feel its warmth or pull his head onto her shoulder and stroke his soft hair—she had resisted. It had been hard, very hard, especially with so much playful banter between them, but so far she'd succeeded.

She'd left the house this morning after breakfast to deposit her unemployment check at the ATM downtown, and then she'd compulsively picked up another bridal magazine at the local convenience store. She'd surprised even herself with this guilty pleasure, but she relished it as well. The magazine was concealed in a plastic bag that swung against her shins as she walked, but she could already anticipate the feeling of cracking it open, scanning the slick pages for possible images to incorporate into her vision, small details that would resonate in exactly the same way the dress had resonated. There was something incredibly fun, enchanting, about acting like a kid, planning her perfect imaginary party.

Passing Andy's Service Station on her way back to Elmhurst, she forgot about her fantasy for a moment and glanced up at the graying sky. The forecast called for snow, four to six inches starting late afternoon and continuing into the evening. The air had the wet and muffled fullness that descends before a snowfall, a hush on the street as people gathered themselves to hunker down inside.

"Storm's coming," called Andy, coming out from behind an idling Buick that was beginning to pull away from the pump. He lifted his eyes to the clouds and then settled them back on her again, a spirited grin spreading across his cracked and brittle lips. Amazing that he was still out here at his age. Larisa liked Andy. When she was a kid, he'd shown her how to put air in the tires of her bicycle, always taking the time to test the pressure with his handheld gauge.

She walked over and gave her best mock pout. "Ugh, I know. The older I get, the less I like it."

Andy shook his head. "Nope, not me. I love a good snow. Feels nice to be homebound now and then, take life at a slower pace. I'll never be a snowbird." He cocked his head and pointed a finger toward her as though remembering something. "Speaking of which. How are your parents? Wintering in Palm Springs, someone said?"

Larisa froze. Had it been Teddy she'd told that to, the day she'd signed on for the flowers? Another lie.

"They're fine," she stammered. "I should call them actually. Thanks for reminding me."

"Well, isn't that just what old friends are for?" He grinned again and put an arm around her shoulders, pulling her in. "And hey, I understand congratulations are in order."

Larisa shot him a questioning frown, genuinely confused. "For what?"

"For what?" Andy nudged her with his elbow. "I bet hearts were breaking all over Essex County when they heard you're all signed up for that wedding come spring."

"Oh, that." She wriggled out of his grip and rolled her eyes, feeling the heat on her cheeks.

"Now don't get all embarrassed. You'll make a beautiful bride," Andy continued. "And hey, I was wondering, might you need some kind of a getaway car for after the ceremony? The old Rolls has been sitting in the bay at home for far too long. I used to take Ursula out for a spin when business was slow. But it's a shame to just let it sit there."

"Oh, Andy, that's so nice . . . ," Larisa started but stopped, not knowing what to say. It was one thing to keep the wedding delusion going for herself; it was another thing entirely to involve even more people in her lies. But again, Andy didn't notice her hesitancy.

"You drive stick, right?" he went on. "Why don't you tool around in it for a few days? I just had her tuned up and the old girl runs like magic. She's a classic. The 1979 Silver Shadow II."

Larisa shook her head and looked skyward. "But the snow."

"Oh, nonsense. That'll be gone in a day or so. I'll drop the car over later this afternoon, settle it in the garage. That way, you can just take her out when you're ready. She's either gonna sit in my garage or yours. What's the difference?"

Larisa knew she should decline. Even if she was actually planning a wedding, she didn't need to test-drive the getaway car. This sort of thing, she thought, would only happen in a small town, where people were too trusting and didn't have anything better to do. But she *had* always wanted to drive a vintage car, and well, when someone was offering a Rolls, how could you turn it down? *Larisa Pearl and the Silver Shadow.* It sounded like a mystery novel. She felt a thrill run through her.

"You're sure?" she finally said.

Andy shrugged and gave his widest grin yet. "Why not? I know where you live. Speaking of which, is that where you and your future husband plan to end up? Elmhurst? After you get married?"

Larisa hesitated. She hadn't told anyone about her plans to sell the house and she wasn't about to now, knowing that if word got out, it would spread all over town before sundown. God, she thought, what would Aunt Ursula say in a situation like this, one that called for some sort of answer?

"Well, that remains to be seen," she finally said, though it wasn't quite right. Her main reluctance lay not in the lie to Andy, but rather in the fact that she still had not even told

Jack her true intentions, her plan to sell. He'd been such an indispensable part of Elmhurst for years, and now he'd been so integral to the renovations that she just didn't know how to break it to him. She knew she should have told him right away, as soon as he'd signed on to the work, but stupidly she'd waited and it had just gotten harder the more time passed. He'd be upset, of course, and she wasn't sure how to weather that. And also, the truth was, the more work they did together, the more conflicted she actually felt about a possible sale. She'd become more invested, both emotionally and financially, than she'd expected. She'd sunk so much time and money in and she knew most people would think it a shame to part with it. But no, she told herself firmly, no. She wasn't going to end up like Aunt Ursula. The house was much too much to manage, especially without her mother. She was going to sell and move on and that was that. She'd have to bite the bullet and tell Jack. Today. Yes, today, she decided as she waved her goodbye and thanks to Andy, was definitely the day to tell Jack.

She arrived back at the house and found him in the stripped kitchen, cutting wood he'd laid over a set of sawhorses. The noise of the saw masked her arrival and so she had a chance to study him before making her presence known. He bent his long, lean body over the project, pressing one hand onto the supported section of the board, his fingers splayed evenly against it. His eyes held their focus on the saw and the shorter piece of wood, unwavering from the task at hand. As always, she felt something pulse inside her as she watched him work. She fingered the spine of the bridal magazine in its plastic bag and stepped into his line of sight. Jack switched off the circular saw and looked up at her from behind his safety glasses.

"Coming together," he said, gesturing around the shell of the kitchen. He pushed the glasses up to the top of his head and gave an encouraging smile.

"Is it?" She stepped back and assessed. To her, it still seemed all torn apart. "Not that it's really going to happen—ha ha—but it would be hard to imagine a wedding here in six months."

Jack scuffed his feet into the sawdust and leaned against the counter, smiling. "Forget the house. You don't even have a groom." He opened his arms to his sides as though offering himself.

Larisa shrugged. They were both joking again about the wedding that would never happen, but he was throwing something else at her as well. A vibe that she chose to ignore. Jack was so fragile still that if she gave the smallest opening, he would make his move. She couldn't let that happen. So when she responded, she avoided eye contact and moved farther toward the other side of the room. "You never know. I might be able to patch things up with Brent."

"Sure." Jack stepped closer, blocking her exit. He leveled his gaze and she caught his suggestive glance for a second even despite her attempt to escape it. "But is that what you want?"

Larisa gave a flustered smile, suddenly remembering the new bridal magazine. She pulled it now from the plastic bag and used it to bat her way out of the room and into the foyer. She stood and breathed for a moment. The day after she and Jack had started working on the house together, Larisa had been so frightened of her feelings for him that she'd actually called Brent. She hadn't spoken to him in over three weeks, but he'd answered on the first ring, sounding interested to hear what she had to say. On the call, she'd done something she didn't often do. She sat in the front parlor, the starched drapes, seafoam green, calming her as she gathered her courage. She had apologized for saying those awful things. For telling him he'd never amount to anything. For saying he was no better than a brainless monkey, swinging around in those trees. For yelling that he had no class, no style, no sense of self. She'd just flat-out apologized, making no excuses. It had been humbling, really. She had felt better about herself immediately.

"Listen," he'd told her. "I'm not ashamed of who I am, how I grew up. I'm not as cultured as your college friends. But I work hard, I pay my bills, I'm an honest man. This is who I am. You can take it or leave it."

Then something else had happened that she hadn't expected. Larisa felt that maybe she might take it, after all. Brent *did* work hard. She respected this about him. He was still helping his younger brothers go through college and he still sent his mother a little extra money for rent when she needed it. And Larisa knew his affection toward her was sincere. He could be a bit goofy, but when he swept her up in his arms, he was never faking it. My God, she thought, here I thought I was being the wrong person with Brent, that it was all my fault. But maybe all we needed was a little space and a little honesty. The call had ended with forgiveness on both sides and they had spoken at least half a dozen more times since. Now that she wasn't living with him, she found that she liked chatting with him, getting to know him in a way she hadn't before.

"How's your mother these days?" he had asked on one such call.

"Too far away," answered Larisa. "And yet I can't bring myself to visit."

"New Hampshire is not that far. *Go*. You'll feel better."

"Every time I go, I feel worse."

"Oh, honey." Brent sighed. "I can go with you if you want. I'll come to Elmhurst to pick you up and we can drive up together."

Larisa stiffened. He was the only one she'd told about the probable sale of the house, but she still hadn't told him about the impulsive purchase of the wedding dress or the June date she'd set with Teddy. And while she had told him that she'd recruited Jack to help her with the house renovations, she'd conveniently neglected to mention that Jack was also living with her at Elmhurst. If Brent came up to visit, did that mean they were getting back together? Something still lingered in her mind, something Jack had said when she'd been questioning her relationship with Brent. *Two years is long enough. . . . If you really wanted to marry him, wouldn't you have known it by now?*

"Let's just take this slow," she had finally responded that day on the phone, and they'd left it at that.

Larisa peeked back into the kitchen. Jack hadn't moved from his spot on the dusty floor. He gave her a quizzical look as their eyes met, still waiting for the response to his question. But instead of answering it, she flicked her head to the side, gesturing toward the front door.

"Come on," she said. "Let's get out of this place. I'll treat you to lunch."

They drove together in Jack's pickup to the Tidewater Tavern, a local joint perched on the edge of a sprawling marsh on the outskirts of town. The clouds were low and dark, gathering in great bunches overhead. The wind had kicked up and the air had grown moist and palpable. The approaching storm was still several hours away but coming fast. They bustled into the restaurant and followed a hostess to a small two-seater by the window. Larisa looked back at the bar as she sat; Jack raised a hand to some of the regulars.

"The *Tread*water Tavern," commented Larisa. "That's what Aunt Ursula used to call this place. Where people come to tread water for a while until they figure out what's next."

Jack acknowledged the comment with a tip of his head, but she could see that he wasn't entirely amused. "They're just people like everyone else," he said.

They ordered and then the waitress brought rolls, leaning over to give Jack a good glimpse of her cleavage. "Hey, honey, haven't seen you for a while," she purred, then swiveled and strutted away. Jack didn't answer but his cheeks flushed red.

"I've lived in this town too damn long," he finally muttered, picking up his butter knife and reaching for a roll.

"Exactly why I can't wait to leave," answered Larisa.

Jack paused mid-spread of the butter. "You're leaving? I thought you planned to stay at Elmhurst."

She froze. Damn it, she'd planned to tell him today about the sale, but this was not how it was supposed to come out. "Well, eventually, I guess. I haven't totally figured it out yet."

"Huh." Jack bit into the bread and chewed, holding his stare. "How's it going with Brent?"

Larisa shrugged. "OK. He's a good guy and he has so much potential. I just wish he would realize it."

Jack shook his head and gave her a look. "You don't marry a person because of his potential."

Larisa gazed back at him. "Why did you marry Holly?"

"That was different. We were young and stupid and horny."

Larisa felt a throb in her groin when he said the word *horny*. She moved her hands from her lap to the table and held them there, feeling her own cheeks warm with color.

Jack kept on with his talk. "We had no idea what it would mean to be married. There's the wedding. And then there's the marriage. Two very different things. One lasts a day, the other a lifetime." He paused. "Or not."

Larisa nodded. The waitress strolled back over and set down their meals. They both started to eat and then Larisa broke the silence, telling Jack about the compulsive purchase of the new bridal magazine and about her conversation with Andy, his offer to lend her the Rolls and her acceptance of it.

"Why do I act like that?" She shook her head at herself. "Pretending this stupid wedding is a possibility, imagining it into being."

"Isn't it obvious?" Jack laid down his fork. "You're lonely. You want companionship. You want . . ."

He let the sentence drift long enough so that Larisa finally filled the silence. "What?"

"You want what I want." He corrected himself when the words fell too hard. "What everyone wants. To share yourself with another person, to see yourself reflected there."

She kept her gaze on him. Is that what she wanted? The wind began to blow at the windows, rattling the panes in their frames. Larisa pulled her arms around her elbows and shivered. She knew she should look away, before Jack said something she didn't want to hear. But he had been right: she wanted to share herself with another person—him—physically, mentally, entirely.

Jack leaned in. "I have to say something. Something I've wanted to say since I've moved into Elmhurst. There's something between us. I know you feel it too."

Larisa nodded cautiously, still determined not to engage. "We've become good friends, you and me."

"No," said Jack sternly. "It's more than that. We've been playing house for over two months now. I don't think I can pretend anymore."

Larisa pointed at the wedding band he still wore on his finger. "You need to go back to your wife."

Jack fingered the ring. "She hates me."

Larisa rolled her eyes. "She doesn't hate you. She's just mad. Women get mad and stay mad."

Jack shrugged. "Even if I could win her back, that doesn't change the fact that there's something between us."

"There's nothing between us." Larisa looked down at her plate, knowing it wasn't true. "Stop trying to seduce me. I don't want to be seduced."

Jack shook his head and leaned back, resigned. "Seduce you. That's not at all what I've been trying to do. I've just been trying to be honest about something we *both* feel. If you want me to shut up about it, then I will. But it doesn't change anything."

He rose abruptly and gestured toward the waitress for the bill. Larisa sighed, releasing the tension that had built up inside her. *What if I'm wrong?* she thought. *What if we both feel this thing that we only ever feel for each other? What if Aunt Ursula had married her true love, following her heart instead of listening to her parents?* But Larisa pushed the thoughts away and followed Jack out of the restaurant. The ride back to Elmhurst was uncomfortable, but they got through it. Before long they'd settled back into the work in the dining room. Jack held the slabs of Sheetrock as she knelt and secured them to the wall, covering up the names they'd penciled there. She and Jack were inches apart, but Larisa relaxed a little, feeling that they had both aired something back there at the tavern and that they'd moved on. She still hadn't told him about her intention to sell, but she'd get to it, she would. And then, just when she thought she was in the clear, that nothing would happen between them, she felt his eyes on her again.

"Hey," he said, grinning, "you've gotten pretty good with that drill."

And without a beat, she had turned, a self-amused smile spreading across her lips as the joke escaped. "Oh yeah? You should see me screw."

It was such a cheesy thing to say, the words flying out of her mouth before she could think, and it could have been the cheesiest of moments. But after Jack's features had settled from the initial surprise, he gave her such a look of yearning, his long lashes softly framing his dark eyes, that it triggered something in her. She recognized this same feeling in herself and so instead of turning away, she held his gaze, inviting him. He reached for her chin, holding it gently between his thumb and forefinger, and pulled her into a long and tender kiss. She sunk into it, the gentle yet firm weight of his lips against hers. There was a rhythm to the kiss, a sense of being in sync. She had expected this and still it sent such a buzz through her body that when they finally pulled apart, she felt immediately impatient for more. He smiled at her and stroked her cheek with one finger.

Then came the knock at the door. They both turned to face it and Jack broke the silence. "Expecting someone?"

Larisa shook her head.

She heard another knock and then a deep voice. "Larisa?"

She gasped. "Oh my God, it's Brent." She wiped her lips and staggered to her feet, stumbling toward the entryway. She paused before opening the door, sneaking a look back at Jack, who had followed her over to the foyer. In response to her panic, it seemed, he had gone back to retrieve the drill, and now stood holding it several feet behind her as though eager to demonstrate no foul play. Larisa swung the door open and faced Brent.

He stood there, a meager fistful of daisies in one hand, a nervous smile frozen on his face. "Hi."

"You didn't tell me you were coming," Larisa chastised loudly, the comment directed to Jack, before enveloping Brent in a hug, avoiding the kiss he seemed to be going for.

"I wanted to surprise you," he said, giving a full grin now. "Surprise!"

"Wow." Larisa accepted the daisies. "You didn't have to drive all the way up here right before the storm."

He shrugged. "Well, work's slow this time of year, so I took a few weeks off. Might be kind of nice to get snowed in together. You know, catch up a bit." He relaxed into a sheepish smile and Larisa had to fight to keep the look of panic from fluttering across her features. Now, of all times, was not the time to be snowed in with Brent. Jack and Brent, both at Elmhurst?

Larisa stepped out onto the front walk and surveyed the sky again. She turned to see Jack hovering in the doorway, so she gathered herself and introduced him to Brent. The two shook hands. Larisa was about to usher everyone into the parlor when she spotted Teddy Beauregard and Mrs. Muldoon headed up the drive, each with something in hand.

"Oh," said Brent, following her gaze and squinting down at them, "there's that guy from the flower shop. He helped me remember how to get here."

Larisa's eyes flared, her heart beginning to pound. "You told him you were coming here?"

"Sure. How do you think I found the place? And that woman was in his shop too. She said she had something for you."

Jack raised his eyebrows at Larisa. "This should be interesting."

Larisa shot him a pointed glare but said nothing. She waved tentatively at the pair as they approached. Teddy arrived first, flapping a folder full of paper.

"Boy, are you tough to get on the phone," he said, pausing to catch his breath. "Now, sweetheart, I know June second is still months away, but it's good to get a head start. I put together a modest proposal. And yes, I know we're friends, but I will still need a deposit."

"Of course," said Larisa, looking back at both Brent, who seemed oblivious, and Jack, who seemed entertained. She reached to receive the paperwork.

"Naturally, there will be changes." Teddy leaned in toward Brent in a mock whisper. "I've never known a bride who didn't change her mind about ten times a week. But at least this will get us started."

Before Brent could respond, Mrs. Muldoon edged her way in and began to unpack a collection of veils from the box under her arm. "Darling, I know how busy you are, so I just brought a few for you to toy with."

"Thank you," whispered Larisa, eager to send her and Teddy back down the hill. But before she could, Mrs. Muldoon homed in on Brent. Watching, Larisa was reminded of the rooster weather vane perched atop the community center, its brass beak snapping forward in response to the wind.

"And you must be the mysterious beau," Mrs. Muldoon declared. "*Where* have you been?"

"I don't think anyone's ever accused me of being mysterious before." Brent laughed and reached out a hand for her to shake. "I'm just Brent."

"You're much more than 'just Brent,'" protested Mrs. Muldoon. She brought her hands to her hips and pursed her lips as though scolding a naughty child. "The whole darn town's been waiting to meet you."

Brent's brows fluttered as he tried to make sense of the moment. Larisa shook her head at him and rolled her eyes toward Mrs. Muldoon, trying to convey that there had been a wacky misunderstanding that she would explain later. But then Mrs. Muldoon selected one of the gauzy veils from her box and draped it over Larisa's head. "Oh, doesn't she look beautiful?" She turned to get Brent's reaction.

Larisa smiled stiffly under the veil, trying to decide whether she could somehow pass all this off as a bit of fun. But as she smoothed the veil out of her face and offered a sheepish grin, she saw a look of realization begin to come into Brent's eyes. He glanced from Mrs. Muldoon to Larisa and then back at Jack. "I don't get it. . . . Wait . . . is somebody getting married?"

Mrs. Muldoon let out a hearty forced laugh. "Ha ha!" She turned to Larisa and nudged her in the ribs. "Handsome *and* has a sense of humor! Now don't you worry, Brent: most grooms get cold feet somewhere along the way, but you couldn't do better than our Larisa. She's a keeper, for sure."

"Right," said Brent, complete confusion consuming his features. "That's why I came."

Larisa swept the veil from her head and reached for Brent's hand. "Well, thanks, everyone, for coming by," she said, an attempt to dismiss Teddy and Mrs. Muldoon. "But listen, Brent only just got here and we really need to—"

Brent interrupted her. "You want to marry me? Is that what all those make-up calls were about?"

Larisa gave a nervous, noncommittal shrug and caught a glimpse of Jack smirking in the doorway. She turned to face Teddy and Mrs. Muldoon, who both looked very uncomfortable. A swell of panic began to rise in Larisa—just what had she gotten herself into?—and she seized onto Brent's arm. "Look, I know we have a lot to talk about. . . ."

She expected him to agree, to somehow finish her sentence, to back her up, but instead he just stood there looking stunned. Mrs. Muldoon cleared her throat and gave an emphatic nod. "So many details to a wedding."

Then Larisa's heart really began to race as her gaze fluttered from face to face. God, she'd done it this time. Until now her deceptions had seemed relatively trivial, unlikely to impact anyone but herself. She'd bought a dress from Mrs. Muldoon, pretending she was engaged. She'd picked a date with Teddy, pretending she was planning a wedding. She'd been joking about all of it with Jack, while she hadn't told Brent about any of it. Each lie had seemed relatively small in the moment, insignificant. And yet she hadn't expected all of her lies to converge on one moment, especially *this* moment, the one in which Brent found out about the wedding falsehood for the first time. Brent, who was the only one who knew the truth about her parents.

Her parents. Facing everyone, she knew she ought to come clean, right here and now. It would be humiliating, but better to come out with the truth than to hide behind the lies. Yet she resisted. Her pride, her sense of privacy, her crazy yearning to hold on to the illusion . . . something was keeping her from full disclosure. As she turned from person to person, feeling the shame and embarrassment build within, she searched for a way out of the situation. If she didn't face it, then she'd need to flee. And that was just what she would do. She'd get as far away from everyone as soon as possible.

"Yes, so many details for us to talk about," she responded to Mrs. Muldoon. She released Brent's arm and began to back away, trying to think of where she could go. "But . . . first I need . . . I need to go see my parents."

Teddy frowned. "I thought they were wintering in Palm Springs."

"No, no," squawked Mrs. Muldoon, "hiking in the Himalayas." She tilted her head, the brass rooster weather vane come to life. "What's the weather like there now?"

Larisa nodded at both of them without really answering either. "They're back now."

Teddy's eyebrows shot up. "At only the start of winter? I thought the point of wintering was . . ."

Larisa laughed nervously. "Oh, you know Clark and Kittie, always on the move."

"What are you talking about?" Brent frowned at Larisa. "Your mother's in no shape to hike the Himalayas."

Larisa gritted her teeth. "That's not exactly public knowledge."

Brent shook her off and turned toward the others. "They're in a retirement community in New Hampshire. Which is where Larisa should be, supporting them, instead of worrying about selling this house."

Before Larisa could explain, Jack was right there, confronting her. "Wait, what? You're *selling* Elmhurst? That's why we're fixing it up? So you can just turn around and sell it?"

Larisa saw Mrs. Muldoon and Teddy exchange a glance. Both took a few steps back and suddenly seemed to scrutinize the stones on the front walk. Teddy bent down to pluck at the weeds.

"I was going to tell you," Larisa told Jack, her voice pleading. "It wasn't something I was certain about."

Jack glared at her. "When? *When* were you going to tell me? The couch fabric will always be Wedgwood blue, you said. The library ladder will always squeak in its track. Our names are behind the wall here. And you're *selling* it? Look, I know it's not my house, but I *have* been the caretaker here for over twenty years. You could have at least been honest with me." He turned on his heel and strode angrily back into the house.

Larisa started to go after him, but Brent grabbed her elbow.

"Larisa, what is going on?"

Larisa twisted free and pounded her fists against her thighs. She looked from questioning face to questioning face, the adrenaline pumping through her. "I need to go visit my parents," she said again, more insistent this time. "I just need to go. Now."

Mrs. Muldoon put a hand on Larisa's arm, but she was looking at Brent. "Storm's coming, dear. Not the best time to leave."

Larisa shrugged out of her grip. "I have to go."

"You don't even have a car." Brent folded his arms. "And no, you can't have mine. At least not until you tell me what the fuck is going on."

"Language," whispered Mrs. Muldoon.

It was true. Larisa didn't have a car; she'd taken the train to town. But then she remembered Andy's Rolls. She glanced down the driveway toward the carriage house to confirm that he had stationed it there, probably when she was out to lunch with Jack. She sucked in her breath. Would she dare? She would. She pushed Brent aside and loped back into the house and up the front stairs to Ursula's room. Her replenished suitcase from her most recent trip to Somerville still sat there unpacked. She threw a few extras into it, zipped it shut, and then dragged it downstairs. Jack sat in an armchair in the parlor, his eyes trained on the Tibetan rug. She paused in front of him.

"I knew you were perpetuating all these lies to everyone else," he said without looking up, "but I didn't think you'd lie to me."

Before she could answer, Brent came bursting in the front door, edging himself between her and Jack. "Larisa, seriously, tell me what's going on."

Larisa backed into the foyer, away from both of them. Through the open doorway, she could see Teddy and Mrs. Muldoon retreating down the hill, each of them stealing backward glances at the unfolding scene. Great, the whole ordeal would be all over town within hours. Larisa wrung her hands. She needed to get out of this place. She turned again toward Jack and Brent.

"I'm sorry," she said, looking pleadingly at them. "Please believe me. I'm sorry. I can't explain it now, but I promise to explain it all. To both of you. Later."

"Wait," they said at the same time, but she had already turned toward the storm and fled.

PART II

WINTER

CHAPTER SIX

Clark and Kittie had the perfect marriage. Everyone always said. Larisa had been hearing it for years. They'd met at a football game their freshman year of college, not long after Clark's father had died suddenly. Clark had grown up quickly then, Larisa had been told, but thankfully the elder Pearl had left behind significant savings and a pension plan, and so the family hadn't suffered. Undergrad and then law school for Clark was paid for, with plenty to spare. In contrast, Kittie had grown up in a frugal middle-class household, and thus wasn't much like the polished debutantes Clark had dated in prep school. But she had a practical and simple grace. She'd taught piano to schoolchildren since she was fifteen and continued to do so as she supported herself through junior college. Legend had it that Clark, grieving for his lost father, had sat through some of her sessions, listening to the young students practice their scales or work their way through a new piece. He'd lie on the couch in the adjacent room, feet on the armrest, releasing his sadness as Kittie, with her soft and soothing voice, guided the children in their finger work or temporarily commanded the keys to demonstrate the gusto with which *The Merry Farmer* ought to be played. With her quiet yet persistent manner, she'd nurtured him back from the brink. Then she'd bolstered him on through law school. Sure, her accounting certification was not quite as complimentary as the liberal arts degrees that were customary for the sorority girls at the sister school to Clark's, but arguably much more useful. And anyway, Kittie hadn't been averse to a more rounded education. She'd learned how to mix his favorite old-fashioned and could soon whip up a proper sauce béarnaise with the best of them. And though Larisa knew that Clark's mother, Grandmother Ginny, had at first refused to accept "oh-so-simple Kittie" for her only son, everyone had eventually moved on in time.

But Larisa didn't have to be told about their exceptional camaraderie. Of course, she'd seen it firsthand—frequent embraces, afternoon walks, a predictable dish routine (she washed, he dried). They consulted each other in everything and though they sometimes disagreed, they never raised their voices. Every night when Clark turned on the evening news, Kittie would settle in neatly beside him with her current needlepoint project. She took care to iron his shirts when he had important meetings; he was certain to bring her a sweater when she shivered against an evening chill. Eventually, when Clark opened his own practice as a public interest lawyer, Kittie became his bookkeeper. People who'd interacted with him only in corporate matters were at first surprised to learn that this quiet woman in the back was his wife. Though not unattractive, Kittie kept herself plain and unadorned. Larisa had always considered her father a little too handsome for her mother, his reddish-brown hair sparking up his playful green eyes. And yet, they were a pair. He allowed her to limit his dessert intake. She permitted him to take the crossword away when it was time for bed. Many times Larisa had watched her parents lean into each other when certain songs came crooning over the oldies station. Oh yes, she knew Clark and Kittie were perfectly matched. They had a marriage that was impossible to live up to. She'd been in awe of it all her life.

But Larisa hadn't seen her parents since the beginning of September. She had refused even to think about them much since she'd started the renovations on Elmhurst, and she only barely allowed herself to think about them now as she skidded down the highway, headed north in the Silver Shadow. The classic Rolls-Royce hood ornament, a shiny winged woman leaning into the wind, looked as though she might leap right into the storm, and Larisa used her, the flying lady, to center the car as she steered. She gripped the textured wheel tightly and tried to remain calm. The snow had come faster and wetter than she'd expected, thick and clumpy against the windshield, the delicate wipers barely keeping up. Her visibility decidedly limited, Larisa did her best to quell the constant, unnerving fear that she might hit a rough patch and inadvertently swerve off the road and into an icy ditch. Thus, less than an hour into the drive, alone in her thoughts, a line of traffic amassing behind her in the slow lane, and the storm menacing from the front, she began to question the choices she had made over the past few months, beginning with her return to Kent Crossing, her purchase of the wedding dress, and now culminating in her impulsive decision to drive to New Hampshire. The trip under perfect conditions would take an hour. In the snow, in a vintage Rolls, it could take three. Oh well. No way but forward now.

Her cell phone had started ringing practically as soon as she'd plunged down the driveway and out onto Main Street. She'd been disappointed to see the number come up as Brent's rather than Jack's, and she hadn't answered even when he'd continued to call multiple times. She realized now how idiotic she had been to keep so many secrets. Why, she asked herself, had she perpetuated all these lies? Of course it was Brent, not Jack, calling. Brent, who'd known nothing about the dress, the flowers, the June date, until now. He'd be buzzing with questions about what she'd been planning with Teddy and Mrs. Muldoon, the state of their relationship, whether she was serious about patching things up, all of it. He was probably already questioning Jack. God, why had she left them alone together in the house? And Jack was another matter, sure to be totally pissed over her failure to be frank about the sale of the house. Which sadly also meant that construction would likely cease and she'd be left with a bunch of half-finished rooms. *Crap.* She hadn't exactly lied to him about Elmhurst. But she sure hadn't told him the whole truth. She shouldn't have pulled him into the project in the first place. And she clearly shouldn't have let him pull her into that kiss.

Here she paused and thought about the kiss—mmm, it had been luscious, better than she'd imagined—before continuing to chastise herself. How could she have been so stupid? A married man. The father of three. The keeper of the house she was planning to sell. She'd have to give it a few days and then summon the courage to apologize. But first she'd have to get through this damn storm.

The wipers swept the windshield in a persistent rhythm; the snowflakes swirled in the wind. Larisa glanced down and for the first time noticed a cassette tape protruding from the player. Great, she thought, a distraction; hopefully some kind of self-help session, ha ha. But when she popped it in, the heavy chords of Mendelssohn's "Wedding March" blared at her so loudly that she jumped in her seat before fumbling to shut it off. She groaned. *Andy.* He must have left the tape in there on purpose, his way of further celebrating her betrothal and forthcoming matrimony, not knowing that none of it had been real. She would have laughed had it not underscored her idiocy even more. She deserved this, she knew, this punishment, this in-your-face kind of irony. And she almost forced herself to pop the cassette back in and listen to the ridiculous soundtrack she had created for herself. But she just couldn't bear it, no. Not after the scene she'd caused back at Elmhurst—Brent and Teddy and Mrs. Muldoon all gaping and sneaking confused glances at one another, Jack sequestered inside. She fiddled instead with the radio dial, trying to tune anything in, but all she got was static. So rather than face the near silence—the watery swish of the tires against the snow, the incessant *thunk-thunk* of the wipers—she seized her phone, despite the snow, and decided at last to call her father. She at least ought to let him know to expect her rather than show up unannounced. He picked up on the third ring, clearing his throat before addressing her calmly in his self-amused baritone.

"Well, hello, stranger. To what do I owe this honor?"

Larisa heard his teasing tone and still she felt herself bristle with guilt. "Come on, Daddy," she answered. "I call you every week."

"Oh yes," he conceded. "But only at the appointed time, dear. Don't get me wrong; I love a woman who sticks to her schedule. Half the reason I married your mother. But isn't it nice to be impromptu now and then?"

Larisa swallowed, her eyes welling with tears. "She doesn't much stick to her schedule anymore."

He drew in a deep breath and let it out in a long sigh. "True," he finally answered. "But that's just the disease."

Larisa could hear the sadness in his voice and she regretted her comment almost immediately. But rather than face it—the disease, everything that had settled over Kittie and their neat and happy little family—she blinked the tears away and decided to change the subject.

"Actually, you'd be surprised. I've been doing a lot of impromptu things lately. Which is sort of why I'm calling. I want . . ." But before she could get the words out, she choked up again, unsure just what she'd been about to say. The words *I want to come home* lingered on the edge of her consciousness, but that wasn't right. Kent Crossing was home, Elmhurst was home—wasn't it?—but no, neither of those places had really been home without her parents. She'd been adrift. Thankfully, her father didn't let the silence consume her for long.

"You sound muffled, darling," he said. "Calling from the bottom of a well, are we?"

Larisa laughed into the cell phone and gripped the wheel of the Rolls with her free hand. "No, from the middle of a blizzard actually and *guess what*. Headed your way. See how impromptu I can be?"

Clark seemed to hesitate before letting his words gush forth. "Larisa, no! In this kind of weather? We'll be thrilled to see you, of course, but are you sure it's safe? I'm looking out the window and there are snowflakes the size of French poodles. Speaking of French poodles, remember that awful one Ursula used to have?"

Larisa started to giggle. "Freddie."

"Ha! Right, Freddie the Fearful. If you even looked at him the wrong way, he'd shit on the rug. Am I right? It got so bad, we each had to come with our own bottle of stain remover for Christmas."

"No," Larisa protested through her laughter. "I liked Freddie. He could look kind of distinguished, actually. Like a statue next to the fireplace."

"Oh, admit it. You only admired him because he was French. It's the Huguenot in you."

"Huguenot?" shouted Larisa gleefully. "He was a French *poodle*, Dad, i.e. *not* actually French."

"Not actually French? *Mais non!* Our Freddie would absolutely shit in his grave to hear you say that."

Here she giggled again at the thought of dear departed Freddie defecating into the tulip beds.

"Good," she finally declared, "better there than on the damn rug!"

Then it was his turn to laugh, which he did with unbridled joy, whooping and roaring into the receiver before finally gathering himself with a series of calming breaths. Larisa loved this about her father—his ability to sense the tension in a situation and turn it into a playful banter. She had been drawn in despite herself. God, it was good to talk to him.

"Oh, sweetheart," he said. "It's been so long since I've

laughed like that. I only wish . . ." His voice tapered off, and she understood, for what was there, really, to say?

"Me too," she managed, and then there was silence.

Larisa swallowed, already feeling the anxiety over facing her mother. At the last visit, Kittie, who had never uttered a crass word in her life, let loose with an incredible string of swears, the words tripping off her tongue as if she were merely reciting a nursery rhyme. She turned to Larisa, who was visiting for the weekend, scowled fiercely, and shouted, "And just when did you become such a supreme bitch?" Clark's eyebrows shot up; Larisa gasped. The word *bitch* and the subsequent silence lingered in the air as Larisa gaped at Kittie, completely unable to respond, while Kittie, oblivious to the entire outburst, calmly bit into her peanut butter and jelly sandwich and nodded so convincingly that Larisa was almost forced to wonder if she *had* in fact become a supreme bitch.

What would come next? Her father seemed impermeable in moments like these, so patient, so steady, as he steered Kittie calmly toward a new task. Larisa knew she should follow his example. But watching her mother spew such vitriol, she just wanted to run the other way. The doctors had warned them that the dementia would progress and they would experience unpredictable moments. She'd understood it would be tough, and she thought she would able to handle it. But this damn disease was depriving her of her mother. She'd realized how distressing it would be for Kittie herself. But what Larisa hadn't been ready for, what really rattled her, was how unmoored it made *her* feel. She'd always thought of her parents as beacons in her life. But when one of those beacons, when one of the coordinates by which she oriented herself, ceased to exist, then who on earth was she? Larisa had no idea anymore.

The Silver Shadow shuddered down the highway through the snow, Larisa hunched inside over the wheel. She'd begun to lose cell phone reception partway through the call and more than an hour had passed since she'd talked to her father. But she was finally nearing the exit that would funnel her into the winding parkway that led to No One's Home. The storm had stopped. The snow had settled into sculpted drifts all along the highway, the wind occasionally whipping the powder up and into the car so that a light dusting speckled the windshield before melting into tiny droplets of water. As the sun set, the roads had cleared under the darkening sky, so despite the deplorable conditions, she sailed smoothly forward now, up and over the hills and through the valleys, flanked only by the occasional plow. The rising moon cast a luminous blue glow over the contours of the snowbanks so that the world looked cool and distant. Gliding through the eerie and unrecognizable landscape, Larisa felt an ethereal calm come over her and she journeyed onward as if in a dream. The muffled crunch of the tires over the snow, the whir of the engine exerting itself on the hills . . . the sounds barely registered as she drifted meditatively through. It was from the distance of this detached dream state that Larisa finally decided to call Brent.

He answered quickly, his voice heated. "You are one crazy girl, you know that? Not for nothing, but you had me worried you'd ended up in some ditch on the side of the road."

"I'm know, I know. I'm sorry. I just didn't expect you to show up out of the blue like that in the middle of the construction."

"Well, how was I supposed to know? You told me you were

renovating, but I thought you meant just a few things. This house is a mess. What have you and Jack been doing here?"

"Nothing. We're just fixing it up." Larisa hoped he didn't hear the hesitation in her voice. What *had* she and Jack been doing? They'd signed their names on the wall. She pushed away her memory of the kiss they'd shared and focused instead on what Jack had said the night he'd arrived at Elmhurst after Holly had kicked him out. *Sometimes you've got to let things get messy before you can build them back up again.*

Brent sighed heavily into the phone, and she could see him holding his head in his hands, slumped into whatever armchair he had chosen. "Things are messy all right. We need to talk."

"OK, I know. But we need to talk fast; I don't have much battery." Larisa palmed the phone in one hand and gripped the steering wheel with the other. "Is Jack still there with you?"

"He left an hour ago to plow the streets. It's just you and me now, sweetheart."

Larisa stiffened at his remark. She began to stutter through some sort of explanation. She told him how she had arrived at Kent's Crossing that fall day, how she'd wandered into the bridal shop; she really hadn't meant to buy the dress. . . . Something had come over her, like she was under a spell. Then her old friend Teddy had called about the flowers, and she couldn't say no. The whole thing had just kind of snowballed out of control. It had become a joke of sorts.

"But I still don't get it," he said. "Do you . . . I mean . . . do you want to get married?"

Larisa tensed, unable to answer. She had fled from her parents and now she was fleeing back to them, away from Brent and the others. Why had she fled? Why had she kept all these secrets? A moment came back to her. A snippet from her last visit with her mother. Though Kittie's short-term memory was shot, her long-term memory was still intact. While it was difficult for her to carry on a conversation about current events, it was not unusual for her to bring up stories from way back, from her own childhood or Larisa's. And that was what had finally thrown Larisa over the edge that last visit. Kittie kept telling the same unsettling story over and over. It was a story about a time soon after Larisa was born. Kittie had driven out to the grocery store, intending to bring the infant Larisa in to do some shopping. But on the drive, before she'd eased the car into the parking spot, the wailing Larisa had settled into a deep and quiet slumber and the young Kittie, exhausted from being up all night nursing, had completely forgotten about her. She'd made it all the way into the store and was comparing heads of lettuce when it struck her that the baby was still in the car. It was a mistake that could have happened to anyone, but still she felt horrible as she ran back to the parking lot.

"I was frantic," she said, "in those few minutes, before I got back to you. Absolutely frantic, my little baby with no one to look out for her. But when I got to the car, there you were with those big blue eyes, sucking your fingers and kicking your feet, totally unharmed. You were fine, but I've never forgotten. The truth is we're all alone." She looked solemnly at Larisa and then started to cry, her chest heaving up and down as her eyes scrunched up and the tears began to fall.

Larisa had felt her throat close up. Kittie had always been the type of mother who spent hours at her side with a cool washcloth when she'd had a fever. Even when Larisa had graduated college and moved into her own apartment, Kittie came by most weekends with extra groceries and a loaf of homemade zucchini bread. She sometimes took Larisa's clothes home to scrub out a stain or iron them. But now she was talking about being alone. Larisa seized her mother's hand. "You're not alone, Mom. You're *not* alone. I'm right here with you. And Daddy's here too."

But Kittie just shook her head. "Alone."

"Larisa," said Brent now over the phone. "I need to know where things stand. Look, I have to be honest with you. I've started to see other people. Nothing serious, just a few dates. And I put it all on hold when you called a few weeks back, when things were looking better—possible—between us. But I mean if you wanted to get married . . . when the heck were you gonna tell me?"

Larisa cringed. The world was rushing by. She couldn't focus, realizing suddenly that she hadn't eaten in hours. Marriage. She had a vision of herself in that beautiful dress, standing on top of the tufted ottoman while Mrs. Muldoon pinned her hair, humming "Here Comes the Bride." Then her mind flashed again to the moment of her kiss with Jack. His lips melding with hers. Oh yes, it had been luscious, better than she'd imagined. Everything was spiraling, swirling around in her head. Brent and Jack and Mrs. Muldoon. She couldn't seem to keep it all straight. When was the last time her mother had made zucchini bread? she wondered. Was she still permitted to use the iron?

"Listen, I can't talk," she said. "My phone is about to die."

But Brent was still prattling on in that puppy dog way of his.

"I messed up, somehow. But if you can just tell me what I did, where it went wrong. I do still love you, you know I do."

Larisa swallowed. She did know. Her eyes pooled with tears at the thought of it. She remembered his wrenching sobs as he'd recounted the loss of his father. How proud he was to have helped raise his brothers. He was so strong, so sweet, in his way. She winced at the thought of hurting him.

"Seriously, Brent, my battery's almost out. It's going to die any second."

"But do you want to give it a go?" he said again. "I know we could be good together. I'd be a good husband."

Larisa thought of the kiss yet again. Jack's lips against hers, so soft and supple. His strong and insistent grip on her arm. The exit was coming up; she could see it ahead and she began to slow the Rolls. Yes, Jack's lips against hers had felt perfect, comforting, familiar. But here was Brent, with so much hope and affection in his voice, and suddenly she wasn't ready to let go of him. She was losing her mother, herself; did she have to lose Brent, too? No, she wanted to believe him, she needed to believe that he was her fate, that everything would be OK again. In this swirling, dizzying moment, she felt like all the elements of her life were streaming by. Like she was clinging, just barely, to a rock on the side of a fast-moving river. And under the force of that pull, she wanted to give in. She wanted to let go, surrender. What if—just what if?—this thing with Brent could work out? And she could be herself again. How magical that would be.

"Do you want to get married?" said Brent, practically shouting now as the snowscape went whizzing by.

Do you want to get married? Do you want to get married? It whirred and whirred and went spinning around in her brain like a roulette ball.

"Yes," she said, "yes. Let's get married. OK?"

Brent didn't answer and she wasn't even sure he had heard her; her spent phone had already started to power down. And now *finally* there was that lighthouse up ahead, its faux tower an unlikely beacon in the wake of the storm.

"Look," she said, though the phone had already died, "I'm here. I have to go. I'm *here.*"

She hadn't meant it, the getting married bit, not really. Of course she hadn't. But melding together with Brent in that moment, giving him the promise of reconciliation, had suddenly felt much better than forging ahead alone. She dropped the phone and accelerated, the lighthouse coming into focus, the flying lady keeping it in her sights. But Larisa had misjudged; in her excitement, she'd taken the turn too fast. She felt the wheels lose their grip; the car went sliding across the ice. She panicked and swerved and slammed on the brakes, but it was too late: she had already lost control. And so instead she braced herself, locking her arms against the steering column as the car began to shimmy and then spin, and the lighthouse went whirring by in the rearview mirror.

CHAPTER SEVEN

Well, at least she hadn't totaled the Rolls. Sure, she'd busted up the tail end pretty good, spinning off into a ditch and nearly rolling the car onto its side before lodging the rear bumper between the rails of the fence that encircled the lighthouse tower. But remarkably, Larisa herself had escaped relatively unscathed and was standing on the sidewalk, already assessing the damage before any of the evening attendants burst out of the front office and into the snow. Shuddering with adrenaline and the chill of the storm, feeling the weight of the staff's arms around her, Larisa knew that the crash could have been much worse, and she silently thanked the universe for delivering her safely despite her incredible foolishness. Yes, her left wrist was throbbing from being mashed against the steering column. True, the back end of the car was a mess and she'd have to figure out how to get it all fixed. But it *was* all fixable, wasn't it? Surely everything could be fixed.

This was how Larisa consoled herself as she lay in the hospital gurney at the rehab center at No One's Home, waiting to be evaluated. The staff had insisted on it and she had conceded—probably wise considering her wrist had now ballooned to twice its normal size. Her cell phone had gone flying in the crash, its screen shattered, but somebody had gone to summon her father and at least no more phone meant no more calls from Brent. Had she agreed to marry him? God, what an idiot she'd been. Lying to Jack and leading Brent on and making such an utter mess of things.

One of the nurses came to check her vital signs and wrap and ice her wrist. The doctor diagnosed a slight sprain, three to five days to heal. He told her she was free to go, but Larisa lingered there for a few minutes, attempting to gather herself. She'd have to call Brent back, though she had no desire to tell him about the crash. She'd like to call Jack. But first she'd have to get a new phone. And in the short term, she'd have to find the energy to face her mother. Just as she had gathered her strength and was about to hoist herself from the gurney, there came her father in a blue bathrobe and slippers, his chin shadowed with unshaven scruff, his gray hair long and tufted, like that of a child's puppet.

"PB&J," he announced, handing her one of two wrapped sandwiches in his hand. "Not much, but the best I could do on short notice."

"Oh, Dad," whispered Larisa. "That's just like you."

"Well, I was so worried. I needed to do *something* to fill the time while I waited for someone to stay with your mother."

"I'm sorry," Larisa answered. "Is she OK?"

"Don't worry, she's sleeping. But my word, Larisa, are *you* OK? What were you thinking, driving through a storm like that? You're lucky you weren't killed."

"What if she wakes up?"

"She'll be fine; she's in a deep snooze." He reached for her bandaged wrist and cradled it in his hand. "Does it hurt?"

Larisa closed her eyes, relieved to have him there but feeling guilty all the same. "Just what you need. Another patient."

"Now, now, it's nothing. Eat your sandwich; you must be starving. And neither one of you are patients. You're my *family*."

Larisa bit into her PB&J. She knew it wasn't nothing. She'd become another burden and he'd already had enough burden, hadn't he? Through the open door, she watched the nurses tend to some of the elderly residents who hadn't quite managed to nod off to sleep. A wizened old man with a walker shuffling so slowly down the corridor, the buxom caretaker by his side patiently slowing her step to match his. A younger white-haired woman in a wheelchair accepting spooned applesauce into her puckered mouth, the nurse gently wiping the dribbled bits from her chin. The hospital staff was so adept at caring for their elderly wards, just as Clark tended so carefully to Kittie day in and day out. She—Larisa—ought to be able to bear it as well. She ought to be able to face her mother, oughtn't she? But the thought of it now filled her with dread. God, what kind of person was she? When the *Titanic* was going down, would she have shoved the others out of the way to leap into the lifeboat first?

"Never mind, dear," her father continued. "You'll just have to hole up with us for a few days to recover."

Larisa had closed her eyes and rested her head against the

pillow, but now her eyes flitted open as she remembered the accident. "What's happened to the car?"

"Towed to the auto body shop next door. We can walk over in the morning." He leveled his gaze on her. "And speaking of the car, do you want to tell me how you ended up out in the middle of a nor'easter in that fancy-pants Rolls?"

Larisa paused mid-chew. She swallowed and wiped at her lips with the cloth napkin he had provided.

"Well . . . ," she started, fumbling for the right entry point, "Brent and I got into a fight. At Elmhurst. Andy had offered me the car earlier in the day."

Here a wave of guilt and panic swept over her. She'd taken the Rolls—Andy's Rolls—out of town completely without his permission and now she'd cracked it up. Shit, shit, shit. Would she have to tell him about the damage or could she somehow fix it before he knew?

"Andy from the gas station?" Clark questioned. "He just offered you his precious Rolls-Royce right out of the blue?"

Larisa bit her lip. "Well, not out of the blue, really." She let out an exasperated sigh, eager to explain but embarrassed by the circumstances into which she'd gotten herself.

"It's a long story. I hadn't planned on taking it out in the storm, but then Brent and I got into that fight and I just needed to get away." She swallowed again, feeling a little tearful, groping for another angle. "I needed to see you and Mom."

Clark reached for her good hand and squeezed. He squinted, considering things more closely. "Andy just gave you the car, huh? Well, I guess I can believe that. Given his history with Ursula."

Larisa relaxed again. She wiped peanut butter from the

corner of her mouth. "Right. He told me he used to take her out for drives now and then."

"Sure," answered Clark as he bit into his own sandwich. "But, you know, I always wondered whether there might be a little more than friendship between them. Something romantic maybe."

Larisa sat up a little straighter in her chair and eyed her father. "Ursula and Andy?"

Clark smiled his toothy grin. "Don't you think? They sure seemed to spend a lot of time together as they got on in age."

Larisa's mind flashed to an image of Ursula and Andy sitting together on the wooden bench at the gas station, each with a glass of lemonade, on a bright summer's day. Or another time in the early spring when Larisa had driven up from Somerville and Andy had come by with a bunch of lilac, newly in bloom. Wasn't it Andy who had dropped in one Christmas Eve with a pitcher full of eggnog? Until this fall, it had been years since Larisa had lived in Kent Crossing, but in thinking about it now, it did seem striking that the few times she'd returned, she'd often encountered Andy on her visits to Ursula. How had she never noticed the nature of their camaraderie before? And why hadn't Ursula ever said anything? Larisa had always just assumed their friendship was platonic, two village elders swapping memories of the good old days. But yes, her father was probably right about the romantic leaning to it. Thinking about it, Larisa smiled. Funny how you thought you knew someone, and then the secrets began to emerge.

Clark patted her arm again. "Well, thank God you're all right. The car can be fixed. With humans, as you well know, it can be much more complicated."

Larisa bit her lip again. She took a breath and released it slowly. "Let's not tell Mom about the accident. I mean, I don't want to upset her, especially since I'm not even hurt, not really."

Clark considered and then conceded with a tilt of his head. "But you'll have to call Andy, of course."

Larisa nodded even though she knew she wouldn't. She had the money; she could just talk to the auto body shop and get it fixed. Then she wouldn't have to tell Andy about fleeing into the snowstorm in his precious car. She wouldn't have to admit to her bad choices, her failures, her mistakes. Her father, of course, would never lie about such a thing. No, he'd be appalled to learn all the lies she'd been telling. But he wouldn't have to know that Andy didn't know. It would all be fixed in no time and no one would ever have to know.

"You look exhausted," said Clark. He beckoned her off the gurney. "Come. Let's get you settled in the guest room."

Larisa tensed and dug the nails of her good hand into the mattress. "Can't I just stay here?"

Clark frowned. "Don't be silly. I thought you wanted to see us. You said that's why you risked your life in this awful storm. To see me and your mother."

"But she's sleeping." Larisa felt another wave of guilt and panic wash over her. She *did* want to see her mother, but, then again, she didn't. How could she explain this to her father, who spent all his days caring for her? Larisa wanted the mother she'd always known. She wanted her life to be clean, organized, predictable. Her mother—so steady, so calm—had always made it so. But this new mother who repeated herself and forgot things and told frightening stories . . . she felt horrible admitting it, but this wasn't the mother she wanted.

She took a deep breath. "You know that story she tells? The one about leaving me alone in the car as a baby?"

Clark shook his head dismissively. "That was years ago. You were fine."

Larisa sighed. "I know. But I just always thought that Mom would be there for me. I know I'm not a baby anymore. I'm old enough to take care of myself. But when I call her to chat, she can't stay focused. When I ask her advice, I'm greeted with silence. And somehow—I just don't know who to be without her."

Clark sat on the side of the bed and put his arm around her. "Don't torture yourself. She isn't gone yet, you know."

Larisa sighed. "I know. Rationally, I know that. But if I stay away, it's almost like she *is* already gone. And then I don't have to watch her deteriorate. I don't have to experience all the awful moments."

"Larisa, honey. You can pretend this isn't happening, but that won't prevent it from actually happening. Those awful moments will come whether you choose to experience them or not. Our lives are different now, yes. But sometimes the truth isn't as bad as you think it will be. In the end, isn't it better to face it?"

Larisa slowly maneuvered herself off the gurney until she came to a standing position. Would her father lend her his car, she wondered, while the Rolls was getting fixed? Maybe she could talk him into it and then she could just go back to Elmhurst in a day or so. But for now she'd try to be brave. She turned toward her father and mustered a small smile. "Well, I did come all this way."

"That a girl. Now let's get some sleep. Everything will look a little brighter in the morning."

———————

Larisa woke early to the sounds of the plows scraping the streets. She lingered beneath the warm blankets, listening. Her neck felt stiff and she had an ache at the back of her skull, but the throbbing in her wrist had lessened and the swelling had gone down. She sat up. Her eyes landed on the undisturbed bed to her right, the pair to the one in which she lay. She hadn't slept in a twin bed in years, she realized. It felt impossibly small and yet delightfully cozy, familiar. In fact, she recognized the set as the same one that had always resided in her childhood bedroom. As before, the two beds were outfitted with matching coverlets and ruffled pillow shams. Larisa remembered that as a young girl she sometimes got confused as to which bed she ought to occupy given that they looked so much alike. Now she was struck with a feeling of order and then disorder as she assessed the one bed neatly made and the other entirely rumpled. But the room didn't feel at all like her old bedroom. The walls were painted a mushroom white and the air smelled like disinfectant and talcum powder. Sniffing, Larisa wondered whether her father sometimes slept in here alone, perhaps to escape her mother's thrashings? Had it gotten so bad that Kittie didn't recognize him when she woke in the middle of the night? Before she could think further on it, the silence of the morning was interrupted by the sharp cries of Kittie herself coming from the master bathroom across the hall.

"No, no, no, no, *no!*" she protested. "I don't need a shower. I just had one."

"Now, now," came Clark's soothing voice. "We'll do a quick sponge bath. Something to freshen you up. Our Larisa is here to see us."

Larisa heard the roar and splash of water against the tub as Clark turned on the faucet.

"Stop it!" yelled Kittie, her voice both muffled and amplified in the acoustics of the bathroom.

"It's OK," said Clark. "I turned up the heat and I'll make the water nice and warm so you'll be comfortable."

"I don't want to," said Kittie. "Why don't you leave me alone?"

"You'll be just fine," Clark assured her. "I'll be right here with you."

Larisa rose and crept into the hallway until she stood outside the bathroom. Clark had left the door slightly ajar, so that peeking in, Larisa could only just see the back of her father's head reflected in the mirror. Her mother was not in sight, but Larisa could hear her continued protests.

"Don't touch me," she snapped. "You get your hands off me."

"I'm going to talk you through this," said Clark. "I'm just going to lift up your nightgown and get you seated on the stool like usual."

He leaned to turn off the water and Larisa caught a quick glimpse of Kittie in the mirror, her lips pursed, her eyes fierce.

"You're going to do no such thing."

"But how are we going to get you clean, sweetheart? Don't you want to get cleaned up and put on a pretty dress for Larisa?"

Kittie seemed to acquiesce. She allowed Clark to slip the nightgown over her head and guide her onto the stool. Larisa felt her own body relax a bit. It seemed the worse her mother got, the better her father became. Kinder, more patient, more brave. But then just when Larisa thought they would get through it without any more discord, Kittie started to scream.

"Help, help me!" she cried, her distress clearly real despite the lack of actual danger.

"Shh, shh," Clark tried to calm her.

Then came the sounds of a scuffle, the absence of words making it almost worse than the screams. Larisa pushed the door wide enough to see her mother flailing at her father, her clenched fists pummeling his thighs. Clark tried to grab her by the wrists, but Kittie, clad only in large white panties, began to kick. Larisa got a full glimpse of her mother's pale breasts, blue-veined and saggy, bobbing incongruously in response to the struggle. Larisa shielded her eyes and withdrew before her parents could see her. She'd witnessed her mother's outbursts before, but this combative behavior was a new progression of the disease, one she'd never experienced firsthand. Larisa cringed. She should help her father, she knew she should. But this was exactly the sort of episode she'd been trying to avoid. Blood coursing through her, her eyes filling with tears, she returned to her bedroom, pulled on some clothes, grabbed her injured phone, and crept into the kitchen. Her father's car keys were hanging on the hook. The streets were plowed now; she'd just head over to the auto body shop and get the work on the car going. Then she'd get her phone replaced.

"Where are you going?"

Larisa swiveled to face her father, glad to see that her mother was not in sight. "I talked with Andy," she lied. "He asked me to take some photos of the damage. You don't mind if I borrow your car, do you?"

Her father frowned. "So soon? I thought we could wait

until after breakfast and do it together. You should give that wrist some time to heal."

Larisa bit her lower lip and held up her shattered phone. "I have to get this fixed too. So I can take the photos. The wrist's fine, I promise. I don't have far to go."

Clark folded his arms across his chest. "How did you call Andy if your phone was still broken?"

Larisa swallowed. "I used the house phone."

Clark looked unconvinced. "Larisa, honey, what's wrong? You don't seem like yourself."

"Nothing's wrong. I just want to focus on getting the car fixed in time for Christmas."

"OK," he acquiesced, "but please, take care."

Three hours later, when she crept back in with her new phone in hand, her father was waiting for her at the kitchen table with a bowl of tomato soup and some sliced apples. Larisa beamed down at him, but groaned a bit inwardly. God, here she was, almost forty years old, and she'd become a kid again.

"They can start work on the car today," she told him. "It's just the bumper really, so it won't take too long."

"Great," her father answered. "It will be wonderful to have you here for a few days."

Larisa glanced anxiously toward the hallway that led to the bedrooms. "Where's Mom?"

"Oh, she takes a dance class every Tuesday morning. Part of her regimen. Eat up and then we'll go catch the end of it."

Larisa felt the familiar tightening of her stomach. She felt heartsick imagining Kittie in some dismal dance class, groups of the elderly shuffling their feet to "Blue Bayou" as some energetic instructor shouted instructions with an abundance of youth and vigor. God, it would be awful. But her father was grinning and looking at her so expectantly—what was he up to?—that Larisa knew she couldn't refuse. And this was her mother, after all. Larisa should *want* to see her. *Sometimes the truth isn't as bad as you think it will be,* he had said. The bathroom scene this morning had been bad, but that episode had passed. Maybe her father was right. Larisa felt the smile stiffen on her face as she nodded. She cleared her dishes and then followed him down the hallway to the class.

"Now," he told her as they neared the door, "just be sure you don't do anything to disturb them. Nadine is quite clear about that. We can watch from the window, but that's it."

Larisa cocked her head. "Nadine?"

"The dance teacher. Oh, you'll love her. She's just marvelous with your mother."

He turned toward Larisa, clamping one hand on her good wrist to stop their progression down the hallway. His eyes were suddenly very serious, concerned. For her or for Kittie? Larisa couldn't discern. The hum of the fluorescent lights filled the silence as she drew in a breath and waited for him to speak.

"I should prep you," he finally said. "She likes to dress up a little. For the class."

"Nadine?"

Clark swatted at the air. "No, no. Your mother."

"Dress up?" Larisa had a hard time imagining her plain-Jane mother wearing anything fancier than a string of pearls.

"Yes," said Clark. "Quite a bit more than you're used to. And oh!" Here he clapped his hands together and gave a self-satisfied smile. "I've given her the perfect stage name." He paused and announced it with some flair. "Rosa Rugosa!"

Larisa frowned. "Rosa Rugosa? Like that bush you used to sing about?" His familiar saying ran through her head. *Rosa Rugosa? There's no Rosa Rugosa here.* She could picture him walking along the beach roses as he sang the words back at her.

Clark grinned. "It's sort of silly, I know, but she loves it." He started down the hallway again.

Larisa didn't follow. She stood immobile, her feelings of fear and guilt and sadness suddenly fusing into a current of anger. The idea of her mother playing dress-up made her feel sick. It seemed so undignified, humiliating.

"Dad, this is demented. I mean, aren't you supposed to be helping her *remember* who she is? Rather than confusing her with some stupid made-up name?"

Clark wheeled around to face her, his face unexpectedly flush with emotion. "Damn it, Larisa. I don't know what I'm supposed to be doing. Who's to say what's real and what's pretend? All I know is that it makes her smile. And that's the best thing in the world to me. If you'd stop thinking about yourself for a minute, maybe you'd see that."

"I'm thinking about *her*," Larisa protested.

"Are you?" Clark shook his head. "I've spent months, no, *years* now, struggling with this. Trying to remind her who I am, who she is." He gave her a pointed stare. "Who you are."

Who am I? Larisa wondered to herself.

"And it doesn't get us anything, anywhere," Clark continued. "We both just end up frustrated and exhausted. She isn't the person she was. She'll never truly be that person again."

"No," Larisa insisted. "She'll *always* be that person to me."

Clark ignored her, suddenly waving his hands in a circle, as though conducting a symphony. "But this pretend stuff is *fun*. It's invigorating. For both of us. We laugh a little; we smile."

He turned his back to her and began to walk away. Larisa trailed after him.

"But it's just wrong," she insisted. "To deceive her like that."

"Why is it wrong?" Clark turned toward her again and fixed her with a knowing smile. "We all have our deceptions, small or large. Are my deceptions more wrong than yours?"

Larisa froze, trying to assess his expression. Did he somehow know something about her secrets but wasn't letting on? She opened her mouth to protest but before she could, her gaze shifted to the viewing window that flanked the side of the dance studio. They'd arrived at the class. Through the closed door came the sonorous voice of Frank Sinatra crooning his way through "It Had to Be You." And there was Kittie, almost unrecognizable in a peony-pink ostrich feather coat, her smoky gray hair clipped stylishly around her ears. She stood in the middle of the room, arms positioned on the waist and shoulders of a wiry woman in black. The class wasn't full of decrepit and depressed old people, as Larisa had imagined. The class consisted only of Kittie and her instructor. And it wasn't loud or patronizing. Rather, Kittie looked exuberant as she rocked slowly around the room under Nadine's guidance. Yes, her arms were impossibly thin and her spotted skin hung down from her elbows as though draped across her bones. But she displayed a magnificent smile that showed most of her teeth and brought color to her cheeks. At first Larisa had almost laughed to see her in the feathered coat, not because it was comic so much as unexpected. Rather, there was something beautiful, regal, *dignified* about the way she held herself. Watching, Larisa felt as though she had never seen her mother so happy.

"That's incredible," she whispered.

Clark put an arm around her shoulders. "Isn't it?"

The pair neared as the song came to its close. Kittie sang the final words in a weak but sonorous voice. Nadine turned and caught Larisa's eye through the window. They finished the dance and both came to the door.

"I didn't know she could still dance," said Larisa, shaking her head and smiling.

Nadine grinned back. "It's something we've been doing to help our dementia patients. To give them back some joy."

"Her short-term memory is not great," Clark filled in. "She might not remember something that just happened, but she remembers the music and starts to move."

He stepped closer and enveloped Kittie in his arms. "Hello, Rosa."

In seconds the two of them were moving softly across the floor, lost to each other. Larisa watched through the open doorway. Clark and Kittie maneuvered around the room until the song ended, and then they approached. Larisa felt the familiar nervousness. As Kittie stepped through the doorway and neared Larisa, her eyes began to cloud up and she blinked without registering any expression. There were times now when Kittie couldn't even remember Larisa's name. But other times, it was hard to tell she was even sick. Larisa never knew which version of her mother to expect.

"Mom?" said Larisa, tentatively offering her hand when her mother hesitated.

"This is Larisa," explained Clark. He patted Kittie reassuringly on the back as he urged her forward. "She's come to visit."

Kittie squinted and looked around the room until her eyes landed on her daughter. "Yes, of course."

Her face still blank, she accepted the proffered hand. She traced the bandages that encircled Larisa's wrist and then peered into Larisa's palm as though seeking her fortune there. She stroked the fingers and kept her gaze fixed on them for an interminably long time. When she finally lifted her eyes back to Larisa's, they were full of wonder and excitement.

"You're getting married?" she said, directing her gaze to Aunt Ursula's sapphire on Larisa's ring finger.

Larisa balked, and pulled her hand away.

"No," she said. "Yes."

Kittie laughed uncertainly and pulled Larisa into a long embrace. Larisa looked over Kittie's shoulder to see her father smirking down at her. "You know," he said in his familiar teasing voice. "I heard a rumor you were getting married. I guess our invite got lost in the mail?"

"You *heard*?" Larisa wriggled out of Kittie's arms, her expression apologetic.

"Well, you know how it is in a small town," answered her father. "It was only a matter of time before somebody tracked us down. Is it true?"

"It's complicated," said Larisa, looking back and forth between her parents.

"Well, then," said Clark. "It seems we have a lot to talk about."

Larisa froze, knowing she'd been caught. She had so much to tell them, she realized, but wasn't at all sure how to tell it, how much to delve into, how much to withhold. The breakup with Brent, the loss of her job, the purchase of the wedding dress, the June 2 date. It might feel good, at some level, to come clean, to spill all the secrets she'd been hoarding for so long. Her father was watching her earnestly now, waiting for her response.

"I don't know what to say," she managed. Her heart began to pound against her chest.

"Try telling the truth," he quipped. "It's easier to remember."

Larisa turned toward her mother. Kittie stood watching with placid blue eyes, patting her hair into place with the tips of her fingers. The gesture was so familiar to Larisa and yet this woman in the pink feathered coat seemed so different from the mother she'd known all her life. Had Kittie been harboring this stranger all along, hidden deep within? Larisa thought of herself in the wedding dress shop that day with Mrs. Muldoon. She hadn't intended to buy the dress and yet she had. The world was topsy-turvy and here were her parents, with their perfect marriage, waiting for an explanation. *Try telling the truth,* her father had said, but once again she felt the urge to lie. No, her father was wrong—it was *not* better to face the truth. Pretending made things bearable when the truth was too hard to take. Hadn't he just proven that himself with this Rosa Rugosa ruse? *Who's to say what's real and what's pretend?* Her father was staring at her, waiting for a response. She suddenly knew what to say.

"Jack," she declared. "Jack and I are going to get married."

"Jack?" her father answered, confusion clouding his features. "Jack Merrill, the caretaker?"

"Yes, *that* Jack," said Larisa, as though convincing herself. She began to speak more quickly, spooling herself into another lie. "I've been fixing up Elmhurst a bit—you know, it's been years since anyone did any real work on the place—and Jack's been helping me. Speaking of which, Daddy, I've been meaning to talk to you about the house. We really need to sell it. It's much too big; it's way too much to take care of."

"But wait a minute, *Jack*? What about Brent?"

"Brent and I broke up at the end of August," Larisa announced flatly. "I've been living at Elmhurst since September. Which is where I encountered Jack."

Clark's eyes widened, and he raised his eyebrows. "But Larisa, this doesn't make any sense. Why didn't you tell us you were getting married? We have to hear about this from our former neighbors? I thought they were kidding; there'd been a misunderstanding."

Larisa swallowed. She tried her best to hold his gaze as she continued to lie. "Well, I've been busy. And I wanted to tell you in person."

Clark shook his head, unconvinced. "But last night you said you got in a fight with *Brent*. That's why you took off in Andy's Rolls-Royce, right? Because you got in a fight with *Brent*."

"Well, right," Larisa stammered. "Brent came by the house unexpected, hoping to patch things up. But I haven't seen him in weeks. It's been over for a long time between us." She tried not to think about the call from the car the night before. Yes, she'd agreed to marry him, but she hadn't *meant* it.

"But isn't Jack already married?" her father asked. "With three kids?"

Larisa nodded. "The triplets. But Jack and Holly are separated. He's been living with me at Elmhurst."

"So he's not even divorced?"

Larisa groaned. "Dad, you don't understand. Their marriage has been rocky for years. It's basically over. He wants to be with me."

Thinking about Jack sent a pulse of energy through her. *There's something between us*, he had said. *I know you feel it too.*

"He's been living with you at Elmhurst? He's there now?"

Larisa shrugged. "Probably. He seemed a little annoyed that Brent showed up out of nowhere." Here Larisa faltered, wondering what had happened to Brent. Hopefully, he wasn't still at Elmhurst too.

Clark looked from Larisa to Kittie and then back to Larisa again. He squinted softly at her. Larisa knew her story wasn't remotely credible. And she knew he probably didn't believe her; his quizzical expression told her as much.

"Marriage isn't a thing you take lightly," he cautioned. "It's a commitment. It's hard work."

Larisa's mind flashed to the article, "Twenty-Five Keys to a Successful Marriage." "I know, I know. Everyone is hard to live with."

Here Kittie chimed in for the first time. "*I'm* not hard to live with."

"Of course not." Clark kissed his wife's cheek and rested a hand on her shoulder. He turned back toward Larisa. She could see him gathering his thoughts before he slowly continued. "You know that story you mentioned? That one about your mother leaving you alone in the car when you were just a baby?"

Larisa nodded, dropping her gaze toward the floor, away from her father. She didn't want to think of that story again.

"I've wondered sometimes why she remembers that one over others. The truth is, she's right. We are all, in some ways, alone in this world. But if you can find someone to care for. Someone for whom you can make life a little brighter, that's the thing. That's what marriage is about. Being vulnerable with each other. I'm the one who tends to her, for better or for worse. First thing in the morning. In the middle of the night."

"I know," Larisa answered. She understood that her father was trying to coax her out of her lie, but instead his words helped illuminate a truth she'd been avoiding. Jack had been right. There was something between them. Something she no longer wanted to ignore. And not just something physical. No, it was deeper than that. Seeing her parents dancing together had brought this into focus for her. She and Jack had shared stories and dinner and a passion for the house they were restoring. They'd written their names on the dining room wall. He had been so kind to her, so easy to talk to. She felt it so fully now—how could she have fought it before? Yes, she *should* marry Jack. Not right away, of course. Only after he'd truly called it quits with Holly and after they'd had time to work through a few things.

"I need to go home," she muttered, more to herself than to her father. "I need to talk to Jack."

"Home?" questioned her father. "You only just got here. You're not going anywhere until you've given that wrist some time to heal."

"*I* want to go home," said Kittie. The pink tendrils of her faux ostrich coat fluttered almost imperceptibly beneath the heating vent.

Clark sighed and fixed his gaze on Larisa. "Going home sounds good to me, too. Home to Elmhurst. With Ursula gone, we could all live there. You could help me with your mother. You said you were fixing the house up?"

Larisa froze. Her father almost never asked for help. She could see his yearning, and yet the idea of Clark and Kittie with her at Elmhurst unleashed panic in her.

She shook her head. "Elmhurst isn't really our home. It's Ursula's."

"Ursula's not here anymore."

"But it isn't the right place for Mom."

Clark sighed. "True. But this really isn't the right place for her either. Not anymore."

"Well, you can't go there now. The house is still a mess, the walls aren't sealed up."

"You can't go there now either," Clark countered. "Your wrist needs to heal, we need to see about the car. And we've got to talk more about this supposed wedding."

Larisa nodded. He was right: she couldn't go yet. But she'd go as soon as she could. Yes, she'd wait for the car to be ready and then she'd head back to Elmhurst to find Jack.

CHAPTER EIGHT

When Jack was a little boy, he thought he'd been named after one of the little ducklings from the classic children's story *Make Way for Ducklings*. He'd been sure of it. Jack, after all, was the *lead* duck in the list of many ducks—Jack, Kack, Lack, Mack, Nack, etc.—and he, Jack Merrill, was the older brother. Even at the young age of five, when this realization had struck, he thought this said something about himself. He had a distinct responsibility for his two younger sisters, who had only been three years old and one year old, respectively. He needed to help take care of them, his mother had said, and he had taken this decree very seriously. He taught them how to maneuver up and down the stairs. He held their hands when walking down the sidewalk to the nearby park. He wiped their tears and comforted them when they fell. This sense of responsibility, this habit of tending to something other than himself, was a practice he had carried with him ever since. So, in a sense, he'd always been a caretaker, even long before Ursula or Elmhurst or this ridiculous nonsense with Larisa. *Larisa.* He shook his head. He thought he knew her, but somehow a stranger had emerged.

After Larisa had raced off into the storm, he'd sat stunned for a solid five minutes in the living room, trying to process. Something—*that kiss*—had finally happened between them and it had felt great, just the way it should. Sure, he had pushed her a little, but she had enjoyed it; he could tell. Then Brent had shown up, and Jack had been caught totally off guard with the news that Larisa planned to sell Elmhurst. Here he'd thought that he and Larisa were aligned, that they had been yearning for the same things. Companionship, culture, a shared aesthetic in the restoration of Elmhurst to her former beauty. But it wasn't the sale that bothered him so much as the deception. He had trusted Larisa. And he'd felt that she had trusted him. Apparently, he'd been wrong.

Eventually Brent, who admittedly had to be even more stunned than he—not about the house, of course, but about the supposed wedding—came stumbling in.

"Level with me," he said, his expression dubious as he slipped off his coat and tossed it onto one of the armchairs. "Do you think she actually wants to marry me?"

Jack shrugged, annoyed. "Beats me. You think I know what women want?"

Brent picked up a decorative bowl from the coffee table and inspected it skeptically before setting it back down and addressing Jack again. "Well, you've been around the house a lot. Has she said anything?"

Jack raised his eyebrows and motioned for Brent to take

a seat. "Yeah, I've been around a lot. I've been *living* here. Didn't she tell you?"

Brent smirked slightly and then paused, as though waiting for Jack to admit the joke. A look of alarm fluttered across his features when he realized Jack was serious. "Living here? With Larisa?"

Jack deflected. Definitely better to not get into it. "Just in one of the back bedrooms. Temporary housing until me and my wife figure things out."

Brent relaxed his shoulders and offered a sympathetic nod. "Ah, so we're in the same boat."

"Except you're not actually married and don't have three young kids to worry about." The words came out more harshly than Jack had expected, and he felt the hypocrisy in them as soon as they came out of his mouth. How could he claim any allegiance to his marriage, to his family, when he'd engaged in that kiss with Larisa only just that morning? Brent had arrived at the doorstep to show Larisa what he wanted. Jack knew he had yet to express the same level of devotion to his wife, even with Holly just down the street.

Brent seemed oblivious to Jack's curtness. He snatched up his coat from the armchair and began rummaging in the pockets until he came up with some papers and a bag of weed.

"Hey, you don't mind, do you?"

He sat and began to lick the paper and pack it without waiting for a response. Jack scowled as Brent tamped and rolled, positioned the joint between his lips, and then flicked at it with his lighter. Jack *did* mind actually. Not that he cared much about marijuana use in general. If people wanted to toke up, that was fine by him. But somehow it seemed so wrong inside this house. Larisa probably wouldn't approve—at least not the

Larisa he knew—and Ursula certainly wouldn't have stood for it. Not by a long shot. But Larisa had abandoned them and Ursula was gone. So, Jack just shrugged again and shook his head. "It's not my house."

"Not really Larisa's house either." Brent gave a conspiratorial grin, his shaggy curls almost entirely obscuring his eyes as he sucked hard, held his breath, and then released his exhale. "Technically her father's."

"I know," Jack snapped, his anger now flaring up again despite himself. Why had Larisa told Brent, her supposed ex, about the sale of the house and not him?

Brent, oblivious, took another hit and relaxed into the chair. He positioned his elbows on the armrests, the joint smoking in one hand, dangerously close to the upholstery.

"She won't answer the phone. I tried three times." He held the joint out toward Jack.

Jack waved the offering away. "Oh, let her run. She'll find her way home soon enough."

"Yeah, if she doesn't kill herself in that car first."

Jack didn't answer. Larisa could take care of herself. He stood and surveyed the scene out the window. The snow had started, though only barely, little flakes skating down the sky and landing softly on the grass. Nothing would stick right away, but if predictions held, they'd be in whiteout conditions by sundown, which meant he'd better get home and hook up the plow to his truck. He didn't officially clear snow for the town, but he'd help out where he could, and he'd also tend to the driveways of the half dozen customers he'd serviced for years.

"I'm headed out on snow duty; it's gonna be a long night," said Jack. He paused. "Look, it's not my house either, but it's probably fine if you crash here. Stay off the roads."

Brent nodded, joint back between his lips. "Sure. I'll keep the home fires burning."

"No fires," said Jack, shaking his head. "And be careful with that joint. One loose spark and this place will go up in flames."

Brent waved his free hand dismissively. "It's just an expression. I'll be careful, I promise."

Jack headed into the foyer and toward the front stairs so he could fetch his gear from his room. "Just take care of her until I get back."

Brent gave a thumbs-up. "Don't worry, bro. You can trust me."

You can trust me, Jack repeated in his head. *Ha. Well, isn't that brilliant, in light of everything.* He charged up the stairs and down the back hallway that led to his small room. He changed quickly, eager to get out of the house, pulling on some fleece-lined snow pants, his winter boots, and a bright orange anorak he'd chosen both for warmth and visibility. As he turned to leave, his eye caught the wedding photo of him and Holly on the bedside table and it stopped him in his place. God, he'd been a fool. Flirting with other women, acting on it more recently. He shouldn't even be thinking about Larisa. His efforts should be centered on fixing things up with Holly and getting back to her and the boys. Holly had been beautiful on that May day, their wedding day, her head tilting back to catch the sun. He had a responsibility, a family. *We're all in this together,* she had said, but he hadn't stood by her the way that he'd promised. Ashamed of himself now, his anger waning, he snatched up the other photo—the one of the three boys—and brought it with him, laying it faceup on the passenger seat of the truck as he drove slowly back to his house.

———

He arrived to find Holly already out salting the walk.

"You should get the boys to help you," he called as he jumped down from the cab and began to hitch up the steel plow blade.

She gestured toward the house with a sweep of her arms. "You want to talk them away from the Xbox? Be my guest. Anyway, I like to get out into the cold air by myself. They can help later when the real snow comes."

Jack finished with the plow setup and approached. Her back was to him as she scattered the salt, and when she leaned into the task, he felt a tenderness toward her that he hadn't felt in a while. How long had they been separated? he wondered. More than two months by now. Actually going on three. Funny how time went by so quickly when they were apart. It had seemed like an eternity when they were in the same household, especially when the yacht club was closed for the winter and he was landlocked until early spring. And yet now he missed the close quarters he'd shared with her. He missed waking up to breakfast with the boys. If she could only find a way to forgive him, to let him back in, things could be better. He just knew it. But he also knew she wasn't likely to give him that chance. She was still so angry and he had no idea how to diffuse it.

"Well, I'm off," he finally said. He made a move toward her, wavering on whether or not to rest a hand on her shoulder, but decided against it. "I'll be back to take care of the driveway."

She turned to face him. Her blue eyes beamed brightly against the dull gray light of the storm, her cheeks wet with softening flecks of snow. Jack couldn't quite read her expression but wasn't surprised when she took a shot. Holly tended to sling arrows when she felt her emotions about to creep in. "Don't bother," she said. "By the time you come back around, we'll be buried. I can do it."

Jack sighed. He had heard this kind of complaint from her before. She'd be last on the list and she knew it. One of the hazards of being married to a contractor was that the chores around your own house were never completed. She'd been asking him to repaint the deck for years. He still hadn't hung up the shelving in the den. The limbs of the big oak tree that hung over the master bedroom would never be trimmed properly. He understood her frustration, but what was he supposed to do, stop working?

"Just wait for me, will you? There's no rush. You know school's already canceled."

"No, thanks, Jack. I can plow myself out."

He knew what she meant—that she'd start up the snowblower and clear the driveway on her own—but still he started to laugh at the obvious euphemism. "Plow yourself out, huh?"

Holly glared. "It's not funny."

"Oh, come on," countered Jack. "It's a little funny."

She folded her arms, stubborn as ever. "I can take care of myself."

"Of course you can. But would it kill you to let me help? My name's still on the mortgage, isn't it?"

"Just come back to get the boys in the morning. They're going to be a nightmare after being cooped up in the house all night and I don't want to deal with them by myself."

Jack turned away. "Fine. I'll be back. But if you start on the snow without me, make sure the boys get out here to help."

As he stepped into the truck, she seemed to nod in conces-
sion. And so he went.

Night came and with it the driving snow. In counterpoint
to the few falling flakes he had glimpsed through the Elmhurst window at the start of the storm, the air was now filled
with thick crystals, cascading from above and blowing at
Jack from all sides as he steered his way through the roads
of Kent Crossing. Alone in his truck, radio tuned to classical, he worked hard, focusing on and honoring the plowman's
maxim to plow early and often. He started each new clearing
with a clean, easy pass, using the controller inside the cab of
his truck to angle the blade this way and that. As the storm
began to build and the powder accumulated, he cut deeper
into the drifts, carving them up and clearing great swaths of
pavement, waving to the bundled children who gathered on
stoops to watch him work. Something about the clarity of the
mission appealed to him, the brute force of it as well. Push
the snow into the bank, raise the plow blade, back the truck
up, shift the gears. Squinting through the icy slush that slid
down his windshield, plow lights illuminating the blanketed
ground in front, he felt powerful, safe, effective. The adults
stomped out in half-laced boots to offer him hot chocolate
and baked goods, which they handed up through the lowered
window, the chill of the air flaring his nostrils before he sealed
himself in again and headed back out to face the storm. He
enjoyed being alone on the roads. The solitude, the feeling
of containment inside his truck, the storm building in force
and tempo so that he was reminded suddenly of the Mahler
symphony he had listened to with Ursula all those years ago.

The orchestrated drama of it, the surge toward the end. Most of the plow guys chose to gather at midnight at Shea's Tavern to grab a drink before last call, but Jack kept at it through the night. He'd had enough of Shea's Tavern; that was what had gotten him into trouble in the first place. The wind kicked up and blew clouds of snow across the roads, but he persisted, meditating on the scrape of the blade, the rumble of the engine, the blinking strobes from other trucks as they passed him in those early hours before dawn.

He plowed and plowed, past the ten-hour mark. The fatigue crept in and he tried to remember the last time he had eaten a full meal. The lunch with Larisa at the Tidewater Tavern? When he'd tried to tell her of his feelings for her? Which he shouldn't be thinking about. No, he needed to focus on Holly and the boys, getting them back. His vision began to blur and his lids fluttered, fighting off sleep, as he urged the truck forward over the treacherous roads. He should stop, he knew, before he got into an accident. But he couldn't. The snow just kept coming and he had wound himself up in the satisfying repetitiveness of the task. Before long, he reached the parking lot to the yacht club and turned in. And though there was no urgency in plowing it now, he began to chip away, moving faster than he should as he made cut after cut into the deep shelf of snow. The truck began to skid. The tires struggled to gain traction and he was getting sloppy with the plow, forgetting to raise the blade before careening backward and then suddenly forward again. *I should stop, I should stop, I should stop,* he told himself. But the snow was still there to be cleared and he wanted to push it all away until there was nothing left. He wasn't able to see clearly now, but he couldn't separate himself from the rhythm of the plowing, and he would have kept going for who knows how long had his vision not been suddenly blinded by the beams of the rising sun. He stomped on the brakes; the truck lurched to a stop and his chest rammed into the steering wheel. But he didn't notice. For the snow had virtually ceased, the shimmering ocean licking at the last few flakes as they floated calmly down, and his gaze was fixated on the beautiful colors—orange and yellow and pink—that were seeping into the sky as the sun did her best to warm the earth on the cold winter day. Watching, transfixed, Jack fell hard into a long, deep sleep.

He woke hours later with a jolt and the immediate feeling that something was wrong. In his exhausted state, he'd left the truck running, heat blasting, and as he pushed himself into a sitting position, blinking through the bright sunlight, he noticed the gas gauge signaling a near empty tank. The photo of the boys had slid to the floor. He reached for it and felt the soreness radiating down his back and neck, the ache behind his eyes. Ugh, he'd forgotten how a night full of plowing could feel.

He glanced at his watch. Already 10:00 A.M. He was late to pick up the boys and he'd never gone back to plow out the driveway, so Holly was sure to be furious as usual. He fished his cell phone from his pocket, but it had died in the night, so he plugged it in to the car charger, shifted the truck into gear, and headed off to Andy's to refuel, passing Elmhurst on the way. The long limbs of the trees were clotted with snow and the front lawn looked clean and white, untouched. There was a stillness to it all, a profound calm that was beautiful to behold. Next to the house, he could see Brent's car, buried but there in the driveway, and Elmhurst still standing, which was good news. But despite the calm, he couldn't shake the anxious feeling that had settled in his gut.

He drove on to the gas station and pulled in next to the pump. As he popped the cap, jumped out of the truck, and slid his credit card into the machine, he heard sirens nearing and he was reminded of Larisa and her trek up to New Hampshire in the Rolls. He wondered if she'd made it safely. Jack was tempted to mention it to Andy now, Larisa's flight in his beloved car. Andy probably didn't even know she had taken it. But Jack thought better of it—best not to cause problems where none were found—so instead just waved to Andy, who sat inside the shop, newspaper in hand, feet up on the counter as he reclined in his chair. Jack turned back to face the road. The sirens were upon him now and the ladder truck went roaring down Main Street. Someone must be in trouble, he thought, and then his stomach began to clench even more as he thought about the boys and Holly alone and vulnerable in the house. He should have been back by now, he chastised himself, and he braced for another argument as he pulled the gas nozzle from the truck, climbed in, and skidded back onto the road. He heard another siren closing in, this one longer-toned, more shrill, and he glanced into the rearview mirror to see the ambulance advancing. He pulled to the shoulder of the road and it zoomed by him down the street, turning up the hill that led toward his house. And now he felt his stomach really seize. He swerved back onto the road and accelerated. The truck shimmied through the snow, throwing up clumps of ice along the running boards. Something was wrong, damn it; he'd known it from the moment he'd woken, and now he couldn't get there fast enough. There were branches in the road and people trying to shovel out their cars and he had to angle around all of it.

And then suddenly he was there and oh God, yes, the fire truck was parked out front, the ambulance workers were dropping the wheels of a stretcher into the unplowed driveway and pushing their way past three abandoned shovels on the walk. But one of the firemen stopped them at the door and they just stood there with their emergency bags and defibrillator, gazing back at the house. Jack couldn't understand it; if something was wrong, why weren't they going in? And then he saw. He couldn't believe he had missed it; he had been so focused on the fire truck and the ambulance, the foreground of the scene. But right there, right in front of him, he now saw that a tree, that big oak that shaded the house on summer days, had collapsed through the roof, its trunk resting on the lower half of the master bedroom window. He slammed the truck into park, cranked on the brake, and before he made it out of the cab, the boys—miraculously, all three of them unharmed—were swarming around him, pulling on his elbow, and jumping nervously about, too scared for tears.

"Where's your mother?" he barked, and he understood without them saying that she was inside the house. He pushed through the picket fence and lumbered up the front walk, his heart pumping, the world spinning around him.

"That's my wife!" he screamed at the front door. The ambulance workers were trying to explain something about the firemen securing the scene before anyone could enter. He was prepared to fight through them, but then Sam Whittaker, the dockmaster, appeared in full firefighter gear—Jack had forgotten that he volunteered during the off-season from the club. Sam, a big man, seized Jack by the arm and forced him away from the door.

"She's OK," he told Jack. "Her leg seems to be broken and she's a little bruised up, but we'll have her out in a minute and off to the hospital and she'll be fine."

Jack looked back to the gate, where the boys had gathered, gripping one another, and he lowered himself to the snow. He knew he should get up to comfort the boys, but in the end, it was them who came to comfort him, patting his back and squeezing his arm.

"Dad, it was so sudden," said Alex. "The tree came down out of nowhere."

"We were outside, shoveling," said Ben. "I called 9-1-1 from the neighbors'."

"She'll be OK," said Charlie. "They said she'd be OK."

Before long, they had Holly out on a stretcher, breathing through an oxygen mask. Her bright eyes found his and stayed there, tracking him as he came to her side, held her hand, and stroked her hair.

"The boys are fine," he told her, knowing they'd be foremost in her mind, "and you'll be fine too." She nodded and closed her eyes and squeezed his hand, a small step toward forgiveness. She had finally given him the sign he'd been looking for, he thought, as he helped to settle her into the ambulance, but my God, he'd never imagined it would come like this.

A broken leg and two bruised ribs. They spent two days in the hospital, the boys there with him for the first night, stretched out on the couches in the adjacent common room, swatting one another with magazines and feasting on Doritos and Sprite from the vending machine. Then his sisters came to collect them and Jack stayed on with Holly. They put a cast on the leg and taught her how to manage the crutches, which wasn't easy with the tender ribs. It struck Jack during those two days that he and Holly hadn't spent that much time together in years, even on vacation. He couldn't put his finger on when or why, but somewhere along the line, they'd lost their companionship. Jack couldn't remember the last time he'd thought of her as a friend. Is this what had driven him to his recent tryst, this emptiness to their marriage? He wasn't sure. But now, for the first time, consumed with guilt and regret, he was ready to face it. He had deceived her, abandoned her, and she deserved an apology. Christ, she deserved much more. And so there, by her hospital bed, he reached for her hand and he told her.

"I spent the night with someone," he confessed, "that night, when I didn't come home. I know you suspected."

She nodded solemnly.

Jack continued. "It was stupid and impulsive and selfish, and it didn't mean anything. I don't know why I did it."

"Jack," she said. "We've been together a long time. We don't have to do this here, now."

"I know," he said. "But I owe you an apology; I have to own up to it. That's not the person I want to be. That's not the father I want my kids to see."

Holly shook her head. "The kids don't know; I didn't tell them."

"Sure, but they're not stupid. They saw me slink in the door that morning."

"Jack, they know you're a good father."

"But do they know I'm a good husband? Do *you* know? I want you to know."

Her eyes were brimming now. "You tried to be. I know that."

"I didn't try hard enough." His eyes met hers. "But now, almost losing you like this . . ."

"You didn't lose me." She shook her head and wiped her eyes free of tears. "I'm fine."

"You're not fine—*look* at you. My God, Holly, if that tree had landed only a few feet over . . . I don't even want to think about it. I should have been there."

She closed her eyes and sunk back into the pillow. "What could you have done even if you had been there? I'm just glad the boys weren't in the house."

"Me too." Jack lowered his voice to a whisper. "But don't you see? This is our chance. To forgive each other. To let go of the anger. To get back to where we used to be."

Holly sighed. "I don't know if we can make it back. Sometimes I have no idea what goes on in that head of yours. And we haven't even lived together in months."

Jack reached for her hand. "I've been distant, I know. But if you just let me come home, I'll tear down those walls, I'll let you in again, I promise. We need to be vulnerable with each other. We need to be brave. Try for me, honey, please try. Maybe if we both try."

He knew it was unfair to lay this on her here, now, in her injured state. But something told him that if he didn't seize this moment, they would be done. The weak flicker between them had illuminated a path forward, but only if they acted now. Holly seemed to sense it too.

"OK, Jack, OK," she whispered. "Let's try." The tears had stopped, and her eyes were full of hope.

"Good." He smiled at her. "Then I'm going to take you home with me."

"Home to where? That house? No, it's fine, I can stay with my mother."

"There's no room at your mother's. And besides, you know she'll drive you crazy. No, I'm going to move you and the boys to Elmhurst."

"Jack," she protested, "it isn't your house."

He paused. He thought about all the years he'd spent working at Elmhurst. He'd come at all times, morning and night, whenever he was summoned. To mow the lawn and trim the hedges, fix the leaky faucets, rewire the outlets, clean the grout between the bathroom tiles. And, more recently, all the time he'd spent on the renovations with Larisa. Larisa, who hadn't even bothered to tell him the truth. Well, you know what? *Fuck Larisa*, he thought. Fuck her and her stupid house. He had more right to be there than she did. Too bad if she didn't like it.

"You're wrong," he told Holly. "It's my house. And I'm going to take care of you."

CHAPTER NINE

By the time the hospital discharged her, Holly's ribs were already beginning to feel better, especially with the help of the pain meds, but the leg would take six to eight weeks to heal, the doctors said, and so she'd be almost fully dependent on Jack to take care of her and the boys. *Don't fuck it up, old man,* Jack told himself as he helped her down from the truck the morning they arrived at Elmhurst. *For God's sake, just don't fuck it up.*

Holly eased her way over the icy walk and maneuvered through the front door and into the dusty entryway. She tilted her head curiously at the piece of pheasant wallpaper obscuring the front hall mirror before moving tentatively around the foyer on crutches.

"Hello?" called Jack into the hushed house. Brent's car still sat unmoved under a pile of snow in the plowed driveway.

That didn't necessarily mean he was still here, but better to find out now before the boys arrived with Holly's mom.

"Jeez, this place is a mess," said Holly, shuffling through the construction debris. She sniffed a bit at the air. "And it *reeks* of pot."

Then Brent emerged from the shadows, his eyes as wide as saucers, clutching the stack of bridal magazines Larisa had compiled over the past few months.

"Man," he greeted Jack, "am I glad to see you. There is absolutely *nothing* to do around here. I would have started putting some of these walls back together but didn't think it was my place." He lifted his arms to show off his load. "So I started in on these instead. You know, so I can maybe help out a little with the wedding."

Jack nodded and watched Brent's eyes pop as he took in Holly on the crutches, her face still swollen and bruised.

"Whoa, what happened to you? Mrs. Jack, right? I recognize you from your wedding photo." He jutted his chin toward Jack. "He keeps it on his bedside table, you know."

Surprise registered on Holly's face as she looked to Jack for affirmation. "He does?"

Jack nodded and then turned to Brent. "Guess you've had time to wander the house."

Brent smiled back and gestured toward the dining room. "I thought about signing my name inside the wall as well. You know, a classic 'Brent was here' declaration or something like that. But I don't think Larisa would like it."

"Why wouldn't she like it?" asked Holly. "Nobody will see it once the walls are sealed up."

"Too permanent," said Brent. "Even after the walls are sealed up."

Holly turned to Jack. "Is your name there?"

Jack felt the heat on his cheeks. He still hadn't told Holly about his kiss with Larisa even after he'd come clean about the one-night stand. He hoped she wouldn't notice Larisa's name on the wall as well.

"Yes," he answered, resting his hand on Holly's shoulder, "but like I said last night, this is *my* house. At least for the time being. My name should be on these walls."

He gave Brent a quick summary of everything that had happened over the past couple of days since the storm had hit.

Brent's eyes grew even wider as he listened. "A tree on your house? No wonder you were gone so long." Brent directed his comments to Jack but then turned to face Holly. "You must be thanking your lucky stars you got out of there alive."

"I am." Holly took him in, a doubtful expression clouding her features. "So . . . you and Larisa are getting married?"

Brent swept his hair out of his eyes and pushed it behind his ear. "I guess."

"You guess?" Holly crutched her way past him and into the parlor. "Well, have you set the date yet?"

Brent followed her, his eyes fluttering toward Jack with a questioning look as he clutched the bridal magazines.

"June, I think," said Jack. Had Larisa actually agreed to this? he wondered. In the last few months they'd joked a lot together about the wedding, but Brent now seemed to think it was real. That seemed unlikely to Jack, but what did he know? Larisa seemed to have her share of secrets.

Holly eased herself into an armchair and squinted skeptically back at Jack. She propped the injured leg up on an ottoman.

Brent dumped the magazines on the coffee table and then

flung himself down across the three-cushion couch next to Holly. He shoved two silk couch pillows behind his head, balanced one of the bridal magazines on his torso, and began paging through. "What do you think . . . cummerbund or no cummerbund?"

Jack rolled his eyes as he sat in one of the side chairs facing them.

Holly considered. "Well, has she picked a color scheme yet? You should match your cummerbund to that."

Brent shrugged and flipped forward a few pages. "I don't know. She likes green."

Holly homed in. "What kind of green? Lime? Kelly? Chartreuse? Kelly green can be tough to take in a tie and cummerbund, unless you're OK looking like a leprechaun."

Brent shrugged as if to say maybe. He twirled his curls around with one finger and grinned. "I think I'd look pretty damn good as a leprechaun."

"Larisa is *not* going to pick kelly green," Jack couldn't help but chime in. "I mean, she has an art history degree. She's going to pick something more subtle."

"True," said Brent, licking a finger and using it to flip the page. "She's artsy-fartsy."

Holly shifted her focus to Jack. "Remember our color scheme?"

"Uh-oh." Jack scanned his memory but came up short. "This is a test, right?"

"Periwinkle and pearl," she answered for him. "Totally classic."

"Periwinkle?" Jack grimaced. "I just remember I was so nervous, I almost dropped the damn rings."

Holly fingered her wedding band. She reached for one of

the magazines and began to leaf through it. "Ooh, this must be important. Larisa underlined it." Holly pointed to a passage and then read it aloud. "'Twenty-Five Keys to a Successful Marriage.' Number twenty-five: 'Everyone is hard to live with.'"

Brent smashed the silk pillows farther under his head with his fist. "That's probably true. I *am* hard to live with."

Jack laughed despite himself. "Well, I guess we'll find out, seeing as we'll all be in the house together for a while. How long do you plan to stay?"

Brent shrugged. "Till Larisa gets back? I mean, I took these few weeks off to be with her."

"Have you heard from her?"

"Not since Monday night. You?"

Jack shook his head. "No. But I left her a voicemail yesterday, asking her to call. I didn't want to explain everything that's happened over a voicemail."

"Huh," said Brent. "Funny she hasn't checked in."

"She's probably taking a few days to be with her parents," Jack offered.

"Well, I hope she knows your work here is wrapping up," said Holly. "Plenty to do at your own house now, what with the roof caved in."

"Right." Jack nodded, wondering whether Brent's hair would leave oil stains on the silk pillows. Oh well, not for him to worry about. He stood, approached Holly, and leaned to kiss her. "The insurance company will send over a crew for the repairs on our place. But you're right: it's time to be done here. I'll get to work right after I make some lunch and get you settled."

Holly blinked up at him and reached for his chin.

But as his lips met hers again, he had to fight not to compare it to the explosive kiss he'd shared with Larisa. No, he told himself, no. The thing with Larisa was over. If Brent could be believed, she seemed to be going through with her stupid wedding. Jack knew he should at least call to tell her that he'd taken over the house with Holly and the boys, but he didn't feel like it—damn it, he was still pissed she hadn't even bothered to tell him the truth about Elmhurst.

"Hey," said Brent, popping up from the couch to follow Jack out, "did someone say something about lunch? I'm starving."

A few more days went by and they'd all settled in remarkably well, actually. The boys had blown in, taking ownership of the house almost immediately: storming up and down the hallways, riding the banister, sending missives to one another down the laundry chute. Jack set Holly up on the foldout bed in the downstairs study so she wouldn't have to contend with the stairs, and the boys were installed in twin beds upstairs, near his back bedroom and not far from Ursula's suite, where first Larisa and now Brent had taken occupancy. Initially, it felt odd to have Brent hanging around, but Jack adjusted. Brent squirreled away the weed even before he was asked, and the boys took to him quickly, chasing him through the many rooms and recruiting him to their sledding expeditions and snowball battles on the front lawn. Brent was handy as well when he wasn't stoned. He stepped up to help Jack with the repairs and the two of them were making such good progress that Jack didn't feel the need to call in his larger crew. At this rate, most of the house would be put back together in a matter of days.

Remarkably, he and Holly seemed to be getting on well too. It felt strange at first to be living together again after so long apart. But the house, it seemed, gave them a new stage on which to set their drama, the accident had given them a new script, and it was invigorating.

"Now I remember why I married you," she said as he collected her laundry and straightened her room. "My Jack. Always so dependable."

He helped her upstairs for a sponge bath in the claw-foot tub, working slowly and carefully so as not to moisten the cast. He massaged her shoulders when she was settled back downstairs in her armchair. Now that she wasn't so angry, it was much easier to be affectionate. He realized that he hadn't sat quietly with her in a long time. Even before the separation, they'd been so caught up in the hubbub of daily life that they'd stopped listening to each other. But now, with the boys back in school during the day and tramping around after Brent when they got home, he'd found time for some tender moments with Holly.

One afternoon, Jack brought the wedding photo down from his room and set it on the table next to her bed. "Remember how young we once were?"

Holly smiled. Jack felt suddenly sad for the loss of passion in their relationship. After long days of working and raising the kids, he had often just retreated, seeking time for himself. It had been hard, even, to kiss her sometimes, never mind make love. And once that fire had died down, neither one of them had tried hard enough to reignite it.

Jack leaned back in his chair, feeling suddenly very serious. "If you could have seen what was in store for us then, would you have still married me? Knowing what you know now?"

Holly's gaze moved beyond him, her eyes seeking something in the corners of the room, some answer hidden there in the shadows. Jack found himself on edge for her response when it came much slower than expected. Finally she wiped the hair out of her eyes and smiled shyly up at him. "I would have. Would you? Regardless of what happens with us now?"

He thought back to it all, their years together, their shared experiences. Hiking as twenty-year-olds in the White Mountains and swimming through the cool pools formed by waterfalls. Packing a picnic and spending a Saturday at the beach, burying their watermelon in the sand. Moving in together to their first apartment, a basement unit that took on water in the rainy spring. Then their engagement and wedding. Their first big fight as newlyweds when, stupidly, he'd insisted on Thanksgiving with his parents instead of hers. They'd laughed together, cried together, shouted at each other. But they'd grown with each other, too, even if eventually they'd grown apart. The stuff he had gone through with Holly had brought him to where he was now and he wouldn't trade it, despite the heartache. And, of course, the boys. She'd given him those wonderful boys. So he smiled in response to her question. "Yes, I would marry you. Without a doubt." But even as he said the words, he knew they offered no guarantee for the future.

One night, when he crept in to check on her, she pulled him down to the mattress and engulfed him in an ardent embrace. Then her lips were on his, her tongue darting, her hands gripping his ass.

"I want you," she whispered lustfully into his ear.

He found himself aroused in an instant but concerned about hurting her. "Not yet, honey. Your leg."

"Soon," she said.

And then it was like when they were teenagers again, making out in the back of his Chevy, groping each other all over, coming to the brink of actual intercourse but stopping short so that the whole thing left them panting and frantic and exhilarated. My God, thought Jack, why had it taken them so long to get back to this place? Had they only needed this new setting to reignite their relationship? Was it something about Elmhurst herself, this house that he had known and loved but never fully shared with his wife? Or was it really the near tragedy, the tree that had struck their home, that had brought them together again?

Now this Sunday afternoon, five days post-accident and with Christmas almost upon them, here they all were. He and Holly had taken the boys to church that morning, not to the quaint Episcopal chapel Ursula had frequented, but to the monumental St. Mary's on the other side of town. They'd invited Brent along, of course, but he had declined, muttering something about being nonreligious and having errands to run.

"Thank God I'm an atheist!" he joked as they headed out the door.

Normally, the boys complained the few times per month that Jack or Holly dragged them to church. But perhaps still shaken by the recent trauma, they went without prodding. They'd been protective of Holly since the accident, catering to her needs almost before Jack could, bringing her tea, stroking her hair, offering frequent hugs. They seemed to want to keep her in their sights, peering over their shoulders at her as she hobbled out of a room. In the sanctuary that morning, they'd been on their best behavior, keeping their hands to themselves and listening attentively as Father Frank recounted the Christmas story—the miraculous birth of Baby Jesus, the Savior. But now, sprawled on the living room rug with Brent, playing a game of Monopoly, some of their usual quizzical commentary emerged. With Holly resting peacefully in her room, Jack couldn't help but smile from his armchair as he worked his way through the newspaper.

"Doesn't it seem weird," said Alex, "that basically the only reason Jesus was born was to die for our sins years later?"

Brent looked up from his tomato soup, eyebrows raised. "See. This is why I don't go to church."

Charlie fiddled with one of his miniature houses on the board. "You don't actually believe that crap, do you? That Jesus rose from the dead?"

Alex shrugged and reached for one of the cards. "I don't know. That's what we're supposed to believe, isn't it? If we have faith?"

"Yeah, yeah." Charlie rolled the dice and ticked his game token—the top hat—forward along the perimeter of the board. "God gave his only son for our sins and all that stuff. Didn't happen. Jesus didn't actually rise from the dead, dummy. If that guy died on the cross, he sure as hell didn't crawl out of some cave a few days later."

Ben sat quietly next to Charlie, paging through his book of M. C. Escher drawings as he awaited his turn. Jack could peer down into the book, and he found himself amazed, as always, by the elaborately sketched illusions—stairs leading to nowhere, rivers streaming uphill, a tessellation of birds transforming into fish. Now Ben looked up and tilted his head thoughtfully.

"What if Jesus was actually an identical twin?"

The group paused to process this suggestion and then Brent's face became suddenly animated. "Oh right! And there was one evil Jesus and one benevolent Jesus."

All three boys responded with baffled expressions.

"Huh?" said Ben. "That is *not* what I meant."

Alex stepped in to clarify. "No, he means the identical twin was hiding in the tomb and he pretended to rise from the dead after the real Jesus died on the cross."

"Whoa," said Brent. "That's heavy."

They all paused and then Charlie shattered the silence with a big guffaw. He swatted at his brothers across the board. "Jesus wasn't an identical twin, you idiots."

Brent started chuckling too. "Oh man. You guys crack me up."

"I *know* he wasn't," said Ben, defensive now. He dodged Charlie and slammed the Escher book shut. "I'm just saying, things aren't always what they seem."

A silence fell over the room. Jack lowered the paper, feeling their eyes on him.

"Wha?" said Brent, looking back and forth between them all.

Jack wasn't sure exactly what was coming, but he'd sensed for days now that the boys had been saving up their questions, waiting for the moment at which they could unleash their emotions and begin to sort through everything that had taken place. He wasn't surprised when the inquisition finally came.

"Are you and Mommy back together?" Alex asked. He peered sideways up at Jack as though shielding himself from the answer.

"I don't know," said Jack. "I think so." His reunion with Holly had been so abrupt that he still felt a fair degree of uncertainty about it himself.

"What's with all these wedding magazines?" Charlie asked. "You said nobody's getting married."

Jack remembered how Charlie had shouted it from the prow of the boat on Columbus Day weekend. *Nobody's getting married!* he had called into the wind, and they had all laughed.

"Brent and Larisa are getting married," Jack answered, looking to Brent for concurrence. Brent nodded, though somewhat unconvincingly.

"Where *is* Larisa?" Alex wondered. "Does she even know we're all at her house?"

"It's not really her house," said Jack.

"I'm never getting married," Charlie told Brent. "Women are too much work."

Brent smiled. "They can be fun sometimes too."

"Fun?" Charlie scowled back at him disapprovingly, but before he could say more, Ben broke in.

"Dad, are we going to be back home for Christmas?" he asked.

Silence fell again as the three boys waited for Jack's response.

"Maybe." Jack tilted his head. "If not, we can have Christmas here."

"Hey, that's an idea," said Brent. "How 'bout I take the boys out to get a Christmas tree? We can surprise Larisa. The gas station down the street is selling them. I saw them when I went out to get some air this morning."

"Oh yeah," answered Jack. "Andy sells them every year.

Want me to drive you over? Easy to throw a tree in the back of the truck."

"No, thanks." Brent looked to the boys. "We can carry it, right?

"Of course," answered Alex.

"I'm a lumberjack and I don't care," Brent chanted as he headed to the foyer and began to pull on his winter gear. He motioned for the boys to follow suit. They made their way noisily out the front door and down the drive. What with Brent being a tree guy, someone who normally worked to *save* trees, Jack wondered how Brent actually felt about buying one that had been chopped down. But seeing as Brent didn't seem too concerned, he decided not to question it. Thinking about the tree, Jack began to wonder when the plants in the conservatory had last been watered. He'd done it the day they'd returned from the hospital, but probably no one had thought about it since, so with the boys out of the house and Holly still sleeping, he decided to check.

With little insulation and limited heat, the conservatory usually felt quite chilly in the winter, but today the sun beamed in, trapping the heat beneath the glass and infusing the room with a warm and radiant glow. As Ursula had gotten on in age, she'd cultivated fewer plants and so the collection was much more sparse than it had once been. But the greenhouse was still edged with a staggered row of variegated ficus and several clusters of potted ferns. A tiered plant stand showcased an assortment of orchids, some with blooms as small as dimes, others as large as teacups. Their colors varied as well—plum purple, mustard yellow, an incandescent white—and the air around them emitted the rich, rusty aroma of wet dirt. Jack felt himself relax among the greenery and as he turned on the water and lifted the hose to give the plants a drink, he remembered his first visit here, the day on which Ursula had steeped him in the Mahler symphony for ninety minutes. The Victrola, he saw, still sat by the French doors, flanked by a pile of records. And there, unassuming in a plain terra-cotta pot on the brick floor next to them, sat the night-blooming cereus, dormant now without a bud in sight, but showing signs of new growth in its limbs. Jack saturated its soil and then moved to turn the water off. As he did so, he heard Holly cantilevering down the hallway on her crutches. He waited for her to appear, hose still in hand, an idea slowly taking hold in his mind.

When she finally arrived at the entryway and looked up, he gave her his biggest smile.

"Come on," he said, gesturing toward one of the cushioned metal lounge chairs. "Lie down. I'll wash your hair."

Holly scrunched her nose and gave a nervous laugh. She took a step forward, glancing around at the exposed windows. "In here?"

"Sure. This place is perfect." Jack gestured with the dripping hose. "Fresh water, a drain in the floor, plenty of sunshine to keep you warm."

Holly's uncertain grimace gave way to a gleeful grin as she staggered over to the lounge chair. "Oh, I would kill to have clean hair again."

Jack went to fetch the shampoo and towels from the upstairs bathroom. When he returned, Holly had arranged herself in a reclining position, her loose shirt pulled down to reveal her shoulders, her head resting on the rim of the metal seat back.

Jack wrapped the cast with one of the towels and draped the other over her torso. "Lose the shirt," he told her, smiling again and tugging on her sleeve. "Come on, the kids are out with Brent. No one else in sight."

Holly looked hesitant but did as told. She repositioned herself, pulling the towel up to the lower wire of her black bra and folding her arms against the chill. Her full breasts swelled beneath the fabric and Jack nodded approvingly. Their evening tryst had been fun, but seeing her like this in full daylight brought a whole other level of excitement.

"Now for a little music," he said. He sorted through the records and came up with one—not the Mahler, of course, but the recognizable "La Cumparsita" tango, with its marching rhythm and staccato strings. He dropped the needle on the vinyl and the music burst forth, strong and sensual with a mesmerizing tone that compelled him to shake his hips comically in time as he strutted over to retrieve the hose and open the spigot. Holly giggled as he approached, still shimmying, and then squealed as the icy water soaked her head and ran down her back, but soon she closed her eyes and leaned into it. Jack lathered his hands with the shampoo and plunged them into her long thick hair, kneading it at the roots and massaging deep into her scalp. He worked the suds up into a foam, smoothing it down the hair shaft, teasing the tresses with his fingers. After he'd worked at it for several minutes, feeling her soften, arms unfolded now, he gave the hair a good rinse, caressed her shoulders, and wiped the water from her brow. Her chest moved slowly up and down, the breasts still bulging out from the halter of her bra, so tempting that he couldn't help but flick a stream of water at them.

"Jack!" she screamed, but she was smiling and laughing, and her blue eyes, open now, glinted mischievously back at him as she seized the hose over her shoulder and soaked his hair and the entire front of his flannel shirt.

"Ha," she countered. "Take that!"

But the cast prevented her from maneuvering and so he easily snatched the hose away and tossed it to the brick where it continued to spew water toward the drain.

"Oh really? Now you're in trouble," he chastised. He came around to the front, leaned over her, and shook like a wet dog so that the droplets of water sprayed all over her bare skin. Screaming now, she attempted to hold him off, but he straddled her on his knees and lowered himself to kiss her neck, her cheek, her chin. He licked the water from her full lips, kissed her hard, and then pulled back to look at her. His Holly. His first love. Staring him down to see what he would do next. The tango music still swelled around them and she grinned up at him with the brightest smile he'd seen in years, urging him to keep going. And so he cupped those breasts in his hands and then reached behind her back to unhitch her bra. Holly shook the undergarment off her arms. Her breasts bounced free, heaving, her nipples firm and erect.

"Oh, honey," he whispered, and he moved to take one in his mouth. But as he did, the record scratched and the music came to an abrupt halt. Jack swiveled to face the door and there stood Larisa, looking totally overdressed in her turtleneck sweater, wool skirt, and boots. Holly gasped and tugged the towel over her body and up to her throat. Larisa dropped her suitcase to the brick, where it fell with a clatter.

"What the hell is going on here?" she snapped, stepping over the threshold and into the room as the water from the hose continued to gurgle down the drain.

CHAPTER TEN

Larisa stood, stunned, trying to make sense of the scene into which she had just stumbled. She'd spent a good portion of the drive back from No One's Home trying to determine exactly what she'd say to Jack to patch things up and convince him to give her another chance. He'd been right. There really was something special between them. She'd felt it all along and just hadn't been ready to face it. Now she was. And so she'd done her hair and she'd chosen her clothing carefully from the limited selection she'd brought along when she'd rushed off to visit her parents. She'd thought she'd prepared herself well. But no. *No*. Neither the advanced preening nor the drive had prepared her for this: Jack and Holly in various states of undress, groping each other on the chaise longue amid the orchids of Aunt Ursula's conservatory.

Jack pushed himself quickly to a standing position on the

brick. He smoothed his shirt and ran his hands through his wet hair, but seemed totally unable to answer. Instead he just gaped at her, a look of anguish in his eyes, and so it was Holly who broke the silence, clutching the towel to her chest, her fingers tangled together around it so that she almost seemed to be praying.

"He was washing my hair," she said.

But it didn't make sense. It didn't make any sense at all. My God, thought Larisa, was she losing her mind, like her mother? And was that a cast on Holly's leg, partially hidden under a second towel? Her own injured wrist seemed insignificant in comparison; she was glad she'd removed the bandages. She looked down at the hose, water still streaming out of its mouth, and eyed the shampoo bottle that lay sideways on the brick floor.

"Washing your hair? Here? In the conservatory?" Larisa floundered in her attempt to assemble the discordant montage into some sort of clear picture. "I thought you two were separated."

Then, in that moment, something almost imperceptible passed between Larisa and Jack. His eyes flared at her. He glanced quickly toward his wife and then back at her, and Larisa understood that he was concerned she might reveal something to Holly about the kiss they had shared. Holly seemed to briefly home in on it too. She lifted her nose like a dog sniffing for an intruder. But unable to locate the threat, she dropped her head and then raised her eyebrows toward Jack.

"I'm sorry," he finally said after a weighted pause. "I should have called to tell you that I brought Holly and the kids here. It's just been so crazy. A tree fell on our house. Holly broke her leg."

"The kids are here too?" Larisa stomped across the brick and wrenched the faucet shut so that the water finally stopped burbling down the drain. She kicked the hose to the side and turned to face Jack and Holly again, her arms folded across her chest. "So you've all been living here without my knowledge?"

"Oh my God," Holly gasped, glaring over at Jack. "You didn't tell her?" She'd taken the moment when Larisa's back was turned to wriggle back into her shirt, and now she pivoted on the chaise so that the cast was fully revealed. "Larisa, I am so sorry. We had no place else to go. I thought he told you."

Larisa glowered at Jack. "He didn't tell me."

Jack shook his head. "I left you a voicemail saying we needed to talk. Too many details to cover in a message. You could have at least called to tell us you were on your way."

Larisa threw her arms to her sides, palms upturned, in anger and disbelief. "I need to call to say I'm coming back to my own house?"

"Although it's not actually your house, is it?"

Larisa countered with her own penetrating stare. "Well, it sure as hell isn't yours."

The three faced one another, the light through the glass dimming as the clouds slid over the sun. Larisa knew she should respond with some sympathy for Jack and Holly—my God, a tree on the house? A broken leg?—and yet something uncontrollable boiled inside her. Jack had brought his wife and kids to the house. *Their* house. The one that she and Jack had labored tirelessly over together. They'd signed their names on the wall. True, neither of them actually owned it and yet each of them could lay a claim. She understood why he'd brought

Holly here, but it felt like an unforgivable violation. Like he'd shared something intensely private, like he'd broken the spell.

On the brink of losing it and afraid of making a scene, Larisa hurried out of the room and back down the hallway into the foyer. She just needed a few minutes alone, she thought, to sort things out, some fresh air to clear her head. But as she approached the front door, Brent came bursting in with the triplets behind, the three of them tugging a netted Christmas tree through the front door.

Larisa skidded to a stop. "You're still here?" When he'd arrived, Brent had mentioned that he'd taken a few weeks off, but she assumed he'd head back to his apartment after she'd fled into the storm.

"There's my bride-to-be!" he called over his shoulder as he took hold of the trunk and guided the team into the parlor.

"Bride-to-be?" Larisa repeated warily, her voice questioning. But it was not truly a question so much as a way of not quite committing. Though she wasn't about to get into it with Brent in front of the others, she at least wanted to throw some public doubt on the subject of their engagement. It was Jack she wanted, not Brent. But Brent seemed oblivious as he and the boys marched the tree into the room and laid it across the hearth. Once he'd unloaded the burden, he lumbered over and enveloped her in his big, burly arms.

"Come 'ere, you," he growled playfully as he gripped her. Then he hoisted her off her feet, spun her around the foyer, and landed a long, sloppy kiss across her lips.

Larisa felt the affection in his embrace, and she tried to relax into it. "Wow, I'm amazed you stayed."

Brent palmed her head in his large hand and stroked her

hair. "Of course I stayed. I've been waiting for you to come back so we could celebrate."

Peering over Brent's shoulder, Larisa could glimpse Jack and Holly emerging from the conservatory, fully composed now aside from the wet hair. Loath to discuss the quasi engagement in front of them, she let Brent's comment go unanswered. Instead she took a deep breath and gathered herself. She forced a smile onto her face as she moved past Brent to approach the two.

"I'm sorry," she said to Jack and Holly. "Really, I'm sorry. I didn't mean to snap at you. That's just horrible about your leg and the house. I'm so glad none of you were seriously hurt."

Jack rested his hands protectively on Holly's shoulders.

"That's all right," he said, though Larisa could see that he was still annoyed. "We're just happy everyone's OK." He gestured toward the boys, who came bounding in from the living room. "You remember my kids. Alex, Ben, Charlie."

"Sure," said Larisa, eyeing the tree on the hearth and their coats strewn across the upholstery. "Looks like you've all made yourself at home."

She meant it to sound welcoming—really, she did—but as the triplets nodded in response, she could see them bristle at the accusatory tone of the remark. Frustrated at herself, her heart pounding in her throat, she closed her eyes, took another deep breath, and released it slowly through pursed lips.

"Hey," said Brent, slinging an arm over her shoulder. "Are *you* OK? How was the visit with your parents?"

Larisa shielded her bruised wrist and spun out of his hold. "I'm fine. I'm just a little overwhelmed. This visit to my parents was hard."

Brent waggled a finger at her. "Which reminds me. I saw Andy at the gas station just now when we went to get the tree. We told him we were bringing the tree to Elmhurst and he asked about the Rolls."

Larisa hedged. "Um, well, the car didn't handle that well in the snow. So I borrowed my father's."

In truth, she'd left the car at the auto body shop and begged for her father to lend her his. Once the bumper was restored to its former condition, her parents could drive it down on Christmas Eve. With any luck, Andy hadn't yet discovered that she'd taken the Rolls out into the storm. She'd have it back before he knew anything had ever happened.

"What did you tell him?" she asked Brent.

Brent shook his head. "Only that you'd check in with him soon. He seemed OK with that. Then he asked if I was the groom. I said, 'Heck yeah!'" Brent smiled widely and exchanged high fives with each of the triplets. At the reference to the wedding, Holly's eyebrows shot up, a flash of realization across her face.

"The wedding—I almost forgot! Well, of course you're overwhelmed," she said to Larisa. "To find everyone here and then a wedding to think about."

Larisa winced slightly and glanced sideways at Brent. "I haven't thought much about the wedding, actually."

"Well, that's OK," said Holly, moving past Larisa into the parlor and gesturing for the others to follow. "Brent and I have been planning it for you."

"That's true," said Brent, playfully nudging Larisa with his elbow. "I found your stack of magazines. I even highlighted a few things."

Larisa ignored him and homed in on Holly in the parlor.

"You've been planning it for me? Brent and I haven't even had time to talk."

"Oh, I know," answered Holly, waving her hand dismissively in the air. "I just meant we've been chatting about it."

"Okaaay." Larisa gritted her teeth. "But we're not anywhere near the planning phase yet."

"Of course, of course," Holly answered. "It's your day. But, seriously, let me help. We've been such an imposition moving in here . . . and then, ahem, that scene in the greenhouse. The least I can do is make myself useful. I totally could have been a wedding planner in another life."

"What scene in the greenhouse?" asked Brent.

"That's so nice of you to offer to help," Larisa cut in with her response to Holly. "But I need some time to wrap my own head around it first." She cleared her throat. "I can't quite believe it's happening."

Brent didn't seem to notice her hesitation. But Jack stood by the doorway, an amused expression on his face. He shook his head and Larisa could see that he couldn't quite believe it either. Then he gestured toward the Christmas tree. "OK if I bring some of the ornaments up from the basement? I already brought the stand up. The kids are excited to decorate."

"Sure," said Larisa. She moved her gaze from one side of the room to the other, taking them all in. "It's been a while since the place has seen so much holiday cheer. I wonder what Aunt Ursula would think."

Brent beckoned the boys into the room and the four of them guided the tree into the stand. They spent several minutes securing it, twisting it this way and that to find its best face. Meanwhile, Larisa and Holly eyed each other from opposing armchairs. Holly's hair was still wet and though she looked almost matronly now, her injured leg propped up on the ottoman, Larisa was having a hard time banishing the lusty vision of her supine in the chaise, Jack astride and leaning in to mouth her breast. My God, she thought, what exactly had been going on here in the few days she'd been gone? Had it really taken so little time for Jack and Holly to reconcile? Surely Jack had been seduced into this intimate encounter. After all, it had only been days since he'd landed the kiss on Larisa and insisted there was something between them. She'd been led to believe that his marriage was on the brink of being over. But now here they all were—his wife and family—taking over Elmhurst as though they'd lived here forever. As the kids rummaged through Aunt Ursula's Christmas ornaments and began to hook them onto the tree, sipping at the cans of soda that Brent had passed around, Larisa found herself at a loss for words. She had expected to return to the quiet but satisfying rhythm she'd been sharing with Jack. She'd expected to move their relationship to the next realm, after she'd broken things off with Brent, of course, this time for good. Instead she'd come home to this. Jack's three kids, his estranged wife, and her own ex-boyfriend-turned-fiancé. None of them belonged here—my God, they didn't even have the sense to use coasters on the fine wood furniture—and yet she couldn't banish them to the street. And thinking about it, she realized, she didn't want Jack and Holly and the kids to go. Because if they went, that meant she'd be stuck here alone with Brent. Who she *did not* want to marry. Yes, she'd thought about Jack on the way home, but she'd thought a good deal about Brent as well. He wasn't right for her; she'd known it for a long time. But she felt awful about having to break it to him.

"I'm hungry," announced one of the boys.

"Me too," said the others in unison.

Jack looked at his watch and then glanced over at Holly. "We have a call with the insurance company in ten minutes. I could go get some takeout after that. We definitely don't have enough in the fridge for everyone."

Brent chimed in, directing his words to Jack. "No way. It's my turn to buy. How does everyone feel about Chinese food?"

Larisa was about to protest—takeout cartons at Elmhurst? Like disposable cups and Continental breakfast, this was a thing of which Ursula would not have approved. But then the boys exploded in a chorus of *"Yes!"*

"Fan-tastic," bellowed Brent. "Get ready for pu-pu platters galore."

"Sounds good to me." Holly pushed herself to a standing position and began to hobble toward the door. "Jack, honey, let's take the call in my room."

"Your room?" questioned Larisa, noticing that Holly had bypassed the stairs to the second floor.

"Oh, that library-looking place," Holly answered. "Easier to get to on crutches."

"The study," corrected Larisa, though Holly was already out of earshot.

Jack headed after Holly but then glanced back at Larisa. "You OK here with the boys? The call shouldn't take too long. It's just a progress update, really. To see how soon we can get back in our house and out of yours."

"Sure," said Larisa, hoping she looked more composed than she felt. Jack seemed calmer now, less angry. She yearned for a chance to talk to him alone. But he disappeared quickly after Holly and then thankfully Brent was gone, too, off to get the food. So Larisa was left alone with the boys. As silence fell over the room, each of the triplets turned to face her. As she blinked back at them, it occurred to Larisa that she'd never really spent that much time with kids. What was she supposed to say to them? She selected a few ornaments from the boxes and began handing them off to the boys—a red-nosed reindeer, a snowflake, a silver sparkly orb.

"That must have been scary to almost lose your mother," Larisa remarked, hoping to break the ice. She was thinking mostly about her own mother, actually, and the illness with which she was grappling. But when all three boys stiffened, she realized her comment had come across as too harsh. One of the kids shrugged, though she wasn't sure which.

"You're . . . Alex?" she ventured.

"Ben."

"Oh right. Sorry."

Then the one she knew to be Charlie piped up. "We're not identical, you know."

Larisa did know. But to be born to the same parents, on the same day. There was a sameness about them despite their differences.

Alex fidgeted with the collar of his shirt. "I was born first."

Charlie gave a self-amused smile before offering his rebuttal. "Yeah, but Dad says I might have been conceived first."

"Ew," said Larisa.

"There's no way to know that," Alex snapped back.

Ben, reflective, glanced at Alex, the firstborn. "One of us will die first. Might be you."

Then Charlie leaned over and punched Ben in the shoulder. "Uh, OK, Dr. Death. Morbid much?"

Ben shrugged. "It's true."

Charlie selected a plastic icicle from the ornament box. He

held it up to his own head and mimed a violent death. Ben grabbed it from him, giggling, and began stabbing himself in the gut.

It *was* true, Larisa thought. One of them probably would die first. But it was odd to think about. And jarring coming out of the mouth of an eleven-year-old.

"Or it could be me to die first," continued Ben, shuffling the icicle from one palm to the other. "Like, what if the tree had landed on me instead of Mom?"

"But it didn't land on you, you idiot."

"But it could have."

"But it didn't."

"It *could* have."

"So?"

"Well, then I might have died. First."

God, thought Larisa, did kids always talk like this? Or was it just because of the recent trauma that they were fixated on the subject of death? Larisa didn't have siblings, so this type of banter felt foreign to her. But despite the strangeness of it, she could see what Ben was getting at. She herself had often been waylaid by what-ifs. At the same time, she could also understand Charlie's point of view. The tree hadn't fallen on the kids. And anyway, Holly hadn't died; she'd only broken her leg. What was the sense in dwelling on what could have happened? Impatient, Alex pried the icicle ornament from Ben's fingers.

"If the two of you don't shut up," he said, "I'm gonna kill both of you. And then you'll both be dead first." He turned to string the decoration onto a branch, and that was that.

With the boys occupied with trimming the tree, Larisa wandered into the foyer. She heard the blare of a blow-dryer coming from the study, which probably meant the insurance call was over. Running her hand up the banister, she stepped slowly up the stairs to the second floor, taking in the framed portraits and photographs, as she always did. The three sisters, the family reunion, the girl with the enormous bow. Just as she reached the upper landing, Jack emerged from the hallway that led to the room where he'd been staying.

Larisa jumped, startled to see him. He must have gone up the back stairs. Her gaze settled into his and they both held it there. Larisa felt the electricity between them. As always, she felt a sense of ease around Jack that she didn't feel with anyone else. She took a deep breath and released it.

"So," said Larisa. "You're back together with your wife."

Jack cocked his head and gave her a quizzical look. "What do you care, now that you're getting married?"

Larisa sighed and shook her head. "I'm not. The whole thing's a huge misunderstanding."

"Oh sure," said Jack, his voice sarcastic. "You bought the dress, you set the date, you've been reading the magazines. Sounds like a total misunderstanding."

"No," insisted Larisa. "I just got caught up in the idea of it. I didn't really want to get married. At least not to Brent."

Jack snorted. "Yeah? Well, you might want to clue him in a little before he blows all his savings on a fancy tuxedo."

"I know," said Larisa, grimacing. "I will. We just haven't had the chance to talk.

"Jack, listen," she added. "I'm sorry I lied to you. About the house. When I first came back to town, I thought I was going to convince my father to sell Elmhurst. But once we started the renovations, I got so caught up in it all that it made me doubt my intentions. I just never got around to admitting it to you."

Jack gave a slight nod, a begrudging acceptance of her apology. "What do you plan to do now? With Elmhurst?"

Larisa shrugged. "I'm not sure. This visit with my parents made me think about a lot of things." She thought back to the dance between her mother and father, the tenderness between them. "Jack, it made me think about what you said."

"No," said Jack, waving her away. "I've had time to think too. I was wrong. Holly needs me. My kids need me. Look what happened when I wasn't there."

"That could have happened whether or not you were there," protested Larisa. "No one knew that tree was going to fall."

"You don't get it, do you?" Jack said. "I could have lost her. I could have lost the kids. Do you know what it's like to watch your wife get hauled out on a stretcher?"

"I don't," Larisa conceded. "But I do know what it's like to watch someone you love struggle. My mother's been sick—"

"Oh, and there's another thing you never told me about."

Larisa winced. "I can barely face it myself."

"Listen," said Jack. "My focus is on my family right now. I'm *responsible* for them. They need me."

Larisa felt her stomach drop. "But I feel something for you. Something strong. I'm finally ready to face it."

"No," said Jack, shaking his head. "That's over."

"I even felt it just now," continued Larisa. "As soon as I saw you at the top of the stairs. That thing between us. I was scared before, I wasn't ready, so I ran away. But I came back to face it. I came back."

"I don't care," said Jack, scowling at her. "Do you hear what I am saying? I. Don't. Care."

Before she could protest again, he pushed past her and stomped away down the stairs.

Larisa watched him go. "But you do," she whispered to herself. "I know you do."

That evening, after the takeout meal, she and Brent made their way awkwardly up the stairs together toward Aunt Ursula's room. Larisa felt exhausted from the drive down from New Hampshire and the series of disappointing encounters with Jack. She just wanted to curl up in a ball and go to sleep. But Brent was waiting, already under the covers in Ursula's bed. As Larisa brushed her teeth and changed into her pajamas in the adjoining bathroom, she knew that *now* was the time to tell him that the wedding was off, that it had been a ruse all along. At dinner she'd watched Jack tend carefully to Holly, refilling her water glass and helping her to seconds. She'd seen the warm smiles between them as they laughed at their kids and discussed the repairs on their house. Though the damaged master bedroom would be inhabitable for another month or more, the workers were predicting that the rest of the house would be fixed before Christmas. Listening to their excitement over the prospect of returning home, Larisa realized that Jack and Holly had a whole life together that she knew nothing about. Stupidly, she hadn't really thought of Jack as a father because mostly she saw him without the kids. But watching him tussle with his boys on the living room carpet after dinner, she saw that it was central to who he was, and it changed the way she thought about him. Her attraction to him had not waned, but even if the tree hadn't fallen on the house, she and Jack might never have had a real chance.

She finished brushing and prepared herself for a moment of truth with Brent. When she emerged from the bathroom, he was no longer in bed but stood by the window instead, his back to her, his oversize flannel pajamas sagging at the waist. This whole thing, thought Larisa, was beginning to feel like a sitcom, the bizarre series of events that had landed everyone at Elmhurst.

"Truly," she quipped, "what would Aunt Ursula say about all of us here in the house?"

She expected Brent to roll his eyes and laugh with her, but as she approached, he turned and went down on one knee, a bashful grin across his face, a small ring lying in his open palm.

"Oh no," said Larisa, the words slipping out before she could stop them. Brent waved his hand dismissively, an indication that she shouldn't worry.

"Look," he said. "I'm no dummy. I know you're not really one hundred percent into the idea of marrying me. And this isn't even a real ring. I just got it from the vending machine outside China Buffet."

Larisa sighed and gestured for him to get up off his knees. "Of course I'm not one hundred percent on the idea of marriage. We haven't even lived together since September."

"I know," said Brent. "It's OK. We can lay off the wedding talk. But, Larisa, listen. It's almost Christmas Eve. And being in this house with Jack and the kids has made me realize something."

Larisa froze, fearful of the revelation and what it might require of her.

"I want a family of my own someday." Brent reached for her hand and held it. "I'd be a good father, I know I would. I don't want to turn into an old man who's too tired to play with his kids."

"Of course." Larisa nodded. "I know how much your own father meant to you."

"That's part of it." Brent gazed solemnly at her. "Look, I need you to be honest with me. If you're serious about working things out, then I'm ready to give it a go." Here he dropped her hand and brushed the hair away from his face. "But don't string me along, OK?"

Larisa stared at him. She hadn't expected this moment of clarity from Brent. She'd been waiting all day to explain to him that the wedding was a ruse and here was her chance to come clean; Brent had handed it to her. But somehow, coming on the heels of her rejection from Jack, she hesitated. She thought of the first time she'd seen Brent, working his magic in the trees, how fascinated she'd been as he moved adeptly from limb to limb. Now his blue eyes had such a look of sincerity about them and she knew that despite the conflict between her and Brent, he had loved her in his way. She sighed again. Brent looked up at her with such a hopeful gleam in his eye that her heart welled with tenderness for the good times they had shared. He didn't know about the kiss with Jack. Was it wrong to keep it from him? She could take in his adoration for one more night, couldn't she? When faced with the prospect of saying goodbye, she found she didn't quite want to. At least not now, not yet. God, she was tired. And so totally confused.

"So much has happened," she said. "Please, let's sleep on it. *Just* sleep."

Brent nodded. "Sleep," he repeated. "But please. Be honest with me."

She switched off the lights. The two of them slid tentatively under the covers. Lying there in the dark, she thought again of Jack, his concern for Holly and the boys. Larisa tried to imagine how she would have felt if Brent had been injured the way Holly had. She would be concerned for him, of course, but would it have resurrected any amorous emotion the way it had for Holly and Jack? She closed her eyes and tried to settle into her pillow. After some time, she snuggled her back a little closer to Brent and allowed him to drape an arm around her torso. It felt nice, she thought, to be in his warm strong arms again, his soft breath against her ear. She surrendered and drifted off to a long deep sleep.

In the morning, when she woke, Brent stood by the window, looking out, his back to her. Watching, she tried to think about what he had said. He would be a good father in many ways, that was true. He was playful and energetic and funny. He would devote himself to a wife and kids. She sat up in bed and switched on the light, prepared to face him. He turned and smiled and came to the foot of the bed. Larisa thought for a minute that things might be all right. But then a gust of wind suddenly sent the windowpanes rattling against their frames and the house itself creaked.

"God," said Brent with a grimace, "I can't wait to go home. This place is creepy."

"What do you mean?" Larisa felt her eyes flare. "I feel more at home here than anywhere."

"Well, most of us don't grow up having tea parties with

our great-aunt Ursula." He sighed. "Don't get all bent out of shape. It just isn't for me. I could never live full-time in a place like this."

He stood again, headed toward the bathroom, and shut the door. Larisa stared after him. His comment had been small, but it brought everything into focus for her. Even if she did sell the house, she couldn't imagine being with someone who didn't like Elmhurst. Brent wasn't the partner she wanted, he just wasn't. She was being a coward, using him to make herself feel better. Larisa knew it was over; the future held no place for them. As the day went on, and they all turned to work on the house, her level of agitation increased, knowing she needed to confront him. *Try telling the truth,* her father had said. She would try.

She found Brent in the dining room securing the remaining Sheetrock. She took a deep breath, about to face him, but as his eyes met hers, she faltered.

Brent seemed to sense her intention. He cocked his head toward the open wall but kept his gaze on her. "That's your name on the wall there next to Jack's, huh?"

Larisa glanced quickly at the wall then back at him. She bit her lip. "Brent, listen. We need to talk."

Brent dropped the drill to his side and closed his eyes. "You're breaking up with me, aren't you?"

Larisa pulled out two of the dining room chairs and motioned for him to take a seat next to her. "You told me to be honest with you," she whispered. "I care about you. I really do. If I could make this work out, I would."

"But you don't want to be with me. You never really did."

"Not never, no. We've had some good times together and they've meant a lot to me." She paused. "But no, I'm sorry. I don't want to marry you. This wedding idea was never real. It was all just a joke that went too far."

"Why would you joke about something like that?" Brent glared at her, incredulous.

"I've been too scared to tell you. I didn't want to hurt you."

"You kept me hanging on because you couldn't stand to face yourself."

"That's not true."

"It *is* true. God, Larisa. You have no idea what you want, who you are. You couldn't find yourself in a hall of mirrors."

Larisa knew he was right. Brent knew exactly who he was and she envied him for it. She tried to find a response but didn't know what to say.

Brent filled the silence for her, his voice suddenly loud. "Look at you, trying to find the right words. The *proper* words." He started to mimic her, his hurt turned to anger. "*What would Aunt Ursula do? What would Aunt Ursula say?* Well, let me tell you something, sweetheart. Aunt Ursula wouldn't say a goddamn thing. Because she's fucking dead."

He stood, strode out of the room, and up the stairs.

Jack, who had been working in the kitchen, came through the swinging door just as Brent retreated. "What was all that yelling about? Are you OK?"

Larisa sighed. "I'm fine. But don't expect to hear wedding bells anytime soon."

Jack raised his eyebrows. "You finally leveled with him, huh?"

Larisa nodded. She stood and reached for the piece of Sheetrock and drill that Brent had left behind. She held it in place and began securing it to the wall. Jack looked as though he might help her and Larisa was reminded once more of the moment they'd had together. She wondered whether it might happen again. But then came a clamor at the front door— the kids arriving. Seconds later Holly limped into the room and announced that their house was ready for them to move back in.

"We're going home!" she said, waving her cell phone around like a victory flag.

Larisa tried not to let her feeling of alarm settle on her face. "Wow, so soon," she managed. "I'll go from full house to empty."

Jack looked briefly at Larisa, a flash of concern across his features, before he leaned to hug Holly. "That's wonderful, honey. We'll be home for Christmas."

The boys finished shaking the snow off their boots and Holly sent them upstairs to pack. She retreated to her room to get ready while Jack stood facing Larisa.

"The work is basically done here," he said. "Just a few minor details that my team can finish up."

"Great," said Larisa with a grim smile. "I'll write you a check before you leave."

"Come on, that's not what I was getting at. I just meant you're in good shape. Whatever you decide to do, sell or stay."

Larisa shrugged. "Might as well pay you now. Especially since you're resigning as caretaker. Isn't that what you decided?"

She went over to Aunt Ursula's writing desk, wrote and signed the check, and then handed it to Jack.

"Thanks," he said, putting it in his pocket and striding back toward the foyer. "I'm proud, actually, of how it all turned out."

"Yes," she answered, her eyes meeting his. "Better than expected."

"Right." He gave her one last look and headed toward the stairs.

"Jack, wait."

Larisa felt the panic well within her. If she didn't try one more time with Jack, she knew she'd regret it. Jack turned to face her, his eyes questioning.

"Listen," started Larisa. "I've been afraid of finding the right relationship for a long time. My parents were always so perfectly matched, I wasn't sure I could ever find what they found. It seemed easier to just settle for something close enough."

She wondered what Brent was up to upstairs, whether he might emerge, but she kept her eyes focused on Jack as she continued.

"But now I look at my father and he's losing his partner in life, the person he loves more than anyone." She shook her head. "I don't want to lose you before I even have the chance to see what we could have."

Jack glanced quickly toward the stairs. "We shared one kiss, that was it."

"We could share a lot more."

Upstairs, she heard drawers slamming and the boys' footsteps on the floorboards.

Jack shook his head. "It's over."

The three boys came stumbling down the stairs and Holly made her way slowly into the foyer on her crutches. They all stood there, ready to say goodbye. Then Brent came down as well, his bag slung over his shoulder.

Holly frowned, a look of confusion clouding her features. "Where are you going?"

Brent didn't answer her. Instead he faced Larisa again.

"One more thing," he told her as he flung open the door. "If you love this damn house so much, why are you in such a rush to sell it? Figure out what you want already."

Larisa bowed her head. "You're right," she whispered. "I will."

Brent turned toward Holly and the boys. "I'm sorry you had to witness that. Listen, it's been great getting to know you all, but my time here is clearly up. Congrats on getting back to your house. I'm looking forward to getting back to where I belong, too."

He nodded toward them all, a brief goodbye, and then stepped over the threshold and left. For a second nobody moved. They stood in an uncomfortable silence for what seemed like an eternity and then Holly and the boys began to gather their things.

"Seriously," said Jack, when they were out of earshot. "Are you OK?"

Larisa nodded. *Don't go,* she tried to telegraph to Jack. Still in shock, she half heard Holly muttering her thanks and good-bye. The boys each shook her hand, Jack patted her on the arm, and then they were all gone, out the door, and piling into the truck. Larisa lifted one hand in a stiff wave and shut the door behind her, the tears beginning now. She sat on the stairs and sobbed into her hands and when she looked up, her eyes landed on the scrap of pheasant paper she'd hung on the front hall mirror, that day she'd first disrupted the wallpaper. The one startled pheasant still peered incredulously over his shoulder, its foot suspended from forward march, and Larisa suddenly realized that the pheasants were the perfect meta-phor for who she had become. She had been so busy looking backward that she had lost all forward momentum. Brent was right. What would Aunt Ursula do? What would Aunt Ursula say? It didn't matter.

Larisa tugged on the paper until it came loose from the mirror and she looked at herself. Her cheeks were still wet and her hair was disheveled. She had dark circles under her eyes.

"Who are you?" she said out loud. She had no answer.

Just then, she heard the sound of a car coming up the drive and then a door slam.

"Jack," Larisa whispered to herself. He'd come back for her. She rushed to the door and flung it open, her face break-ing into a wide smile. But of course it wasn't Jack. Instead she was greeted by a small group of Christmas carolers haloed by the half dark of dusk, all of them fully decked out in old-fashioned garb—velvet breeches and fitted bonnets and fur-lined muffs. One of them blew into a pitch pipe and they all broke into song, conducted by a jubilant Mrs. Muldoon.

We wish you a Merry Christmas
We wish you a Merry Christmas
We wish you a Merry Christmas
And a happy New Year!

PART III

SPRING

CHAPTER ELEVEN

When Larisa was a small girl, she'd gone often to Elmhurst, especially on the weekends, to visit with Aunt Ursula and to play with her three older cousins, also girls. Together, they'd scamper up and down the grand staircase and twirl around the checkered floor of the old-fashioned kitchen. They took turns balancing a silver tray with dollhouse teacups, heaving their way through the swinging door that led through the pantry to the dining room. During a game of hide-and-seek, a pair of them would huddle in the scullery cabinet beneath the stairs, communicating with clasped hands and hot whispers, feeling the dizzying thrill of shared concealment as the baffled seeker hunted them all over the house.

As Larisa grew older, she and her cousins were invited to sleep over. After a formal dinner, during which Aunt Ursula would instruct them all in the nuances of proper etiquette, they would settle themselves into their shared beds, giggling and chattering long into the night until sleep prevailed and they drifted slowly off into their separate dreamworlds. On one such night, not long after her tenth birthday, Larisa came to Elmhurst for one final sleepover, a special night with her cousins before their parents moved them cross-country. From the moment Larisa stepped over the threshold into the house, the evening felt different from the others before it—fraught with the angst of the pending farewell, yet also alive with the excitement of a last hurrah. But as Larisa watched her cousins frolic and sashay around the foyer, she knew this night was special for yet another reason, it being the eve of the wedding of Lady Diana Spencer to Charles, Prince of Wales, heir to the British throne.

Aunt Ursula had been a longtime fan of the royal family. The buildup to the wedding had been great and so the girls had been hearing about it for months—Diana's dress, her hairstyle, her flowers, the horse-drawn carriage that, escorted by cavalry, would deliver the royal couple from St. Paul's to Buckingham Palace. Each of the girls had dressed for the occasion in frilly frocks and fancy shoes, their hair neatly styled, and Aunt Ursula had arranged for an elaborate roast dinner, complete with Yorkshire pudding and minted peas.

The girls could barely contain themselves. But doing their best to keep their hands to themselves, their bottoms in their chairs, they nibbled demurely at their bread rolls and chirped pleasantries in approximate British accents.

"How do you do?" and "Such a lovely time for a wedding, don't you think?"

Aunt Ursula watched primly from the head of the table. A

bemused smile toying across her lips, she allowed their prattle to go on longer than usual. But not too long, for the wedding would take place very early the next morning—just after 11:00 A.M. in London, which meant 6:00 A.M. Boston time!—and so they all snuggled into bed before eight o'clock. Ursula awoke them at dawn and they straggled sleepily into her bedroom to gather around the small TV she'd already tuned to the coverage. She offered them tea and crumpets and miniature Union Jack flags. She fitted them with makeshift veils made from gold cardboard crowns and tulle curtain remnants, the fabric hanging well below the waists of their summer nightgowns. In them, the girls processed merrily around the room. Some of them exchanged impromptu vows with deep curtsies and mimed kisses. Others couldn't help but peek coyly at themselves in the oval mirror over the dressing table. But eventually, as the decked-out Diana arrived at St. Paul's and stepped slowly from her coach, a hush settled over the children and they clambered up onto Ursula's bed and leaned in to watch the pageantry.

To the eyes of most young girls, the scene must have seemed like something out of a fairy tale. A magnificent dress, a glittering tiara, the handsome prince in his crisp naval uniform. And yes, it had been exciting, interesting, this celebration. But even then, Larisa had detected a disturbing falseness in all the pomp and circumstance. Watching the scene unfold, she'd felt a bit protective for the soon-to-be princess, who made shy sidelong glances at the esteemed guests all the way up the aisle. As the ceremony ended and the church bells chimed, the crowds went bananas. *But what for?* wondered the young Larisa. How could all these spectators possibly care so much about the joining of these two lives? And how could it matter to Charles and Diana that so many eyes had born witness to their union?

And now, so many years later, waking up in Ursula's room the morning after Jack and Brent had both left, Larisa eyed her stack of bridal magazines, and wondered just how she'd gotten to this point. She thought back over her return to Kent Crossing and the events of the past several months. First, on a lark, she'd bought a dress—ha ha!—and then she'd made up a pretend date—June 2! It had started as a prank, yet somewhere along the line she'd gotten caught up in the pretending. A magnificent wedding had been Ursula's fascination, not hers. She sank back into the bed pillows. The house was so still. No voices, no shuffle of footsteps on the stairs, the silence broken only by the occasional hiss of a radiator or a heap of snow sliding off the sun-warmed roof. Huddled beneath the covers, Larisa felt the profound hollowness that comes from being left behind. With no tears left, she sighed. Jack had not chosen her. Of course he hadn't; it had been foolish of her to think he might. She let this realization sink in, feeling it pool in her depths. Before she could think on it further, her cell phone trilled from its spot on the nightstand. She glanced over and managed a slight smile. Her father. Surely he would know just what to say to set her back on course.

"Hi, Daddy," she said, trying to sound cheerful.

"Hello, darling, just calling to let you know we're almost there."

Larisa frowned into the phone. "Almost where?"

Her father laughed. "Almost to Elmhurst, of course. It's Christmas Eve. Aren't you expecting us?"

Larisa flinched, remembering their agreement that he would

drive the Rolls back down once it was fixed. Crap, she'd completely lost track of time.

"Of course," she said into the phone, trying not to stammer. "I just didn't think you'd be on the road so early."

"Well, with your mother, the earlier the better. So we can get settled and have some semblance of order before her mind begins to drift."

Larisa paused before answering. "How is she?"

"Well," said Clark, "she is how she is." Larisa imagined him glancing over at Kittie on the seat next to him. "Sometimes here, sometimes not. But right now she's dozing."

"That's good," said Larisa. "It'll make the ride go by faster."

"Ha! For her maybe. Not me. The car may be restored to her former glory, but I plan to take it slow. Last thing we need is another accident. Anyway, we'll see you soon."

Larisa hung up the phone and sat up in bed. The threat of her parents' impending arrival gripped her with panic. Being with Kittie at No One's Home had been hard, but at least it had been on Larisa's terms. At Elmhurst, Larisa would just have to sit and watch her mother fade away. She'd have to respond repeatedly to the unending cycle of questions, the recurring confusion. This required such patience, such calm. She was ashamed to admit it, but she absolutely dreaded the visit. And yet, at the same time, she felt an incredible longing as well. A great yearning to recover the mother she had lost. For if she lost her mother for good, if she could no longer relate to this woman who had been so pivotal in her life, how could she hope to ever find herself again?

———

Thirty minutes later Larisa still lay in bed as her parents pulled up, their arrival signaled by two toots of the car horn. She rose, peeled off her pajamas, pulled on a sweater and jeans, and hurried downstairs. She stepped nervously to the front door, gripped the knob, forced a smile, and swung open the door. And then there they were: Clark and Kittie and the Silver Shadow, looking like something back in time. Kittie wore a long skirt under her camel-hair coat and she'd covered her head with a brightly patterned scarf tied neatly under her chin. Clark, Larisa knew, often opted to drive without a coat, and today was no exception. He'd chosen dark corduroys and a medium blue cardigan over a button-down shirt with a tie, and he stood beside the car holding a potted poinsettia.

"Merry Christmas, sweetheart!" he said, stepping forward to embrace her. Over his shoulder, Larisa had a good view of the repaired car bumper.

"Wow, the Rolls looks great," she said, accepting the poinsettia.

"Doesn't it? And she drives like a dream."

As her father leaned to remove the suitcases from the trunk, Larisa saw that he looked a bit more worn than usual and she felt a flutter of concern, but then she noticed the confusion beginning to cloud her mother's face.

"Hi, Mom," said Larisa, trying to sound cheerful. "How are you?"

Kittie accepted Larisa's hug and kiss on the cheek and then gripped her own arms and shivered.

"I'm . . . ," she started, but seemed to struggle for the word. "I'm . . ."

"Cold?" answered Clark for her. He took her elbow and guided her toward the front door. "Don't worry, darling, we can fix that. Let's get you warmed up inside."

"Yes," said Larisa, following her father's cue and helping them both inside.

Kittie removed her scarf and held up her arms as Clark helped her with her coat. She peered suspiciously into the dining room. "Where are the pheasants?" she asked, glaring toward the room where the wallpaper had once been.

Before Larisa could answer, her father stepped in. "Remember I told you, darling, Larisa's been doing some renovations. The pheasants are no longer here. Let's take a look at what else she's done."

Larisa wasn't sure her mother understood, but she did seem to relax as she obediently followed Clark into the kitchen.

Clark gaped appreciatively. "My word, what a difference. This place was in sore need of a face-lift."

Kittie frowned. "Where's Ursula? We ought to say our hellos."

Larisa and her father exchanged a look. As she remembered her great-aunt, Larisa's mind spun through a carousel of images: Ursula, smoothing a spoonful of lemon curd over crisp wheat toast; Ursula pouring water from an earthenware pitcher. Without Ursula to preside over things, she realized, the house had taken on a different tone, and not just because of the renovations.

"Don't you remember, Mom?" said Larisa, patting her mother's arm. "Ursula died last June."

"Died?" echoed Kittie, her eyes flaring. "Why didn't you tell me?"

Larisa looked at her father again, but he was gazing sadly at the granite countertop.

"We *did* tell you," answered Larisa. "You were there at the funeral with us."

Kittie looked horrified, embarrassed. "I don't remember."

"It's OK, darling, you were there. Even if you can't remember." Clark reached for her hand and squeezed it. He turned to face Larisa. "The real question is where's Jack?"

"Jack?" questioned Larisa, remembering his hasty departure the night before with Holly and the boys.

"Sure," answered her father. "You said he was here living with you, right? I want to congratulate him on your upcoming wedding."

"Larisa is getting married?" said Kittie.

"That's what she's told us," answered Clark, his expression slightly skeptical and a tad amused.

Larisa froze. Could she back out of this gracefully? she wondered. Explain that she and Jack had decided to take things more slowly, that they weren't quite planning the wedding yet? But no, that wouldn't work. Jack and Brent were both gone. There was no engagement; there had never been one. She should come clean and tell her father, she knew she should, but something held her back.

"He's with his kids," she bluffed. "Getting some last-minute shopping in."

Clark still seemed doubtful. "We'll see him later then?"

"Later," echoed Larisa. "Though maybe not tonight."

Kittie's eyebrows quivered. She glanced uncertainly around the room. "Will Ursula be here soon?"

Larisa sighed, her stomach in knots over both her lies and her mother's confusion. She found herself unable to answer.

"No," said her father softly behind her. His words were firm, but kind.

"Oh," said Kittie. She moved out of the kitchen and into the living room, where she positioned herself at the window and glanced furtively out. Larisa had the strong sense that she was still looking for Ursula. She wasn't sure she could stay and watch this much longer. She needed to get out of the house, clear her head, and figure out how she was going to explain things to her father.

"Dad," she said, "I'm just going to go downtown quickly to fetch us some lunch. We've got almost nothing in the fridge."

"Great," he answered. "We'll go with you."

"With me?" Larisa had already begun to retrieve her coat from the front closet and she paused as she pivoted to face him. "But what about Mom?"

"She takes a walk with me most days. It will be good to get some fresh air."

Larisa shrugged, trying to release the tension that had settled there. The last thing she wanted was for her parents to follow her down to Main Street, where they were sure to run into someone they knew. But she couldn't rebuff her father. "If you want," she managed.

They bundled up in coats and hats and made their way out onto the front walk. Outside, the sunshine stunned Larisa. She squinted into its bright beams and trudged reluctantly along behind her parents down the long drive away from Elmhurst. Most of the snow from the big storm had dissolved, and the air felt warm and moist on her cheeks, tinged with just a touch of the chill that was more typical this time of year. Kittie, her elbow draped through Clark's, seemed content to be guided along and she pointed in wonder at a flock of children as they sledded down the small hill behind the elementary school, the oversize pom-poms on their knitted hats shaking through the brief turbulence of the ride.

Reaching Main Street, they tramped through the gritty slush that edged the road and dribbled noisily through the sewer grates. As they rounded the corner toward the gas station, Larisa spotted Andy holding up a straggly Christmas tree for prospective buyers. She moved to her father's side, hoping to block his sight line, but Clark had already seen him. He paused in the walk and attempted to wave hello. Andy, obscured now by the tree, didn't notice him.

"Oh, let's not bother him now," said Larisa, urging them forward. "Not when he's with customers.

Clark cocked his head at her. "But you did tell him about the repairs, didn't you?"

"Of course," insisted Larisa, avoiding her father's glance and ushering them on.

Downtown was a bustle of last-minute activity, a line of traffic clogging the street. The Salvation Army volunteer clanged his bell and tipped his Santa hat. Shoppers scurried past, scant few of them stopping to drop spare change into his shiny red kettle. Closer by, a young couple ambled past, cradling cups of steaming cider in their mittened hands. Next door, a flustered woman emerged from the convenience store, clutching several rolls of brightly colored wrapping paper, and Larisa had a sudden memory of helping to wrap Christmas gifts as a little girl, holding one finger over the looped ribbon so that her mother could tie a tighter bow. She sighed again, feeling anguish once more over her mother's decline.

But when she turned to survey her mother's state of mind,

she saw that Kittie's eyes were fixated on the awning of the wedding dress shop.

"Ooh, a bridal shop," cooed Kittie. Her eyes met Larisa's. "Let's go in and look at the dresses, just for fun."

"Yes," agreed Clark, "we can look for one for your wedding."

"Larisa's getting married?" questioned Kittie, her eyes aglow.

Larisa swallowed and patted her mother on the arm. She turned toward her father.

"Actually, I've already bought a dress here," she announced with some degree of confidence. The wedding might be a sham, but at least the dress part was true.

"Oh really?" questioned Clark. "Well, then let's go in and see it. They'll have it here, won't they? For alterations?" He pointed to a flyer affixed to the door. "And it looks like they're hosting a craft fair today. That would be fun to see."

Larisa wavered on the threshold, remembering the thrill she'd felt over the purchase of the wedding dress, how fun it had been to pretend. But today wouldn't be like that. If she went into this shop, it would be a disaster. All her lies would be exposed, and her mother was sure to become overwhelmed and make a scene. Soon the whole town would know about Kittie's illness and then Larisa would be forced to face it as well. But her father was already turning the knob and holding the door for her mother. Larisa had no choice but to step in after them. The little bell tinkled the same way it had on that mid-September day, and her gaze landed on Mrs. Muldoon and her daughter, Sally, dressed in matching green elf outfits. They stood behind a large folding table covered with various holiday wares from painted seashells to crocheted sweaters to flavored popcorn and knitted stockings.

"Larisa!" chirped Mrs. Muldoon. "And Clark and Kittie! How wonderful to see you." She waved them closer and then leaned in, holding a finger to her lips. "Shh—don't tell! We're just two little elves, escaped from Santa's workshop to bring the world some holiday cheer!"

"Yes," said Larisa, glancing at the goods and remembering that she had only just seen Mrs. Muldoon in a different incarnation, caroling at her front door the night before. "Looks as though you've been busy. Hi, Sally, it's been a long time."

"Oh, hey," said Sally, rolling her eyes at her mother and tugging at the shirttails of her elf vest. "It *has* been a long time. I heard you were getting married!"

"Larisa is getting married?" Kittie turned toward her daughter, her eyes both excited and questioning, as though hearing this news for the first time.

Mrs. Muldoon responded with a confused frown. Larisa cleared her throat. "My mother's been having some trouble with her memory," she whispered. Mrs. Muldoon bit her bottom lip and glanced uncertainly toward Kittie.

"Oh," said Kittie, seemingly sensing Larisa's embarrassment. "Did I forget?"

"Yes," said Clark. "It's OK. We've come to see the dress."

"Oh, yes, the *dress*," gushed Mrs. Muldoon, suddenly animated. "It's *perfect*. Just wait till you lay your eyes on it." She disappeared into the back room while Clark settled Kittie into a chair in the corner. Larisa felt her eyes widen in alarm. What would she do when Mrs. Muldoon produced the dress? Would she be required to try it on? Part of her felt a deep yearning to wear it again—the fitted bodice, those lovely beads—but if she tried on the dress, she'd be perpetuating her lies even further. Before she could formulate a plan, Sally came out from behind the counter with a clipboard in her hands.

"You know," she said, "I've been working part-time for a travel agency."

"Yes," managed Larisa, "your mother mentioned."

Sally lifted the clipboard and pointed to a brochure. "No pressure, of course. But have you thought about your honeymoon yet? We're having a really good promotion right now if you book before New Year's."

Larisa pulled the brochure from the clipboard and began to page through. *God, it would be so nice to get away,* she thought as her eyes landed on the photos of beautiful beaches and sunset vistas.

Sally continued. "You're getting married in the summer, right?"

"June," declared Mrs. Muldoon definitively as she re-emerged from the back room with the dress in hand. She hung it on a metal hook and began to carefully unzip it out of its plastic garment bag. Larisa felt her entire body tense.

"Well, Paris is fantastic that time of year," continued Sally, "or Nice, of course. Or if you wanted some more adventure, you could think about the Galapagos or even Thailand."

"Thailand?" repeated Larisa, hesitantly.

"Well, sure," gushed Sally, "as long as you avoid the rainy season. Is your fiancé a beach bum or more of a mountain climber?"

Larisa stared uncertainly at Sally and then turned to face her parents. Clark stood assessing her with a bemused grin, but Kittie's eyes were on the dress, which Mrs. Muldoon had only just extracted from the bag—oh, it was lovely, the beadwork spectacular. Larisa's heart began to pound. By now she'd spent so many months engaging in these deceptions that it had almost become second nature. She had to fight the impulse to indulge in more lies. But the truth was, there would be no wedding. She glanced back and forth between Mrs. Muldoon and Sally—the mother-daughter sameness of them amplified through the identical Christmas elf costumes.

Just then her mother stood. She squinted and looked around the room until her eyes landed on the dress. She looked up at the others in confusion. "I'm sorry, there must be some mistake," she said. "This isn't my dress."

"No, no," Mrs. Muldoon assured her. "This is the dress for *Larisa*."

Kittie fixed Mrs. Muldoon with a bewildered expression. "Larisa," she repeated, her eyes flitting from side to side. "I forgot. I forget so many things lately." She sank back into the chair and started to sob quietly, her face an ugly grimace beneath the tears.

Watching, Larisa cringed and shook her head vigorously as though attempting to shake off her emotions the way a dog might shake water from fur. She couldn't stand it, she just couldn't; her frail mother, so alone in this illness. It was torturous, excruciating, to watch her mother falter; it released something so primal in Larisa, it made her want to scream. Yes, *this* was what she had been avoiding, filling her mind, her days, with distractions so that she wouldn't have to face her mother's illness. The wedding, the engagement, the collections of lies—it had all been an unconscious effort to avoid the awful truth. That her mother was failing. That she would not get better. In fact, she would get worse. And it would be even harder to bear. All the emotion that had been building up for the past day began to bubble within her and she had to fight her own tears from falling. God, she thought, what on earth would make her feel normal again? Standing in front of her parents and Sally and Mrs. Muldoon, surveying the miniature Styrofoam snowman ornaments scattered across their craft table, and faced with the temptation to lie once more, she finally realized that she had a choice. She could go further down the road of deception, tell them all another falsehood. Or she could come clean and face her own impersonation of herself. Larisa could *choose* to return to reality at any time; her mother no longer had that privilege. She'd been so selfish, so cowardly, completely self-absorbed; she detested the person she'd become. But she could put an end to that now. She could share her fears, her disappointments, *herself*. And even though she'd had this choice the entire time—no one had forced her to lie—the realization struck her now as pivotal, the only way back to some sense of normalcy. She took a deep breath and decided at last to come clean.

"It turns out," she said, "that I'm not actually engaged."

Mrs. Muldoon looked stricken. The jingle-bell tip of her elf hat quivered and she clapped one hand over her mouth. "Just like Ursula," she muttered, more to herself, it seemed, than to Larisa.

Sally shot a sideways grimace toward her mother and then rested a hand on Larisa's shoulder. "I'm so sorry."

"No," said Larisa, shaking her off. "No, it's fine actually. I never really wanted to get married. Not yet." Almost immediately, the certainty of the statement sunk in. It felt so good to say it out loud. Sally and Mrs. Muldoon gaped at her, but Larisa turned away to glimpse her father's reaction. He nodded reassuringly and smiled but refrained from speaking.

"Well," said Sally finally, "if it's not what you want . . ."

Mrs. Muldoon bit her lower lip. "Sweetheart, I don't know how to say this, but you know the dress was—"

"I know, I know. All sales final." Larisa shrugged. "I'll probably get married sooner or later. I'll just save it till then, I guess."

They stared at her. Larisa could see them each grappling for the right response. She let them struggle for a moment in silence.

"Well, *why* not?" Mrs. Muldoon finally said a little too emphatically. She patted Larisa's arm. "I'll have the dress sealed up in one of those preservation boxes for you. Just come back down to the shop when you're ready and we'll get it taken care of."

"Thank you." Larisa turned toward her mother, who sat quietly in her chair. "Now let's get you home, where you belong," she said.

Back at the house, they settled at the dining room table with the lunch options they'd picked up at the market before returning to Elmhurst. Larisa asked her father why he hadn't seemed surprised at her revelation.

"Well, I had a feeling it was all a bit of a hoax."

"You did?"

"Sure. I know my daughter, don't I? It's not typical of you to rush into something like this. You like things to be planned, predictable."

"True." Larisa pondered his response. "But I haven't really been myself lately. Why didn't you say something?"

Clark set down his fork and smiled gently at her. "Larisa,

for God's sake, you're an adult. I can't scold you every time I suspect you're telling a lie. I thought it better to wait until you were ready to face the truth."

Larisa nodded. She turned toward her mother, but Kittie seemed to dislike the focus on her. She put down her fork, pushed her chair away, and wandered off toward the living room.

Clark leveled his gaze at her. "Listen, sweetheart. There will be a time, not that far off, when she just won't recognize you. You'll never know when that moment will come, but it will come sooner than you think. She simply won't know who you are." Clark wiped his eyes. "Take the time *now* to be with her."

"I want to," Larisa answered. "I finally want to, but I don't know how to talk to her, what to say."

Clark rested a hand on her shoulder. "Honey, you just need to meet her where she is."

"Where is she?" whispered Larisa. "And how do I get there?"

Clark sighed. "She may not always remember what you said five minutes ago. But she will remember how what you said made her feel. If you snap at her, she'll just feel hurt, defensive. But if you're kind to her, she'll come away feeling loved. That's the best advice I can give."

Larisa nodded again, but still found herself frozen at the table.

Her father stood and beckoned her into a standing position as well. "I don't always know what to say either. Sometimes I just read her nursery rhymes from the book she read to you when you were a little girl."

Larisa frowned. "Nursery rhymes?"

"Sure. You know, Peter Piper picked a peck of pickled peppers . . . she thinks it's hilarious."

Larisa raised her eyebrows, skeptical. "But it doesn't mean anything."

"So what? She likes it. *That's* what it means. That's all it needs to mean."

Then Larisa smiled, getting the gist of it. "Rosa Rugosa?" she said. "There's no Rosa Rugosa here."

Clark smiled back. "Exactly. It's like improv. You have to be OK not knowing what will happen."

Larisa nodded, remembered her days doing high school theater. The cardinal rule of improv: accept the reality you're given. If you negate the reality, you kill the scene. "Join her in her reality when she can't join me in mine."

"That's it," he assured her, moving to clear the dishes from the table. "Give it a try. Put on some music. Maybe light a little fire. Think about the things that will make her feel safe, happy."

He headed toward the kitchen with the dishes and left her alone to face her mother. After a long pause, Larisa entered the living room and settled her mother in an armchair in front of the fireplace. She laid a log with some paper and kindling, as her father had taught her, and lit the match to start the fire. Then she fetched the Victrola on its cart from the conservatory and dropped the needle on a record. The opening tones of Pachelbel's Canon rippled through the room. When Larisa turned back toward the hearth, she saw that her mother had homed in on the pile of bridal magazines Larisa had carried down from the bedroom that morning. Kittie had selected one from the top and was already paging through.

"Oh, I love a good wedding," she gushed. "Is somebody getting married?"

"Oh, well, no," answered Larisa, rocking on her heels as she searched for an answer. "They were just fun to look at."

But Kittie didn't seem to be listening.

"'Here comes the bride,'" she sang, her tune clashing with the opening arpeggio of the classical violins from the Victrola. As she belted out the words, she gestured with the magazine so that the cover bride seemed to march comically down the imaginary aisle. Oblivious to the discord, Kittie stood and kept on singing. "'All dressed in white!'"

She dropped the magazine to the carpet and took up a pose in the middle of the room, something between classical ballet and magician's assistant. She began to turn herself in a slow circle around the center medallion of the rug. Watching, Larisa was reminded of a fragile mechanical figurine, spinning only on her own axis. She felt the inevitable distance created by the presence of a person who was already part gone. She seemed so alone, so unreachable. How could Larisa possibly penetrate that world? But she remembered what her father had said—she needed to meet her mother where she was—so she stepped into the circle and proffered herself.

"May I have this dance?" she asked.

Kittie smiled and giggled and then clamped herself onto Larisa's arm and waist and they moved slowly together. It struck Larisa as funny that now, after coming clean with all her deceptions, she was engaging in a new kind of deception with her mother, this improvised moment. But in this new moment of deception, the oddest thing happened. Larisa began to recognize herself again. It was so basic, so elementary, this gesture of kindness. And yet in it, Larisa had a glimpse of the kind and nurturing soul she wanted to be. *If you can find someone to care for,* her father had said, *someone for whom you can make life a little brighter, that's the thing. That's what marriage is about. Being vulnerable with each other.* Yes, she realized, in these confusing months—Ursula's death, her fallout with Brent, her mother's illness—she'd lost track of humanity. She'd acted out; she'd lied to the people around her; she'd turned from her parents in their time of need. Her mind flashed back suddenly to the moment she'd scrawled *FU BITCH* on the mirror at work. My God, she thought, if only she had peered a little more closely into that very mirror.

As she stepped forward into the dance, Larisa had expected to feel her mother's frailty, but Kittie's grip was strong and forceful, insistent. In her arms, Larisa found that she was the one who felt weak, broken, and as the music began to swell, tears gathered and slid rapidly down her cheeks. She felt all of the emotions she'd been holding in for months and before she could stop herself, she broke down into deep, throaty sobs. The violins were going crazy now, building to their crescendo, and the tears came and came, but her mother still held her, saying "Shh, shh, don't cry." Larisa nodded and wiped at her eyes with the sleeve of her sweater.

Kittie looked searchingly at her. "What is it?"

Larisa shuddered through the last tears. When she quieted herself, she gazed intently back.

"Do you know me?" she asked. "Do you know who I am?"

Kittie rolled her eyes and let out a tsk. "Do I *know* you? Of course I know you. You're my Larisa. What kind of question is that?"

Larisa took a deep breath and released it. Now was the time to step toward the strife, to face it. Her mother's disease was hard. It was awful. But it would be better to feel it, to experience the grief and pain, than to be absent entirely from the experience. She sank back into her mother's arms and they swayed around and around. The fire was crackling now and they danced in its heat as the music unwound itself down to the final chord.

Kittie's eyes were bright and beaming. "Let's do it again."

Larisa nodded and smiled back. But before she reset the record, she picked up the bridal magazine that Kittie had cast to the carpet. She turned toward the hearth and fed it to the fire.

CHAPTER TWELVE

Three months had gone by since Jack had moved back in with Holly, both of them hopeful that their rekindled flame would continue to flicker. And it had, for a time. The first weeks had gone well, with him and Holly settling comfortably back into their long-established routines. Jack felt glad to be back in his own cozy home, relishing in the antics of his adolescent boys, giving only a little thought to Larisa Pearl and the house he'd left behind. He did wonder a bit whether she would indeed sell the house, especially now that the supposed wedding was off, Brent having fled. But he hadn't talked to Larisa since Christmas and had no intention of contacting her. He couldn't worry about her any longer, he couldn't worry about the house, sad as that made him feel. Instead he focused on tending more carefully to his wife and kids, knowing how easily things could break apart. They celebrated Christmas with few presents but a fair amount of cheer, and then Jack turned his efforts to directing the ServiceMaster team assigned by the insurance company to complete the repairs on the house. He found it funny, but refreshing, not to be doing the repairs himself. And he enjoyed the free time to cook meals, clean up, and help out with Holly's home day care. So yes, he'd been proud of their reentry. It felt like old times, almost.

Holly got her cast off in early February and then came Valentine's Day. Jack greeted her with his usual box of chocolates— Holly never wanted him to waste the money on roses—and she reciprocated with a Hallmark card. By then, their master bedroom had been restored, redecorated with new drapes and a fresh coat of paint, and the boys had gone to her mother's for the night, so they had no hindrances to their romantic evening. But though they had made love after his home-cooked meal, their movements had felt forced, mechanical. Holly had seemed annoyed at him ever since and they'd fallen back into an old pattern. Every interaction became a struggle, every other comment a dig. Thus, short on tinder, their flame had been all but snuffed out. Weeks went on with little improvement, nothing to reignite them. And so by now, on a Friday evening in early March, Jack felt more distant from Holly than ever.

The boys had already turned in for the night. He and Holly sat at opposite ends of the living room couch in front of the TV, the clock winding down on the third period of the Bruins game. Jack feigned interest. Sure, he'd grown up shooting the puck around on the frozen lakes and rivers near his house, but he'd never really been much of a hockey fan. Something about the sheer brute nature of it repelled him; and anyway, baseball had always been his sport. In contrast,

Holly's zeal for the game had been instilled from an early age by her father, a season ticket holder. She'd seen her first face-off before she could walk, and she'd even participated in a youth league for a number of years.

"Come on, Bs," she muttered now under her breath. "Time to put the damn puck in the net."

Jack glanced at the game but said nothing. He returned his focus instead to the nautical knot board on his lap, his framed display of hand-tied knots arranged in rows and labeled by name, a project he'd started several weeks earlier to fill his free time. As a seasoned sailor, knot-tying was not new. He'd first practiced knots as a young boy—something to do on a rainy day during sailing class—and it was a hobby he'd carried with him since, so that by now most of them were second nature. Some were simple, basic knots he'd use every trip out on a boat. Bowline, Clove Hitch, Figure 8. He liked these knots because they had definite purpose. Others were more elaborate and lesser used. The Sheepshank, the Carrick Bend, the Monkey's Fist. And some were so elaborate as to be just decorative. The Turk's Head. The Ocean Plait. They were beautiful, these knots. But what he liked best about them was that it took time and practice to figure out how each knot worked. As a child and later as a young adult, it had felt like something worth doing. But he'd never collected them like this on a board before and he found there was something quite satisfying about organizing each of the entanglements and labeling them by name.

Ah, his entanglements. On the night they'd left Elmhurst, Jack had felt the urge to turn back almost as soon as he'd stepped out the door. He'd dismissed it, of course, and turned his focus instead on the right thing to do: go home with his family. They needed him, he told himself; he needed them. Holly could have lost her life in that crazy accident and that wasn't a small thing. He owed it to her to give the marriage another chance, like he'd said he would. These were the thoughts that had propelled him forward.

But as the New Year came and days went by, with lots of time on his hands, he had other thoughts as well. What if there had never been an accident? Would fate have pushed them further apart instead of closer together? Would it have given him the chance he'd craved with Larisa? Jack had married Holly partially because it was what was expected. But my God, they'd been so young, so naive. He'd thought they'd been in love, but what had he known about love? In the beginning, he found that he just liked the way that she looked at him. From there, and through the haze of teenage lust, their relationship grew. But now years of hindsight made him wonder, had he just been in love with her unfaltering adoration? Was this the lost sentiment he hoped to resurrect every time he returned to the marriage?

Outside of Elmhurst, as his marriage began to fizzle, Jack only barely allowed himself to ponder how he would have felt if Holly had died in the accident. Would it have made his life easier? After the shock and grief had dissipated, would it have eventually given him the fresh start he'd been hoping for? No, no, he chastised himself, what kind of man thought that way? Soberly, he answered himself: the kind of man who knew his marriage was over and was afraid to admit it.

We're all in this together, Holly had always said. But they weren't. They just weren't. At least not anymore.

Lost in these thoughts, Jack hadn't noticed Holly's eyes on him, but as he looked up from the knot board, he saw now that she'd been watching him, the hockey game having played itself out. She clicked off the TV and faced him. Jack set the knot board aside and met her gaze.

"They win?"

Holly crossed her arms and clenched her jaw. "You don't have to pretend to be interested."

Jack rubbed his temple and sighed. "Sorry, my mind was elsewhere."

Holly gave a slight nod but continued her stare, something clearly on her mind too.

"I saw your buddy Larisa today," she finally said.

"Oh?" Jack did his best to feign indifference. "I haven't seen her since Christmas."

Holly nodded, her eyes trained on him. "Across the parking lot at the grocery store. I thought she saw me, too, but she walked off so quickly, I didn't even have a chance to wave. It was almost like she was avoiding me."

"Huh." Jack fingered the ends of the knots on his board. "Why would she be avoiding you?"

"Beats me." Holly flared her eyes and shook her head to demonstrate her bewilderment. "But it made me wonder."

Jack knew what she was getting at and he waited for the accusation.

"Did something happen between you and Larisa? Something intimate?"

"No." Jack swallowed. He and Larisa had only ever shared that one kiss. Holly didn't need to know he'd ever wanted more.

Holly bit her fingernail and watched him. "Those two

months before my accident, when you were living with her in that house. Nothing happened?"

"I don't want to fight," said Jack.

"So something *did* happen?"

"*No,*" said Jack. "It didn't." He hoped his insistent tone would convince her. But Holly had a look on her face that told him she knew she was on to something and wasn't about to let it go.

"Then why do you look so guilty?" she asked.

"Jesus," said Jack. "I don't look guilty." He moved closer to her on the couch and rested his hand on her leg, an attempt to quash her inquisition. "Why are you trying to start something?"

Holly sighed and pulled her leg up under her, away from his reach. "I'm not trying to start anything. I'm just trying to figure a few things out."

"What things?"

Holly closed her eyes, took a deep breath, and then opened them again.

"Jack, let me ask you something. Why did you come back to this house after my accident, after we'd been separated?"

Jack hesitated before answering. "I wanted to be with my wife and my kids."

"OK." Holly nodded slowly, deliberately, as though responding to one of the toddlers from her day care. "You wanted to be with your wife and kids. But why did you come back to the *marriage* specifically?"

Jack tilted his head and fixed her with a droll smile. "Well, I said till death do us part, didn't I?" His answer had been an attempt to cajole her out of attack mode, but he saw immediately that it had been the wrong thing to say. Holly thrust her head down into her hands and raked her fingers through her hair. She looked up and drilled him with her eyes.

"See, that's just the problem, Jack. That's it right there. It's not a joke." Her voice had reached an uneven tone that amplified her emotion. "I don't want you to stay with me because you *said* you would. I want you to stay with me because you love me. I want to feel the attraction between us the way I used to."

Jack threw his hands up. "Oh, Holl, come on. It's more complicated than that and you know it. Every relationship goes through its ups and downs." He tried to move closer to her again, but she squirmed away.

"And what if death had parted us, Jack? What if that tree had killed me?"

Jack shook his head, trying to prevent the inevitable next words.

But she persisted. "Would you have been happy to get your freedom back? Would you have been glad that I died?"

Jack widened his eyes at her. "Christ, of course not. That's not what I meant."

She let the moment hang, and then composed herself and spoke calmly. "Then what did you mean?"

Jack tried to choose his words carefully, though as they came out of his mouth, he knew they sounded thin. "I just meant that I made a commitment. To support you. To stand by your side no matter what."

"No matter what. That's great, just great." Holly gave a scoffing laugh. She flashed her eyes sternly up at him. "But I want more than that. If you're going to be with me, you have to *want* to be with me. Not just because of some vow."

"Holly, honey, I know." Jack tried to move closer yet again, but she bristled.

"You *don't* know." Her eyes welled with tears. "I can see that you *want* to be in love with me. But that's not the same as actually being in love with me. Not the same at all."

Jack sat stunned. She was doing that woman trick again where she could see right through him, voicing his thoughts before he even knew he had them. Yes, he wanted to be in love with her partially because it would make things easier. They'd been together so long that true love seemed like a relative idea. Obviously, he cared about her. He always had. But could he fall in love with her again? Had he ever loved her as deeply as he'd wanted?

Holly struggled to hold back her tears. "I know I'm fatter than I used to be. My hair is turning gray. I look old."

Jack winced at the pain in her eyes; he grappled for the right response. "Oh, come on. Look at me, I'm no spring chicken."

She responded with a sullen pout. "Fuck you, Jack. You look practically the same as when you were seventeen."

"That's not true." He stood to get her some tissues.

She wiped at her eyes. "Practically."

"I don't want to fight," he whispered as he came back to sit with her.

Surprisingly, Holly's face softened with a look of understanding. "Believe it or not, I don't want to fight either. I don't. But I also don't want to live like this, with this void. It's not good for us. It's not good for the boys."

Jack swallowed. *The boys.* He thought of them now, oblivious in their beds to the unraveling of their world. There were days he felt he would do anything to see them smile. And other days when they could be just the biggest pains in his ass. But even on those latter days, as soon as they were out of sight, he found himself craving their company. Just to tousle their hair, just to toss the ball around, just to get one last glimpse of their boyish wiles. But Holly was right: it wasn't fair to give them such uncertainty. Kids absorbed this kind of thing into their souls.

Holly took a deep breath and let it out. Her eyes were kinder now but very serious. "Look, if this is over," she said, "let's just face it. Maybe there's some chance I can meet someone else and even be happy again."

"Someone else?" whispered Jack. "*Is* there someone else?" He was surprised at how possessive the prospect made him feel. He didn't want another man flipping flapjacks for his family on a Sunday morning. And yet, given his past behavior, he had no right.

"No," said Holly. "There's never been anyone else."

"Well, then why are we talking about other people?"

She sighed, exasperated. "Because we just can't seem to make it right between us. That thing we had before Christmas was nice. Really nice. And it worked for a while. But I just don't think we're right for each other anymore. Let's be honest. The only reason you came back is because I broke my leg."

"That's not true."

"It *is* true. If not for the accident, you'd still be at Elmhurst. Our marriage doesn't seem to work without some kind of drama. But I don't plan on breaking my leg again. And anyway, I'm tired of the drama. It shouldn't be this hard. You either have it or you don't, and we just don't anymore."

Jack stared at her. Holly was normally a woman who liked to spar. He was so used to her coming at him with swords drawn that it was unsettling to see her so calm. They'd developed a dance together, a routine: She'd grow frustrated and cast him out; he'd eventually reel himself back in. But now she was changing the pattern, forging a new path.

"I don't know what to say," he said.

"Don't say anything," she answered. "We've said all there is to say."

They both leaned back into the couch. And they sat there, shoulder to shoulder. Eventually Jack stood, reached for her hands, and pulled her up off the couch to go to bed.

The next morning, Saturday, Jack felt the pull of the water more strongly than usual. He felt this way every March, when it was too cold to haul the boat out of winter storage but warm enough to imagine the sun on his back, his hand on the tiller. Holly had left early for her gym class and so he'd slept in. Now, as he stretched his way out of bed, Jack glanced out the window toward the view of the bay. Sure enough, winter had not yet waned. The ocean still had that icy blue about it and the wind struck the water in staccato gusts, as though flogging it, the waves flinching in response. It would be a few more months before he'd make it out there. Until then, he'd have to make do with the here and now.

Still in his pajamas, he headed downstairs and was greeted by the wedding photo, restored months earlier to its place on the foyer table. Seeing it, he tried to work his way through the thicket of confusion his conversation with Holly had created. What had they decided the night before? Were they together? Were they not? He wasn't sure, but he felt like something had shifted. There had been a slow but momentous break-ing apart, like the fracture of a giant land mass into tectonic plates, a permanence to the separation, a final release. But as he approached the kitchen, he decided not to face all that for now.

Alex and Ben were huddled around the dining room table, fully engrossed in the role-playing required by a Saturday-morning session of Dungeons & Dragons. As Jack made coffee and poured out some cereal, he could tell that Alex had assumed the authoritarian role of Dungeon Master.

"OK," he told Ben, overly serious, "after traveling for days, lost in the Valley of Slumshire, the adventurers come across a trapdoor hidden at the foot of a giant oak tree."

As Dungeon Master, Alex's job was to guide the story and determine the fates of Ben's motley crew, which usually consisted of a dwarf, some elves, a halfling, and a human or two. Jack could see them represented on the table by a collection of miniature metal figurines.

Ben selected one figurine from the group and maneuvered him forward. "I open the trapdoor," he said.

"There's no handle," retorted Alex, his eyes bright with the clever thwarting of movement.

"He's a druid," answered Ben. "He uses a spell to warp the wood in the door."

"OK." Alex took some notes on his pad of paper. "Out jumps a Mind Flayer."

"Mind Flayer?" questioned Jack as he entered the room. "Speaking of Mind Flayers, where's your brother?"

Both boys regarded him coolly from their positions at the table.

"Charlie's not a Mind Flayer," said Ben. "He's more of a Bugbear."

"Or a Hobgoblin," snickered Alex.

"He's still sleeping," said Ben, and they returned to the game. They were calmer, Jack always noticed, without Charlie there to rile them up. He'd always found it fascinating how their dynamic became so different depending on the makeup of the group. Charlie was only one person, but his presence had an impact.

Ben chose one of his fighters to face the Mind Flayer. Alex selected the twenty-sided die from his collection of polyhedral dice. He studied its sides, manipulating it between two fingers before casting it down and sending it clattering across the table. Ben hovered eagerly over the table, waiting for the die to settle and determine the outcome of his fighter.

"Eighteen," he announced. "That's a hit."

If only life could be that easy, Jack thought—your fate determined by a flick of the wrist. No deep thought or action required.

"It's a hit," agreed Alex. "The Mind Flayer is mortally wounded."

"That's it?" said Jack. "Dead after only just one hit?"

Alex gave a matter-of-fact shrug. "It was his time. No one can live forever."

"But he can *die* forever," crowed Ben triumphantly. He manipulated his figurine up and down so that it appeared to stomp savagely across the battle grid.

"Well, duh," answered Alex. "That's what death is, stupid. Forever."

Jack wandered away from the boys and into the living room. His mind flashed back again to the conversation he'd had with Holly the night before. Was it really over between them? Over *forever*? Relationships had their own life and death cycles, like plants blooming in the spring and withering in the fall. Some of them didn't make it through the winter. Maybe there just wouldn't ever be any more life to his marriage. *People don't change,* he had told Larisa. Maybe he just ought to know when to walk away.

He thought about Larisa, Elmhurst. Why had he felt the tug back toward them both the night he left, just before Christmas? The hasty departure had not allowed for a proper good-bye with either of them. But it was more than that. He had a history with the house, and Elmhurst had provided a refuge for him and his family in a time of need. There was part of him that had felt worried the magic between him and Holly would wear off once they'd returned to their own home. It was irrational, he knew, but now look what had happened. Outside of Elmhurst, their relationship had deteriorated.

And then there was Larisa. He missed the rhythm of their days together. He missed sharing his morning cup of coffee and passing the paper back and forth. He missed the electric buzz between them, the feeling of mutual attraction that was missing from his marriage. But did he just crave it as a contrast to the void between him and Holly? The days that he'd shared with Larisa at Elmhurst hadn't been real. They hadn't carried with them the finality of marriage or anything like it and maybe that was the only reason it had worked. If he did end up with Larisa, who was to say he wouldn't tire of her the same way he had tired of Holly? Maybe he and Larisa were only destined to have that one moment together, that one kiss. Thinking about it, he was reminded of the exquisite flower on the night-blooming cereus: there for only one night, gone by morning. He sighed. The love you keep and the love you forsake. How to determine between them?

Out the window, he glimpsed Holly's Jeep moving steadily

along the road and then slowing to turn into their driveway. He waited for her to shuffle up the front walk and then elbow her way through the front door, her arms burdened with her gym bag, her water bottle, and the mail she'd collected from the mailbox. Her eyes met his as he reached to help and they hung there for a moment, each of them waiting to see what the encounter would be.

Jack broke the silence. "Good class?"

Holly shrugged and seemed to relax a little. "Gets the job done. The leg feels a little stronger, I think."

Jack nodded. "Good. But don't push it too hard too soon."

"No."

Just then Charlie came pounding down the stairs, a spray of hair fanning over the right side of his head, the typical off-center plumage created by lounging in bed all morning. He stopped long enough to loop an arm around his mother and slap his father a high five before joining his brothers in the dining room. Jack grinned toward Charlie's retreating form.

"Did we create that beast?" he questioned jokingly as he swiveled back toward Holly.

Holly nodded, smiling. "Scary, isn't it? And he's not even close to full grown."

"I heard that," bellowed Charlie as he wedged himself between Alex and Ben at the table.

The boys settled themselves back into the game and Jack and Holly were left facing each other.

"Hey," said Jack. "Let's grab some brunch so we can talk a little more. The boys will be OK here for a few hours by themselves."

Holly's smile faltered, but she agreed to go. They drove in Jack's truck to the Tidewater Tavern, where the hostess seated them at a small table by the window, not far from where Jack had sat with Larisa only months earlier. Jack found himself momentarily hypnotized by the movement of the marsh, the water trickling slowly by, so calm compared to the ocean he had watched from afar that morning. He turned to face his wife.

"You asked about Larisa?" he said.

Holly bit nervously at her thumbnail. "Umm-hmm."

Jack paused, bolstering his courage before speaking. "I kissed her. Once. That's all that ever happened between us."

Holly's expression tightened, an attempt to control her reaction. She raised her eyebrows over the menu as she gave her terse response. "You invited me to brunch to tell me you kissed another woman?"

Jack sighed, ashamed. "You asked, and I wanted to be honest with you. I thought it might be better to tell you in a neutral place."

Holly folded her arms and leaned back in her chair. "You were afraid I might start screaming, huh?"

Jack shrugged. "Maybe."

The waitress came and took their order and then they continued.

"Just one kiss?" asked Holly.

Jack kept his eye contact. "There was talk of more, but never more."

Holly's eyes began to well with tears and she wiped at the sides of her eyes with the palm of one hand.

"We were separated," said Jack, "before your accident. It wasn't at all clear what was going to happen between us."

"OK." Holly blew her nose and gathered herself again. "So why are you telling me now?"

Jack cleared his throat. "I need to be alone again for a little while. Not at Elmhurst. Not with Larisa. Really alone this time. To get my head right, to wrap my mind around a few things."

Holly nodded. "OK." She moved her gaze to look out over the marsh.

Jack studied her, trying to gauge her thoughts. "Why aren't you screaming?"

Holly turned her gaze back toward him. "Like I told you last night. I'm tired of fighting. If this is over, let's just call it over."

Jack nodded, fighting his own tears now. He felt hollow inside, beat. "I'll move out, get an apartment."

They waited for the food to come.

"Let's talk about how we'll tell the boys," said Holly.

Jack nodded as they huddled into the table together.

CHAPTER THIRTEEN

April brought an early spring, the grounds around Elmhurst bursting with color from the eager blooms. First came the crocuses and grape hyacinths, their soft purple and white buds peeking shyly out from under the crumpled autumn leaves. Then the bright yellow flare of forsythia. The miniature pansies shivered through the morning frost, half hiding their skewed faces from the regal daffodils with their imposing collared necks. Aunt Ursula's pussy willow had begun to sprout its funny fuzzy buds. Soon the tulips would push their tapered heads through the soil, the lilacs would hang their long noses over the fences. How did each flower know just when to bloom? Larisa wondered. After a long winter withdrawal, they each somehow recognized the exact moment at which to reemerge. Maybe humans could rouse such instincts as well.

After months of isolation, Larisa had sought out the world. The visit from her parents at Christmastime and the tumultuous events leading up to it—Jack, Brent, Holly, the boys—had shaken something loose in her. And though it had taken some time to absorb all that had happened—all that was still happening with her mother, the disease—by early spring she had the sensation of finally unclenching her fists. Of opening up, letting go. In the end she couldn't be sure just what had edged her back out to reclaim her life. Whether it was the precious moments with her parents, the cool flip of the breeze through the budding trees, or the earthy scent of loam steaming up from the grounds, something had changed. She wasn't so angry. She wasn't so afraid of the uncertainty. She was tired of being alone.

"I guess I kind of went a little nutso," she told Teddy. Her old employer and friend had hired her to help out at his greenhouse a few days a week. The two of them chatted as they worked, shaking tiny young seedlings loose from plastic six-pack trays to pot in bigger containers.

Teddy eyed her from under the brim of his floppy canvas sun hat. "Honey, you're not the first bride to lose her cool."

"But I wasn't even really a bride. I was just pretending." Larisa raked her hand over the roots of one of the seedlings, a technique to promote growth in the new soil. She'd forgotten how much she liked working in the greenhouse among living, growing things.

Teddy tsked. "Such a shame. The whole town was waiting to see you in that dress."

"Well, they'll just have to keep on waiting." Larisa thought of the dress, hanging now in the Elmhurst front hall closet, pristine in its preservation bag. When, if ever, would she get to wear it?

"Well, no one wants you to marry the wrong guy," Teddy continued. "We just want to see you happy."

"I know," answered Larisa, smiling. "I am."

She peered down the length of the greenhouse and breathed in, experiencing the calm yet incredible beauty of the place: all those bright petals lining the metal benches, row upon row of them, illuminated by sunbeams through the clear glass panes. The plants would incubate here for a few more weeks before the spring gardening frenzy began and they'd get snatched up by eager homeowners. Some would flourish well into summer while others would be neglected, forgotten and left to shrivel on a back porch. Some just wouldn't do well regardless of the love and care given them and still others would prosper despite poor odds. Such was the cycle of life. Unpredictable, indiscriminate, yet quietly forgiving at times.

Kittie's illness, of course, had continued to progress. This was no surprise. Yet Larisa found that since Christmas, since her epiphany then, her orientation to it had changed. For starters, she spent a lot more time visiting her parents and helping with her mother's daily routine. In addition, she'd begun to talk to other people about the disease. And once she started talking, she couldn't stop. The words spewed out almost without cognition, carrying with them a fluency all their own. It struck Larisa that when she'd arrived back at Kent Crossing in the fall, she'd felt an overwhelming desire to just be spontaneous, to stop trying to control the minutiae of her life. But had she lived impulsively? Had she thrown caution to the wind? Not really. Her various deceptions had really just been another way to seize control, an attempt to mitigate the fallout from her breakup with Brent, the death of Aunt

Ursula, the loss of her job, that damn disease that gripped her mother. Actually facing the uncertainty and the fear, letting things unravel, feeling the emotions. Well, that had been a different experience entirely.

"And listen," Teddy went on, "you had every reason to go completely nutso. My mother sneezes twice on the phone and I practically fall over with guilt for being so many miles away. I can't imagine going through something as horrible as dementia."

Larisa looked him in the eye. "Neither can I, even though I'm in the thick of it. It's surreal."

Teddy continued. "I'm thinking about flying down for a visit, actually. To my mother's. To just take care of a few things, spend some time with her."

Larisa patted his shoulder. "You should. In the end, we only get so much time to spend with the ones we love."

Teddy responded with a pained expression. "That's what I'm afraid of."

Larisa shook her head. "But don't be afraid of it; that's what I've learned. You need to face it, *feel* it, and just make use of the time you have."

Teddy nodded. He wiped his dirty hands across his work apron and met her gaze. "What's it like now with your mother? Does she still recognize you? Does she know who you are?"

Larisa shrugged. "Well, I try to see her as often as possible—at least once a week—and that helps. Most of the time, yes; she seems to know me, though not always by name. Her grasp on reality is starting to slip more and more. She wanders a lot, as though looking for something, and she can't always articulate what she's experiencing, so my father and I usually have to figure out what she needs."

Teddy shook his head sympathetically. "Poor Clark. How's he holding up?"

Larisa shifted a seedling from one palm to the other. "Well, he's a saint. I don't know how he does it, but he seems to hold it together. They're coming down for a visit today actually."

"Oh?"

"My father wants to look at some care places closer to home. Soon she'll need a full-on memory care unit. You know, a place that's really prepped for dealing with dementia. And it would be a heck of a lot easier to visit if she's close by."

"She's lucky to have you," said Teddy.

"No." Larisa shook her head. "I'm lucky to still have *her*."

Every time Larisa saw her mother, she could feel the presence of the illness, like a hawk circling. This awareness of sheer vulnerability—the feeling that her mother could be snatched up at any moment in the talons of the disease—had created an intense feeling of obligation in Larisa. Whereas in the past she had been unable to face her mother's confusion, she knew now how critical her caregiver role could be. She couldn't prevent the disease from progressing, but she could mitigate some of the fallout. Kittie needed to be guided, protected, coddled. Larisa could do this for her. They weren't alone in this world, as her mother had said. They never had been. They had each other. And they needed to recognize this, now more than ever.

After work, late afternoon, Larisa took her time on the walk back home to Elmhurst. She stopped in the doorway of the Little French Bridal Shop to wave hello to Mrs. Muldoon and she paused to chat with Andy at the gas station. After Christmas, she'd finally come clean with him about the fiasco with the Rolls. He'd seemed stunned at first that she'd carried on a cover-up behind his back, but when she'd elaborated about the wedding falsehood and her moments of doubt and confusion, she saw a flash of recognition and then forgiveness on his face.

"I know how it is," he said. "Weddings have a way of either bringing out the best or worst in people. Ursula and I knew that firsthand."

"Ursula?" Larisa asked.

"Well, sure. Where do you think she got that ring?" Andy pointed at Larisa's hand.

"*This* ring?" Confused, Larisa fidgeted with the sapphire on her finger.

Andy nodded. "Ursula always had a thing for the color blue."

Larisa took a moment to comprehend what Andy was saying. And then it hit her. "Oh my God. You're the lost love. The one the family never accepted."

Andy grinned back at her, neither confirming nor denying.

Larisa recalled the story she'd been told. How Ursula had fallen for a local boy, but the family found him unacceptable and so hustled her off on a cruise to Europe. By the time she'd returned, a different marriage had been arranged, only to be broken off months later. Andy, Larisa saw now, had been the one she'd left behind. She gaped at him. "How have I never figured this out before?"

Andy shrugged. "We didn't tend to talk about it."

"But why didn't you get married later? I mean, when the arranged marriage didn't go through."

Andy shook his head. "We'd missed our time. I'd gone off to the navy. Life went on. By the time I returned, I was a different man. And anyway, marriage didn't matter as much as it once had. Our friendship was the thing we cared about. That's why I gave her the ring, to commemorate our lifelong friendship. First it was only a pretend one, out of a Cracker Jack box. But I saved for years for one that looked like the ring from the royal wedding. You know she was always obsessed with Charles and Di."

Larisa heaved a big sigh. "But then you should have it back. It's rightfully yours." She started to tug the ring over her knuckle, but Andy clapped his hand over hers before she could.

"Keep it." He nodded to convince her, his look gently imploring. "It's yours now. What the hell would I do with it?"

He was right, she realized. What *would* he do with it? Sell it like some castaway trinket at a pawnshop? Find another woman to court? Wasn't there some relative to whom he could pass it on? But before she could ask, he'd excused himself to tend to a customer. She'd stood there stunned for several moments before going on her way.

Now, as she moved beyond the gas station and headed up the hill to Elmhurst, Larisa thought of that post-Christmas conversation again. *We think we know the people in our lives,* she thought, *but no one person can ever be privy to all the knowledge.* In the asymptote of knowing someone, different people became curators of different information, each of them experiencing a unique facet of the same person. Knowing someone, then, became a collective experience and in this deep complexity lay both the joy and the heartache. Ursula's ring would remind her of this, always.

As she approached the house, she noted, happily, that her parents had arrived. Clark stood in the front yard, yanking the leftover Christmas lights off the boxwoods and piling them in clusters on the lawn. Larisa felt a tinge of guilt, knowing she should have done this herself weeks earlier. But then, her father liked to keep busy. Kittie stood nearby, teetering uncertainly between the front steps and the piles of lights, her face obscured by the brim of a large woven hat. Though the morning had been sunny, an evening fog had begun to roll in. It settled in a thick mist around the trunk of the elm and dissipated up through the treetops. Larisa felt the soft moisture on her cheeks and heard the low, steady moan of the foghorn emanating out over the ocean waves. Her parents, she realized, hadn't yet spotted her. Clark leaned into the bushes to extricate a section of lights while Kittie bent to pick up one of the discarded strands. She considered it curiously for a few moments, fingering the tiny bulbs in shaky hands, before beginning to wind the entire string around her neck like a scarf. As she wound, the lights got caught up on the brim of her hat and she began to bat at them, letting out small staccato distress cries. Clark swiveled to face her, his features immediately consumed with a look of annoyance and frustration.

"I need you to take those off," he said sternly. "Please, darling, you're going to hurt yourself."

Kittie jerked on one end of the strand, which only caused the loop to cinch more tightly around her neck. "Leave me alone," she howled, though it was unclear whether she was addressing the lights or her husband.

Clark approached. "I need you to take them off," he snapped. She shuffled to the side to avoid him, but he brusquely cornered her against the bushes. "Please would you take them off? *Please* would you take them off? Take them off, God damn it!" He raised his hands almost as if to strangle her and then thrust his arms down to his sides before striding angrily away. Kittie sat on the ground and began to cry, the lights softly clacking in rhythm to her chest heaves. Clark remained several feet away, his eyes closed, his hands blocking his ears.

Larisa froze. She'd rarely heard her father shout, and certainly not at her mother. But it wasn't just that. She'd rarely seen him so agitated. Clark had always been the type of guy to see the glass half full, to keep his calm in a moment of storm. But now he looked haggard, undone, his chin unshaven, his hair untrimmed. Larisa knew how deeply her mother's illness had affected *her*, but she hadn't quite realized the toll it had been taking on *him*.

"Dad," she called, waving and hurrying to greet him. "This looks challenging. Let me help."

"Who do you think you are, speaking to me like that?" snapped Kittie. "Where's Ursula?"

Clark opened his eyes, his expression grim. "Yes, we're having a moment," he conceded as he lifted his hand in hello.

Kittie continued to wail for Ursula from the bushes. Clark kept his distance and so Larisa approached her mother, crouched down next to her, and spoke in soft, soothing tones. "Shh, there, there, let's just get you untangled." She gently removed the lights and helped Kittie to her feet. As she struggled to stand, Kittie inadvertently knocked the sun hat off, revealing a greasy chunk of hair plastered to one side of her head.

"Wow, Mom," gushed Larisa as she patted Kittie's shoulder. "Look at your new hairdo! It looks *great*." Larisa had learned to say things that made her mother feel good, even if they weren't true.

Kittie beamed and accepted Larisa's kiss on her cheek.

Clark grimaced and shook his head. "She rubbed hand lotion in it again. She just gets into things before I have time to stop her. This morning, she dropped a piece of trash into the toilet."

Larisa put a finger to her lips. "Shh. She looks great. She's Rosa Rugosa, remember?"

Clark looked sadly off toward the water. "Rosa Rugosa? There's no Rosa Rugosa here."

Kittie peered suspiciously over at him. "That's what my husband used to say." In this ever-changing phase of the disease, Larisa realized, Kittie could only remember a younger version of Clark, not the aged and unshaven one who stood before her. Thus, the confusion. Larisa knew that she might be next. She hadn't yet aged the way Clark had. Still, Kittie might recognize her one moment, only to succumb to memory loss in the next.

The two of them faced each other, Clark and Kittie, a dreadful air of discomfort between them. Clark looked to Larisa; then Kittie did too. Both of them stood there waiting for her to give her cue. Larisa flashed an apologetic smile to her father and then steered her mother toward the house.

"Come on," she said. "Let's get you inside. It's chilly now that the sun's going down and we don't want you catching a cold."

Together, they made their way toward the front door. Kittie snuck a backward glance at Clark and clung tightly to Larisa's arm. Once inside, Larisa guided her mother toward the upright piano, where Kittie settled habitually onto the bench and immediately began to play a simple rendition of *The Merry Farmer*, a tune she'd often selected for beginning students. She'd played the piece so frequently over the years that it had become part of her procedural long-term memory, something that was second nature to her. Larisa went back outside to tend to her father.

"I'm sorry," he said, shaking his head. "I shouldn't have lost my temper. I'm just not myself anymore around her."

Larisa pulled him into an embrace. "It's understandable. I know you don't break down often, but you *are* human. And this is *not* easy to deal with."

Clark's eyes welled with tears. "I never thought I would have to 'deal' with my wife. I mean, I love her as much as ever, but sometimes I just can't stand her."

"It's not her," answered Larisa. "It's the disease."

"I know that," said Clark, "but that doesn't make it easier."

"No," Larisa answered softly. "It's like watching someone slowly fade away."

Inside, the rendition of *The Merry Farmer* came to an end. Kittie transitioned to playing up and down the scales in an even, measured manner. Larisa had listened to this countless times as a young girl when her mother was teaching new students, who would repeat the scales, usually less fluidly, in the higher octave. This imperfect mimicry had always struck her as sweet, but now the absence of the counterpart saddened her. She turned to her father.

"Take a break, Dad. I can be in charge for a while. When is the last time you got some time to yourself?"

Clark blinked back at her. "I don't remember."

"Go then." She waved him away as he hesitated. "She'll be fine. I promise."

Clark shook his head. "She's too much to take care of by yourself."

"You do it all the time," Larisa countered.

"Yes," Clark agreed, "but I'm used to it. I know how to handle her."

Larisa raised her eyebrows at him. "Like you did just now?"

Her father crumpled before her. She hadn't meant her comment to land on him the way it had, but then, she reasoned, maybe it would be good for him to realize how much strain he was under.

"Daddy," she said, "you've been a saint to her. Incredible. But it's OK to step away now and then. Let someone else do the caretaking."

He nodded. "I did want to go visit those care facilities."

"Great," said Larisa. "Do that. But do some things for yourself, too. Stop for a cup of coffee. Take a walk on the beach. Do something impulsive."

Clark smirked at her. "Like buy a wedding dress?"

"Ha ha. See—at least your sense of humor is still intact."

Clark shrugged as he blew her a kiss goodbye and headed toward his car. "Barely. But I guess it's keeping me sane."

Larisa went back up the front walk and through the front door. She took a moment to admire some of the renovations she'd done in the dining room and front hall, work she'd done together with Jack. She wondered briefly how he was doing. She'd heard murmurs around town about a separation between him and Holly, but she hadn't heard from him directly since he'd moved out of Elmhurst. And anyway, as she well knew by now, rumors could just be rumors. She'd decided to focus her feelings, for now, on her mother.

Kittie stopped playing as Larisa entered the living room. She looked up from the piano and surveyed her daughter somewhat uncertainly. She looked down at the keys and thrummed them lightly with her fingers, so lightly that no sound was emitted. Then she squinted back up at Larisa.

"Are you here for your lesson, dear?" she finally asked, her voice wispy and thin.

Larisa hadn't noticed outside in the dim light of dusk, but she saw now that her mother's outfit was completely mismatched—a blue tone paisley skirt with a green-striped oxford. This was the sort of thing that had begun to happen more often. The staff at No One's Home had explained that this was typical, that it was better to let her maintain her sense of independence than edit her outfits. Any attempt at correcting her would just lead to a negative interaction. Larisa understood, but still she found it unsettling. Kittie had always been such a neat and careful dresser.

"Yes," she said as she sat down beside her mother on the bench. "What are you going to teach me today?"

Kittie responded with a wavering half smile, her eyes searching. She couldn't quite find the words. This also happened often now, when Kittie was asked a direct question. Larisa had learned to provide the answer for her.

"We were working on arpeggios last time," she said. Larisa wasn't an accomplished pianist, but she knew enough to goad her mother along.

A look of clarity settled across Kittie's features. "Yes. Let's start with C major and then G and D, and so on." She positioned her fingers on the keys and played the corresponding arpeggios in one fluid movement.

Larisa repeated the arpeggios several times as a warm-up, then she looked for further instructions from her teacher. But Kittie's mind had wandered; her eyes focused now on a photo of ten-year-old Larisa, hair pulled back in blue and white ribbon barrettes for her school picture.

"Larisa will be home from school soon," she said. She lifted the photo from its spot and ran her hands lightly over the frame. "I should get her snack ready."

Larisa leaned in and examined herself in the photo. She had to stifle a laugh at her collared shirt and feathered bangs, fashion trends from a time gone by.

"What does Larisa like to eat?" she asked Kittie.

Kittie tsked. "Well, she'd subsist on jelly beans if I let her, but usually I make a nice zucchini bread. Something a little healthier."

Larisa smiled. It was true. As a child, she'd gone through a total infatuation with jelly beans. This was something she hadn't thought about in years. So funny that a moment like this would remind her of a former incarnation of herself.

"Oh, I always loved your zucchini bread," gushed Larisa. "We should make it! I think I might even have the ingredients."

She stood and tugged gently at her mother's hand to encourage her off the piano bench. Kittie snatched up the photo of the schoolgirl Larisa and followed the adult Larisa into the kitchen. Larisa knew by now that she would need to give her mother a task. Kittie was only capable of focusing on what was right in front of her. A task made Kittie feel useful, engaged. And though Kittie did not always complete the task successfully, that wasn't the point. She could line up shoes in her closet, though the pairs were often mismatched. She could clip coupons, not with scissors but by ripping them out with her hands. Of course, the newspaper usually ended up in shreds, but so what? Kittie didn't notice and it kept her busy for a few moments if Clark and Larisa needed to talk to the doctors about her care. Kittie had always liked to fold laundry, the task appealing to her neat and orderly nature, and so Larisa produced the laundry basket now and filled it with dish towels. Kittie dumped them into a pile on the kitchen table and plunged her hands in. Her fingers automatically began to pluck at the cloths and crease them into approximate rectangles. Larisa assembled the ingredients for the zucchini bread, long ago having committed the recipe to memory. She could remember where her mother forgot. She turned on the oven to preheat and began to beat the eggs with the oil and the sugar in one of Ursula's earthenware bowls.

Gazing out the window, Larisa glimpsed the budding greenery of the Rosa rugosa bushes that bordered the great lawn. They weren't in bloom yet, but they would be soon, their peak usually coming in early June. She could imagine the sweet, pungent aroma filling her nostrils. Could Kittie remember the scent if she was asked? One of the most disarming things about the disease was that one could never quite determine what the sufferer would or would not remember on a given day. In the middle stages she was in, Kittie might forget something one minute only to remember the forgotten details mere minutes later. Or she might not remember that she couldn't remember and this could lead to all kinds of frustration.

"Well, it's about time to start dinner," Kittie had announced one day when Larisa was visiting.

"No, dear," Clark tried to correct her, "we've just had dinner."

"I didn't have dinner," Kittie protested.

"You did," Clark tried to assure her. "Larisa and I were right there with you."

"I did *not* have dinner!" Kittie shouted.

The more they corrected her, the more agitated she became until they finally managed to change the subject. As a result of this type of interaction, Larisa had learned to let Kittie be right. And now that she understood much more about the disease, she found it much easier to manage. She didn't feel the need to curate the relationship with her mother the way she once had. Sure, she found it necessary to give her mother direction, but she could let the moment go where it would. As long as Kittie was safe and engaged in a positive interaction, that was what mattered. It took patience, but it didn't take much else to allow her mother to ask the same questions and make the same comments over and over. When Larisa knew what to expect, she found it less troubling.

Larisa grated her zucchini into a separate bowl. She measured and stirred the dry ingredients and then mixed them and the zucchini in with the wet ingredients. By then, Kittie had lost focus on her laundry task and began to home in again on the photo of the young Larisa, which she had recovered from under her pile of dishcloths. She studied it with some intensity before holding it up toward her daughter.

"Larisa will be home from school soon," she said. "I should get her a snack."

"Yes," answered Larisa. "We're making zucchini bread for her."

She showed the batter to Kittie and then began to pour it into the greased bread mold.

Kittie nodded approvingly. "That's her favorite."

Larisa led Kittie back to the table and dumped the laundry

again. Kittie returned to her folding. Larisa put the bread in the oven and set the timer. She'd grown comfortable with the new kitchen that she and Jack had built. She'd made herself at home in the house, too. And by now she'd pretty much decided that she would stay. Of course she couldn't sell Elmhurst. It seemed crazy now that she had even considered it. Clark would need a home once Kittie moved to the care facility. And anyway, it was his house, not hers. She would stay with him here until she got her life back together. She'd work at the greenhouse and become the new caretaker at Elmhurst.

With Kittie engaged in her laundry task and the bread beginning to bake, Larisa wandered into the conservatory. In the chaos of her winter, she'd neglected to care for the plants the way she ought and so some of them had perished. But Teddy had come one day to help her clean up the place and revive any remaining flora. They'd trimmed and pruned and watered and now several of the orchids were bursting with bloom and even the ficus tree seemed to be making a full recovery. Larisa had been playing the records on Aunt Ursula's Victrola almost daily. She'd started the music as a way to counter the awful silence that had descended after Jack left, but now had to wonder whether the classical music had contributed to the plants' recovery.

"Everyone is hard to live with," she'd told the plants as she dropped the needle on the first record. "Even oneself."

But by now she'd settled into a routine of which she felt proud. She enjoyed caring for her home, sweeping the kitchen floor after dinner, running a damp cloth up and down the banister, wiping the cobwebs from the windowpanes. She'd grown comfortable with herself once more. She felt a calmness that she recognized and welcomed. Who knew? Perhaps the plants could recognize it as well.

Larisa squinted now and cocked her head at the night-blooming cereus on the bottom tier of the plant stand. She moved closer. Was that a bud beginning to emerge from the vein of the leaf? Larisa hadn't seen it bloom in years. Now wouldn't that be something.

Back in the kitchen, Kittie had stood and was opening and shutting the cupboard doors.

"Larisa will be home from school soon," she muttered to herself. She yanked open the oven door and then slammed it shut again. She went to the fridge and did the same. Larisa approached slowly.

"What are you looking for, Mom?" she asked.

At the word *Mom*, Kittie jerked her head, almost violently, toward Larisa, still clutching the photo in one hand. She reached her free hand to Larisa's shoulder to steady herself and peered with wide eyes at her daughter. She looked from the photo to Larisa and then back again. In that moment, she seemed to understand both that the child in the photo was Larisa and that the person in front of her was Larisa, yet she was no longer capable of consciously connecting the two. Larisa could feel the tenuous presence of her younger self, somehow still in existence, suspended in a different moment in time. The two personas bobbed in the room like sailboats tethered to their moorings, separate yet pulled by the same current.

Kittie leaned farther in, her eyes searching. "Do you *know* Larisa?" she asked.

Larisa gripped her mother by the shoulders. They could go on like this for the rest of the afternoon and well into evening. Kittie would continue to ask her questions and Larisa would continue to answer, caring patiently for her mother the way she ought. Kittie now had trouble, sometimes, recognizing herself in the mirror. It was shocking when it happened, yet this type of incident didn't sadden Larisa the way it once had. Not when she could understand it from her mother's perspective. Kittie wasn't expecting to see an old lady in the reflection; of course she didn't recognize herself. And as to the question of who she—Larisa—was, *her* identity. Well, she wasn't so fixated on that anymore. The answer: The self isn't static. It's always changing, evolving, like the plants to which she tended at Teddy's greenhouse. A new bud would form and then bloom and then fall away again to make way for new growth. She was not the same person as when she was younger. And yet she was. Her eyes landed once again on the photo of her as a schoolgirl. Peering down the hallway, she could just catch the reflection of her adult self in the hallway mirror, the same mirror she'd obscured with the pheasant wallpaper months earlier.

Do you know *Larisa?* Kittie had asked.

Larisa smiled.

"Well, yes," she answered as she pulled her mother into a calming embrace and eased the old photo from her grip. "I do."

CHAPTER FOURTEEN

Jack Merrill had been the one to find Ursula Pearl in the conservatory the day she died. She'd taken her tea in the late afternoon as she always did, and when Jack finished his work and came in search of her, there she lay, cozied into the chaise with the music surging around her, looking as peaceful as always. So peaceful that it took Jack a moment to realize she was gone. Sure, he had registered it intuitively on some immediate level—she had a stillness about her that was deeper than sleep—but it took some time to sink in. The idea of someone dying in her sleep seemed both fantastical and too simple, in a way. He was glad it hadn't been painful, of course, but with a woman like Ursula Pearl, he had expected something more dramatic. What, he wondered, would cause one's body—one's being—to just give up like that? Alive one moment and completely expired the next. Hadn't she only an hour ago asked him to trim the roses and water the lawn? It didn't follow that she would just lie down and die when there were new blooms to cultivate. But then he thought of the dry and crumpled petals he had swept that morning from the flagstone patio. New blooms would come, yes. But then inevitably they would go.

He stood now, coffee cup in hand, on the rocky beach of one of the small coves the sea had sculpted over time. The tide was going out, and as the water reached and receded, reached and receded, slowly revealing the flat and speckled slab of sand beneath—the rhythm distinctly different from the pounce and strike of high tide—he marveled that just over a year had passed since he'd found Ursula that late-May day. And Christ, what a year it had been. Two months ago he had moved out of the home he'd shared with Holly and the boys, squatting first at his parents' house until the fog had lifted and he could find his bearings. He had enjoyed being back in the comfort of his childhood home, allowing his mother to fret over him, his father to fill the silence with corny jokes and the customary platitudes. But the twin bed was too small, the TV too loud, and really, an adult man could only live with one's parents for so long. And so he was relieved when Sam Whittaker offered him a very generous rate for the cottage overlooking the cove. Once an oversize in-law apartment, it had a small kitchenette, a decent master bedroom, and a second bedroom with just enough room for his three boys. Only a week had passed since he'd moved in, but already it felt like home, the early morning routine of walking down to this beach by now well established.

"Hey, Dad!" came a call from the bluff behind him. Charlie, leading the pack, the others skidding to a stop behind. Barefoot and lanky, still in their pajamas, they clutched their arms against the chill and scrabbled over the rocks to his side.

"Hey, you bozos," Jack greeted them, cuffing each playfully on the shoulder as they lumbered by. "How'd everybody sleep?"

"Good." Both Ben and Alex smirked and shifted their eyes toward Charlie.

"What?" yelled Charlie. "I was *not* snoring!"

"Aha," quipped Jack. "So that's what woke me up. Sounded like someone was jackhammering the street."

"Ha ha," answered Charlie with an exaggerated and overly goofy grin.

Alex had started selecting flat stones to skim out over the water and Ben was shifting his balance between his feet on the peak of a large rock. The boys seemed to be doing well for their first night in the new place, Jack thought, but then only time would tell. There would be an ebb and flow for sure.

Back in March he'd been so nervous about telling them he was leaving yet again, but when he and Holly sat them down for the somber conversation, they hadn't seemed so surprised. Charlie had tapped his foot in a steady rhythm against the shag carpet, but, uncharacteristically, said nothing.

"Will you live at Elmhurst again?" asked Ben.

Jack shook his head. "No, not this time. My work there is done."

"Then who will you live with?" said Alex. His glance, Jack saw, flitted quickly toward Holly and then away again. Concerned for her feelings, it seemed, should Jack suddenly reveal he was moving in with another woman.

"By myself," Jack answered firmly. "I'll move in with Nana

and Poppa until I find my own apartment, but then I'll be on my own."

"When will we see you?" whispered Ben.

Jack felt his chest tighten, his heart aching for his boys. He hoped the divorce would be better for them in the end. After all the emotions were aired, after time and routine had given it the tint of normalcy, they would see that this was the better choice. For everyone. But he knew it wasn't great now. He was relieved, at least, that they had one another.

"We haven't worked out the schedule yet," Holly answered for him. "But it will probably be a couple nights a week and every other weekend."

Part of the reason the boys were reacting so calmly was because of Holly. Where in the past she'd been bitter and angry, launching continuous missiles at him, never mind if the boys were within earshot, now she maintained an almost impenetrable calm. She had a new resolve about her, as though now that she and Jack had set this course—now that they'd had their frank conversations—she was determined to maintain an even keel, keep them all afloat. Hadn't that been *his* job once? Jack was grateful for her composure, but he couldn't help but feel a bit adrift. But he knew however calm Holly seemed, it must be strange for her, too. Heck, neither of them had gone into the marriage imagining it would end someday. So yes, they would go their separate ways, though they'd forever be part of a linked choreography. He was glad, at least, that they weren't fighting anymore, glad to finally be on the same page with this woman for whom his faded love was no longer enough.

"Dad!" Charlie's voice brought him back to the present. "Do you have any breakfast for us?"

Jack glanced over to see his son slapping his gut. Ah yes, the bottomless pit. Jack remembered his own insatiable stomach at that age.

"Wha?" He feigned surprise. "I have to *feed* you?"

The boys came grinning to his side. Jack focused his gaze out over the shoals and toward the horizon one last time. In the stillness of morning, the sun, a brilliant gold disk, seemed amplified, only just out of reach. Jack was more accustomed to being on the boat looking from the ocean in; sometimes on his sails he even went so far as to lose sight of the mainland. But there was something gratifying now about being here onshore, grounded, with his boys, watching the last wriggle of water against the sand, the tide softly tugging.

"OK, everyone," he finally said, "can't stand around all day when there are pancakes to be made."

"With chocolate chips?" asked Charlie.

"Blueberries," suggested Ben.

"All of the above," answered Jack.

"And maple syrup," Alex filled in. "I saw it on the counter."

"See? I'm not as helpless as you all thought, huh?" Jack turned away from the water and headed back up the path, beckoning for the boys to follow. As he stepped up to the bluff, he smiled to hear the buzz of the bees back in the rose hips, which meant summer was on its way. Yes, things came in cycles for sure.

When Jack had thought of Ursula over the years, when he'd heard her name come up in conversation, when other townsfolk mentioned her, his mind always flashed to an image of her padding slowly across the freshly mowed lawn toward him, that first weekend he'd worked at Elmhurst. She'd carried a tall glass of iced tea on a silver tray. Her future still unknown. Watching her approach, the cubes of ice clinking softly against the side of the glass, mid-melt, he could never have imagined he would be the one to find her years later in the chaise. She hadn't gone there directly; the path hadn't been obvious. And yet—who could have known?—all along she had been steadily advancing toward this final moment, like a sailboat tacking back and forth until it reached its mark. There was a feeling of inevitability and yet still he felt surprised. Had this outcome always been determined—predestined—or had it come about by chance? Standing there, moving his fingers nervously over the grit of his gardening gloves, he hadn't known what to do at first. He hadn't felt the need to try to resuscitate her—she was ninety-six, after all—but should he call 9-1-1 or just the local police number? Would it be better to call someone from the family first? Ironically, Ursula might have been the one to instruct him on such matters had she still been alive. He searched his memory. Had she ever talked anything like this over with him? Had she left any kind of end-of-life instructions? No, he finally decided, she hadn't. And so, he first called the local police number—it would be silly to get everyone all worked up with sirens and, anyway, Ursula would have hated that. Thankfully, after he explained things carefully to the deputy, he was transferred to Chief Sullivan, who offered to call the family directly after the death had been confirmed.

He sat with her and waited for the authorities to come. What else was he to do? He felt afraid for a fleeting moment to linger so boldly with death. But once he'd lowered himself into the chair next to her, he relaxed. There was a quiet elegance, an intimacy, he realized, in being with someone this way, just sitting with the shell of the woman for whom he had cared so many years. Keeping her vigil. Around her, the flowering plants had begun to bloom, small slivers of color—pink and yellow and white—peeking out from the folds of the buds. The afternoon sun winked behind the trees, glinting through the panes of glass into the conservatory. The record played to the end and then the arm of the needle retreated to its cradle. A heavy silence embalmed the room so that all he could hear was the draft of his own breath. In. Out. He reached at one point for Ursula's hand, but it was cold and he was struck suddenly by the definite absence of her. She had been there, alive, at lunch this afternoon, peering with amusement at him over the steam of her baked shrimp scampi. But now she was missing, the spirit fled from her body. Where, he wondered sadly, had she gone?

Back up at the cottage, after breakfast, the boys began to help him settle into the new place, digging through the boxes he'd packed over a few afternoons at the old house, when Holly and the boys were out. He'd already unpacked his clothes, but there were books and CDs, a small model of a tugboat given to him by his grandfather, and the knot board he'd started in March.

Alex pulled the board out of the box and ran his fingers over the looped cords, landing finally on the one empty spot. He glanced up at Jack. "Why haven't you finished this?"

"It's taking longer than I thought." Jack reached for it. "When I mess up, some of the knots are almost as hard to undo as they are to tie in the first place."

He lifted his gaze to meet that of his son, but Alex's eyes

had landed on something else in the box. The wedding photo, swiped along with the group shot of the boys, from the front hall table. He'd taken them with him, two moments in time among countless others. Jack slipped the photo of the boys out of the moving box and positioned it on the ledge of the living room window. He reached for the photo of him and Holly, not sure just what he would do with it, but Alex refused to let go. Eventually he set the photo down on the couch beside him, and looked squarely at Jack.

"You and Mom aren't going to get back together this time, are you?"

Jack felt the room go into a slow spin. He and Holly had already explained that they had decided to divorce—they had been very clear about that, emphasizing that it was nothing the boys had done—but of course he could understand how the boys might be slow to accept it. Ben and Charlie were staring at him now too, frozen in their tasks, waiting along with their brother for his response. He could lie, he knew. Spin some soft words about how relationships were tough, but things might work out if they worked at it. But that wouldn't be right, that wouldn't be true. He sat down on the couch next to his son and reached for the photo, taking one last gaze at long ago. Then he set it back into the box, facedown.

"No," he said. "It isn't going to work out this time, no."

Alex persisted. "But you've been separated before. You could get back together."

Jack shook his head. "No, Al, that's not what's going to happen. I'm sorry."

He watched them each react in their various ways. Alex evaded his father, plucked a soccer ball from one of the boxes and began practicing maneuvers, dribbling the ball and flicking it into the air and across the kitchen floor. Charlie began kicking at the back of Alex's knees as Alex handled the ball. Ben turned back to the spices he'd been organizing, seeking order in the unease. After a moment he came to the edge of the room and stood, shifting his weight from one leg to the other. He bit his bottom lip and stepped closer.

"Did you fall in love with that lady?"

Jack frowned. "That lady?"

"Larisa." Charlie answered for Ben, launching one last kick at the back of Alex's knees and then leaping onto the couch next to Jack. His eyes fluttered nervously, not quite able to look at his father.

"No," said Jack, a little too quickly. He took a deep breath in. How to explain all this to these boys, who were still so young, who had never been in love, who didn't—couldn't—understand the peaks and valleys of a romantic relationship.

Alex booted the ball down the hallway toward the bedrooms and then came to the doorway to face Jack. "Then why were you always smiling when she was around?"

Jack raised his eyebrows at his sons. It seemed they had picked up on it too, the buzz between him and Larisa. Of course they had.

"I thought Larisa was marrying Brent," said Ben.

"Remember they got in that fight?" answered Charlie.

"Even if she was gonna marry Brent," said Alex, "that doesn't mean Daddy can't fall in love with her."

"What do you know about love?" giggled Charlie, poking Alex in the ribs. "Just because you have a crush on Ashley Higgins, doesn't mean you know anything about love."

Ben smirked over at his brothers. "Ashley Higgins doesn't even know you exist," he told Alex.

Alex wrestled Ben into a headlock on the chaise arm of the couch and began rubbing his knuckles into Ben's hair. "But *you* know I exist, don't you?"

Charlie stood on the sidelines, nipping with hands at his brothers' ankles. Watching them enact the old routines in this new place, Jack realized they *were* still all in this together, even Holly. But there was no denying it was a new reality for all of them, one that they were all still tentatively stepping through, its parameters not yet clear.

"It's true, actually," Jack said suddenly. "I started to fall in love with Larisa."

All on the couch now, they snapped their attention toward him and listened. The tide, Jack saw through the window, had already started to move back in, ever on its endless circuit, erasing the patterns on the sand.

"I didn't mean to," he said, "but your mother and I were fighting. I've known Larisa a long time and we became good friends when I moved into Elmhurst."

They stared at him. There was a pause as the boys considered whether they should question him further. Jack knew from past experience that they would ask only what they were ready to hear, nothing less and nothing more. He knew better than to offer unsolicited information.

"Are you still friends?" asked Charlie.

Jack considered this. "I don't know. I haven't spoken to her since Christmas."

"Really?" said Ben and Charlie at the same time.

"Well," said Alex, shoving Ben into the cushions one last time, "at least she knows you exist."

There was a release of energy then, a settling in the room, like a stack of lit fireplace logs shifting under a hot flame as they splintered slowly into ash. Something had been acknowledged between them, Jack and his boys. Something felt more permanent than it had before. From this place of tentative acceptance, they would go forward.

Even though Jack had not spoken to Larisa since Christmas, he *had* seen her. In a small town, that was inevitable. Once from a distance at the hardware store, another time walking down the road toward the public beach. And then, on the way back from dropping the kids at Holly's Sunday night, he spotted her again, this time crossing the road in front of Palmer's Market with her mother. Larisa was intently focused on Kittie, guiding her gently by the elbow over the crosswalk and toward the store, and so she hadn't noticed Jack stopped in his truck at the corner. But Jack, watching, was struck by the care and patience she took with her mother. Struck both by the need for it and by this new role for Larisa. Jack had heard about the illness, but he hadn't seen Kittie since Ursula's funeral. She was a woman of small stature, but she'd always radiated a quiet strength and sense of self-assurance. As she leaned on her daughter, taking small shuffling steps across the road, Jack was saddened by how frail she seemed, her final moments beginning to come into focus. Kittie stumbled and then fell against her daughter and Larisa jolted her free arm up so quickly that her purse fell to the road, some of its contents spilling across the blacktop. Jack put his hand on the door lever, almost propelling himself out of the truck with his natural instinct to help, but then he held himself back. Others were there already with quick hands and kind words. Kittie and Larisa collected themselves and went on. Watching mother and daughter disappear behind a building, Jack thought of Ursula again, the men from the funeral home lifting her gently from the chaise. Andy, Jack now recalled, had been there too, and he realized suddenly and with amazement that the two must have meant something to each other. How had he not noticed that before? Most of the stories Andy told included Ursula in some way. *In the end,* Jack thought, *we are all reliant on those around us.* For love, for care. Friends and family became the keepers of collective memories, memories that allowed the ill and deceased to live on. What, he wondered, would his memories be? What memories would he imprint on others?

Sunday night, after dropping the boys back at Holly's, Jack picked up the knot board again and began to work on the knot for the final spot. He had a book with detailed illustrations that gave step-by-step instructions to completing each knot, and in the past when he'd paged through, he'd thought about choosing the Spanish Bowline, a knot that resulted in two loops, one that was often used in rescue work. He had always prided himself in first learning the intricacies of each knot, tying and untying them until he could do them without the guide. Only then would he complete the final knot and affix it to the board. He had planned the same for this remaining knot. But after he'd sat and worked it out, the two loops looked a little too much like nooses hanging from a center tangle—one each for him and Holly at the end of their marriage, he thought wryly to himself—and so he pulled it apart. He turned instead to the end of the book to the Endless Knot, also called the Eternity Knot, an elaborate weave that was not particularly nautical, but which symbolized the continuous cycle of birth, death, rebirth. This, he decided, would be the one.

He sat and learned the knot in the low light of evening, glancing intermittently out over the bay to watch the slow approach of a summer storm, the toss of the seawater against the rocks, the swaths of darkened ocean. In minutes came the shudder of rain against the windowpanes and the long, low call of the foghorn. He tied the knot, he untied the knot, he tied it again. He began to think about Larisa. Why had he held himself back from jumping out of the truck to help her? Why had he held himself back from calling her over the past several weeks, months? He wasn't angry with her anymore— had he ever really been angry at all?—and now that he was definitely single, wouldn't it be natural to reestablish the friendship, to at least see where it might lead? What was keeping him away? The fear of getting close to someone? The fear of the stigma of guys like him, guys who moved on to the next relationship when the prior one was only barely over?

He tied the knot, he untied the knot, practiced getting it right. Over the past six months he'd had a lot of time to think about Larisa, and it always left him feeling confused. He had felt so in sync with her until Holly's accident. But that was partially because Brent had shown up out of nowhere. Even then Jack could see that would never last, Larisa and Brent. Why, he wondered, were some relationships so hard and others so much more natural?

He tied the knot. He untied the knot. He thought about Larisa. His feelings for her, he realized, were caught up with his feelings for the house, which he also missed. Holly had been the reason he'd quit the caretaker job, but now that their marriage was over, might he be able to go back to that role, assuming Larisa had decided to keep Elmhurst? He'd been focused on a few contracting jobs to keep him going, but it would be easy to free up his schedule and, anyway, Elmhurst was a labor of love he would welcome. But then he'd surely be back in Larisa's orbit. And suppose he did embark on a romantic relationship with Larisa that started off full of passion and then died down to nothing. He would have been foolish to start it in the first place.

Jack put the knot board aside and headed to bed early. But when he rose the next morning, his mind was still consumed with thoughts of Larisa, even after he'd dressed and eaten breakfast. He toyed with the knot once more and then shoved the loose entanglement into the pocket of his jeans. Christ, why was it so damn hard to be in a relationship? Why, for that matter, had Ursula never married? Because, Jack thought, smiling to himself, remembering the quip from Larisa's bridal magazine. *Everyone is hard to live with.* Well, now that he was alone, he didn't have that problem anymore.

On impulse, he found himself suddenly moving out the door and up the street, toward the center of town. He came to the public beach and crossed through the parking lot. There was a man up near the seawall throwing a red Frisbee to a mangy dog. He'd seen that man before. They came to the beach almost every day, their relationship solidified by their routine. How would they both feel if they stopped coming to the beach as he had stopped going to Elmhurst? In the distance, he could hear the ice cream truck cruising the neighborhoods near the beach, the blare of "Maple Leaf Rag" out of its speaker. He had chased that truck as a child, or one like it. The familiar sound, he realized, gave him a feeling of belonging. But where did he belong now that his world had been upturned? Ursula was gone. There would be no more lessons, no more teatime chatter. But the sun would rise and fall, the tides would come and go as they always had. He would allow himself to be swept up in their current.

He turned from the beach and started toward Elmhurst. He wasn't sure where things would go, but there was one thing he knew for certain and he'd felt it watching her cross the street with her mother. His attraction to Larisa had not waned. Yes, he still felt her pull, strongly. Before long, he was making his way up the driveway, toward the house. He had no idea what he would do, what he would say. It didn't matter. He fingered the Endless Knot in his pocket, grasped and released it, grasped and released. He raised his hand and knocked.

CHAPTER FIFTEEN

The house had taken on a different presence. Larisa couldn't quite put her finger on it, but something felt subtly though irrevocably different, and not just because of the renovations. Elmhurst felt every bit as grand as when she'd arrived in the fall, but it had lost that impression of omniscience. No doubt it had seen its share of secrets through the years and it held a certain hidden knowledge within its walls. Over the past nine months some of those secrets had spilled out. Surely others remained, some never to be revealed. But Larisa no longer felt, as she had then, that the house was shielding something from her. She had taken down its walls, she had penetrated its outer mystique, she had reached its inner core. And, of course, in the fall she had still felt like a visitor, the house only a stopover along her way. Now it felt like home.

Larisa had risen early, before her parents. She and her

father had been planning a family portrait for several weeks, something they had done every year at the start of spring ever since Larisa was a little girl. They had an album full of such portraits, usually taken in various spots on the Elmhurst grounds, each shot chronicling Larisa's development and the small tweaks to their hairstyles and dress fads through the years. This year, the lead-up to the portrait had felt more somber to Larisa, given that they were now also capturing Kittie's deterioration on film, and this morning she already felt a tightening in her gut as she braced herself for the emotions that might surge. But now, as she rummaged through the front hall desk for a pen, she came across Aunt Ursula's date book, which she hadn't seen since late September. She sunk into the desk chair, turned the page to the beginning of June, and began to laugh.

Clark, on his way down the stairs, paused and raised his eyebrows, one hand palming the balustrade. "What's so funny?"

Larisa held the book up toward him and smirked. "June second. Today is my wedding day." She explained how back in the fall, before she'd given up her ruse—before it had really started even—she had arranged a pretend date in a flustered response to Teddy's questioning.

"Aha." Clark smiled and then cocked his head toward the front hall closet. "I noticed that dress is still boxed up in there. What are you planning to do with it?"

Larisa shrugged. She thought of that cold sunny day she had arrived in Kent Crossing at the end of September. "I'm never getting married," she had announced to that prissy mannequin in the window of the bridal shop, before she bought the dress. Her head had been in such a different place then, her thinking clouded with the confusion of her life choices, Aunt

Ursula's death, her mother's disease. She'd meant it—the not-getting-married part—but still, somehow, she'd impulsively bought the dress. Her world had felt so unraveled then, so unclear. The dress, the wedding, all of it, had just been a way to be someone else for a while, to avoid the realities she didn't want to face. Now that she was no longer avoiding the circumstances of her life, she didn't feel the need to pretend.

"Well, maybe I'll get married someday," she told her father now. It didn't matter one way or the other.

Clark contemplated for several moments. Then his face lit up with an impish grin. "Well, why not today, dear?"

Larisa frowned back at him. "How am I supposed to get married today, Dad? I still don't have a groom, remember? And anyway, I've kind of been enjoying my independence."

"That's fine; you can keep your independence."

Clark went on to explain how he had heard of other families staging special moments with their loved ones who were coping with dementia.

"Of course, there's no rush for you to get married," he told her, "but if it's too long from now, she might not be able to participate. This is a way for her to see you in your wedding dress before her dementia becomes too severe. We had the photo shoot planned anyway. We'll just kick it up a notch."

Larisa shook her head. "Isn't that kind of nuts? And pretty lacking in sincerity. I'm not sure I could fake a moment like that. It wouldn't feel fair to Mom."

Clark held up his hands. "I know, I know. It sounds crazy, but the people in my support group have said it's been really meaningful. The point is not to capture the real wedding moment but to capture the emotion behind such a real moment. That's wherein the sincerity lies."

Larisa thought about it. She riffled haphazardly through Aunt Ursula's date book, as though she might find some direction there. She noticed for the first time that Andy's name was penciled in on almost every Tuesday. A standing date between them, it seemed. Funny how something like that could be right under your nose and go unnoticed. Larisa stood and let her eyes travel up the stairwell toward her father. Her gaze landed as always on the family photos that adorned the wall. The small girl with the enormous hair bow. The three sisters on horses. Her parents on the front steps of the church on their wedding day. How would her mother have fared without her father to tend to her? The importance of their companionship had been amplified by Kittie's illness. The choosing of someone to be with, for better or for worse, was a momentous thing. Well, thank goodness, at least, that she had called it off with Brent.

Larisa heard some movement from the floor above, the sign of her mother waking. She turned to mount the stairs.

Clark put a hand on her arm. "I'll go."

Larisa shrugged him off. "No, no. Let me do it this time."

She found her mother seated on one of the twin beds of the guest room where Clark and Kittie stayed when they came to Elmhurst. Larisa had offered them the queen bed in Ursula's room, but Clark had waved her off, and Larisa had realized that they probably hadn't slept in the same bed in months. She had heard from her father that her mother sometimes woke in confusion in the middle of the night, frightened of "a stranger" in her bed. Now, as Larisa entered the room, Kittie was running her hands over the rumpled patchwork quilt and padding her feet softly against the floor. She didn't seem to notice Larisa. Instead she gazed out the window, smiling and watching the birds flutter in and out of the treetops. Though Larisa appreciated the moments in which her mother was calm, she struggled with how unreachable Kittie seemed, trapped in her own impenetrable world.

Larisa came to sit beside her on the bed. "How are you, Mom?"

Kittie turned toward her, a frown clouding her visage. Her eyes searched her daughter's face for a moment, orienting herself. "What?" she asked. "Where's Clark?"

Larisa felt her stomach clench. She braced herself for a challenging moment. "How are you, Mom?" she repeated.

Kittie shook her head, her frown still present, though a little less severe. She mostly just seemed annoyed that Larisa had disturbed her.

"I'm fine," she said, pushing her daughter away. "I'm fine." She turned back to watching the birds.

In that moment, Larisa remembered a recent visit to the doctor's office. She and her father had been discussing the middle stages of the disease with him.

"She will be fine," the doctor had assured them. "She won't know that anything is wrong, because she just won't remember." He had paused and patted Larisa gravely on the arm. "I'm truly sorry to say it, but it's *you* who won't be fine. You and your father, because you'll be witnessing her deterioration."

At the time, Larisa had been taken aback by the bluntness of his remarks, but in the ensuing weeks, she had witnessed how prescient he had been. Larisa left her mother to the birds and returned back down the stairs. She found her father in the kitchen, making coffee.

"The wedding photo," she said. "We could stage it in the conservatory, where she'd feel comfortable. Teddy could still be the photographer, like we planned for the original portrait."

Clark nodded. "The conservatory, yes. As long as there's not too much light in there."

Larisa glanced out the kitchen window. "It doesn't get too sunny in there until the afternoon. And anyway, the day's a bit overcast."

Clark took a look for himself. He stood beside her, grinning. "Good. And I'm sure we could find your mother a dress out of Ursula's old wardrobe. Something festive enough for the occasion."

Larisa smiled, remembering her great-aunt's penchant for dress-up. "And maybe a hat?"

And so that was how it had started. As always, Larisa and Clark did their best to keep Kittie's routine as normal as possible, feeding her breakfast and settling her in the living room with a pile of cloth napkins to fold. Teddy had agreed to be the photographer, planning to arrive at Elmhurst at noon, so they just had to prepare Kittie. They reminded her repeatedly about the family photo shoot, a concept to which she was already acquainted, and they explained that Larisa would be wearing a wedding dress. There wasn't much need to explain further, as she just nodded with an amicable smile and continued with her folding. Larisa dug into Ursula's closet and emerged with a peony-pink jacket and matching skirt for her mother. She brought them down to the living room, where Clark was sitting quietly next to Kittie. When he saw Larisa approach, he nodded and stood and held out his hands to his wife.

"I'm going to get you ready now," he told her.

"Why?" She peered around the room as though she might find her answer there.

"It's a special day, dear. Larisa is getting married. We've got to put on our pretty clothes."

"Larisa is getting married," she repeated, nodding, though her face was blank. She began to rub one hand nervously over the other but gave no visual cue that she actually understood what she had said.

Larisa watched her father gently ease her mother to her feet. Once she was standing, he put his arm around her and stayed by her side as she slowly shuffled toward the stairs. Their ascent would take some time, and so Larisa took the back stairs up to her room. Earlier in the day, she'd taken the dress from the front hall closet, removed it from its box, and hung it from one of the drapery rods. It hovered there now, illuminated by daylight, neatly framed by the large window.

She sat on her bed and surveyed the dress from a distance: the beautiful beadwork, the tiny gray pearls at the neckline, the final flare of the skirt at the hem. As the sun peeked momentarily out from behind the clouds, the silver beads glinted at her. *Are you really going to go through with this?* they seemed to ask. Larisa remembered smoothing the gown down over her hips that first time, how regal she had felt stepping around the bridal shop, ceremoniously trailed by Mrs. Muldoon. But today was not about how she would feel. The point was how her mother would feel. As Larisa turned away from the dress, she worried about this. She couldn't say her mother had worsened over the past few weeks, but she certainly hadn't gotten better. She often became agitated when Larisa or Clark tried to convince her to change her clothes. She still asked repeatedly about Aunt Ursula. She shouted at them as they tried to coax her to eat. But then they had experienced some tender moments as well.

Larisa sighed. It was already half past ten, so she really ought to start to get ready if she wanted any kind of hair and makeup, but she hesitated. She stood and squared off with the dress, remembering how magical she had felt in it at the bridal shop. Was there something taboo about wearing one's wedding dress for an occasion other than one's wedding? No, that was silly. She stepped closer and sniffed at the fabric. She pinched the pendulous beads between her fingers. The magic she had felt that day in the dress shop had only been a reflection of her longing for things to be in alignment. She had purchased the dress knowing she was only pretending. The dress was just a costume, and she'd be playing a part today, just as she did most days—every day?—now with her mother. Would she wear it one day for her actual wedding? She didn't know. And she realized now that it didn't matter. It was just a dress. She could cut it into pieces and it wouldn't mean anything other than a waste of money. But in conjuring the possibility of her own wedding, her mind did turn very fleetingly to Jack. His lips against hers that one time. His hands gripping hers. The kindness of his glance.

But Jack was not here.

She slipped the dress from the hanger, laid it on the bed, and stepped into the bathroom to get ready.

An hour later, hair swept into a French twist and face made up, she slipped into the dress and came down the stairs to check on her parents. She looked to the right. They weren't in the living room. She looked to the left. They weren't in the dining room. Peering in, Larisa thought of the hole she had made in the wall. The repeating pattern of the wallpaper was no longer there to greet her, no more silly pheasants looking backward over their shoulders. She heard a murmur of voices then and pivoted toward the sound, down the hallway that led to the conservatory. She came to the doorway and waited for them to notice her. Kittie sat primly on the wicker love seat in front of the plant stand, looking radiant in her cheery pink suit, and Clark stood in his suit by the Victrola, flipping through a stack of records. He settled on one, removed it from its case, and positioned it on the turntable. But before he dropped the needle on the record, his gaze shifted to Larisa and his eyes lit up.

"My goodness," he gasped. "Well, just look at you."

Larisa smiled and twirled slowly into the center of the room.

Kittie noticed her now too and came alive again. As Larisa neared her, Kittie held up her hands to Larisa. Larisa sat beside her and Kittie reached up and stroked Larisa's cheeks and looked intently into her eyes.

"Oh, isn't it wonderful?" she said. Larisa wasn't sure how much she understood about this day, about what they were doing, but she felt compelled to respond positively.

"Yes, it's so wonderful," she said.

"I picked you some peonies," her father said. He handed them to her now, a big clump of them. "Your bouquet, darling."

"Do I . . . hold your hand?" asked Kittie tentatively, shyly, by her side, and in that moment, that tender moment, Larisa felt that she couldn't possibly love her mother any more. These moments and the hope that they might come again, made the deception worthwhile, didn't they? She accepted the bouquet from her father and felt happy there with her parents, just incredibly happy that they had decided to have this time together. But as her father turned back to the record and the sun came out from behind the clouds and drenched the room in light, she suddenly felt overexposed. Her mother's cheek had a wet sheen to it, like the skin of a white onion, and her lips were trembling, her eyes were losing focus. Larisa felt as though her happiness—now and forever—somehow teetered on the brink of this one moment. *It's you who will not be fine,* the doctor had said. Summer would come and the Rosa rugosa would bloom and her mother would retreat further into confusion. And it would be unbearable. She would not be able to stand it. She and her father would each have to bear it alone.

"Excuse me," she said. "I've forgotten my lipstick."

She stood and tried not to flee too quickly from the room. She stopped in the hallway to gather herself, her breath coming in quick bursts. Teddy would be here soon, and he would help her hold it together. He would take their photo and she would survive the moment and the doctor was wrong, damn it, she *would* be fine. She looked up and glimpsed herself in the hallway mirror then. She smiled at her image, how beautiful she looked. Was if awful to recognize one's own beauty, however fleeting? And as she surveyed herself, her mirror image, it occurred to her that no one could ever actually see oneself. A mirror image was a reversed reflection of an actual thing. Even a photo could not capture the full dimensions of a person. It took another person to really see you. She felt immensely comforted by that thought.

A knock at the door shook her out of her reverie. Thank

goodness, Teddy had finally arrived. She swung open the door, excited to show off her dress to her friend, but it was Jack who stood at the door. Jack in his flannel shirt and work boots.

"I have a question for you," he said. But he didn't pose it. Instead a look of incredulity overcame his face. "What are you wearing?"

Larisa felt the color travel up her cheeks. "Oh God. It's not what it looks like. It's so stupid, really. Well, not stupid but—here." She grabbed his arm and pulled him in. "Let me explain."

And she told him. About her mother, the disease, the confusion. Her words came hot and fast and quick. And during that time, Teddy did actually arrive with Mrs. Muldoon in tow.

"My assistant," Teddy explained.

"Oh, honey, you look beautiful," cooed Mrs. Muldoon. "When Teddy told me about the shoot, there was no way he could keep me away."

Larisa waved her hellos, but she had so much to say to Jack, so much catching up to do, that she barely paused in her narrative and so Teddy and Mrs. Muldoon went on to the conservatory. Eventually, after she'd managed to get it all out, she paused and peeked up at Jack.

"You must think I'm absolutely crazy."

Jack had been listening quietly the whole time, one hand in the pocket of his jeans. He smiled now and clasped both of her hands in his and shook his head. "No," he said. "This is better than I expected."

Larisa smiled back. "Come and say hello to my parents."

In the conservatory, the record was already playing the

song that Clark had chosen for Kittie: "Unforgettable" by Nat King Cole. Teddy had set up his tripod and camera in front of the love seat, but Kittie had moved to the chaise, her thin legs stretched out in front of her.

"Are you the groom?" she asked as Larisa brought Jack over to say hello.

Jack responded with a warm and wry smile. "No, I don't think he's arrived yet."

"Well," cooed Kittie. "I'll tell you. She's a keeper, this one."

Clark grinned as he came to shake Jack's hand. "That sounds like something Aunt Ursula would say."

"Ursula," said Kittie, furrowing her brows. "Where *is* Ursula?"

"She couldn't make it," answered Larisa, coaxing her mother into a standing position. "The important thing is that you're here now."

Kittie began to hum to the music as she shuffled over to the couch, still supported in Clark's arms.

Larisa turned toward Jack. "What were you going to ask me? You said you had a question for me when you arrived at the door."

Jack smiled. "'Twenty-Five Keys to a Successful Marriage.' Number twenty-five: 'Everyone is hard to live with.'"

"OK." Larisa raised her eyebrows. "So what's the question?"

"What are the other twenty-four?"

Larisa started to laugh. "I don't remember. I don't think I ever actually knew them, really. Seems like number twenty-five is the only one that stuck."

She moved to take her seat on the couch between her

parents as Teddy positioned himself behind the camera, Jack on one side of him and Mrs. Muldoon on the other, watching, committing the moment to memory.

"Everybody ready?" called Teddy. "One, two . . ."

He stopped before he reached three, and came out from around the camera, squinting at something behind the love seat. He stepped closer.

"The night-blooming cereus," he said, pointing at the lower tier of the plant riser. "It has a bud that's beginning to open."

A gasp went up around the room as they all rose to huddle around the plant. Larisa thought about that night, years ago, with Jack and Ursula, the first time they had seen it bloom. *It only blooms once a year, at night, and only if you're lucky,* Aunt Ursula had said. They'd spent all day waiting for that damn plant to bloom, watching it unfurl. But oh, when it finally did, it was marvelous. A bloom as big as a pie plate and that delicious jasmine smell that filled the room. Larisa turned to Jack, who was crouching next to her, leaning in to the plant. She could see that he remembered too. In the morning the bloom would drop off and might not come again for many years. But they would have this night, at least, and it would be glorious. Clark had risen and pulled Kittie up again into a close embrace. They stood in the center of the floor and swayed to the words of their song. Teddy and Mrs. Muldoon returned to the bench to watch. But Jack stayed by her side, facing the plant. She felt the heat of his body next to hers.

Almost breathless, she turned to him. "Do you think it will bloom again?"

Jack took her hand and smiled. Shifting slightly in her crouch, Larisa felt the tug of the wedding dress against her body, she saw the fragile tilt of her mother's head against her father's chest.

"I don't know," said Jack. He winked. "I guess we'll just have to wait and see."

ACKNOWLEDGMENTS

My kindergarten report card read: *Jennifer doesn't want to talk to anyone; she just wants to sit in the corner and read.* Truth be told, I still mostly want to sit in the corner and read (though I do now also want to talk to people). I am so grateful to my late mother, Kathe Hill Dupee, for fostering my early love of reading, for recognizing my flair for creative writing, and for instilling in me the strong work ethic needed to actualize my lifelong dream of becoming a published writer. Thank you also to my father, William Dupee, for recognizing and encouraging my persistent nature and my love of books and puzzles, all of which I needed as I grappled my way through the multiple drafts of this novel. Thank you to my wonderful stepmother, Judith Forrest Dupee, for cheering wholeheartedly from the sidelines. And to my triplet siblings, Andrew Dupee and Lisa Staton, for being there (literally and figuratively) from the very beginning and for providing a lifetime of love, laughter, and memories. When we were younger, I always thought it was important to periodically remind you that I am the oldest (by maybe five minutes). But you, my "younger" siblings, have each taught me more than I can say.

I am also indebted to my brilliant agent, Jacques de Spoelberch, for believing in me and for championing this book and for finding a perfect home for it. To my fantastic editor, Leslie Gelbman, I am so honored and privileged to work with you and feel so lucky to be paired with someone with so much experience and so much knowledge about the industry. Your wisdom and insight have been invaluable and have made this book infinitely better. Thank you for taking this chance on me! To the talented and hardworking St. Martin's team (Sally Richardson, Jennifer Enderlin, Tiffany Shelton, Michael Storrings, Kaitlin Severini, Chrisinda Lynch, Brant Janeway, Jessica Zimmerman, Marissa Sangiacomo, and many more behind the scenes), thank you for taking such good care with my debut and for helping to shepherd it into the world. A special shout-out to Michael Storrings, art director extraordinaire, for the fantastic cover design!

The GrubStreet writing organization in Boston has long cultivated a thriving writing community, and I have been so privileged to be a part of it and to have found my fierce and loyal writing group, The Salt + Radish Writers, through its community. To the Salties—Anjali Mitter Duva, Crystal King, Henriette Lazaridis, and Kelly Robertson—thank you from the bottom of my heart for always encouraging me to keep going, for picking me up after disappointing news, and for providing such good company and such good food on a regular basis. And a special thanks to all my fellow authors who were so kind, generous, and supportive. I truly appreciate it.

Thank you to Melissa Hobbs at The Emerson Inn in Rockport, Massachusetts, for giving me a small roll of the pheasant wallpaper from the Grand Café. My budding novel really gained momentum when I spotted this wallpaper in the café one morning and found myself fixated on it. I still have a piece of it pinned up in my office!

Thank you to my dear friend Viktoria Shulevitch for reading early drafts and for your unwavering enthusiasm, quirky sense of humor, and adventurous spirit. You have inspired me from the moment we met.

I have been blessed to have some very remarkable and animated relatives, who filled my childhood with an incredible mixture of wit and whimsy, erudition, and creativity. Though they are no longer with us, I would be remiss if I did not recognize their great influence on me and on the world of this book: Constance Turner Dupee ("Dee Dee") and William Arthur Dupee II, Margaret and John Hill, Clara and Andy Lindsay, Jeannie Dupee, and Howard Turner and Robert Hertzberg. I miss you all!

To Josh, my husband and love; this book could not have been written without your ongoing love, support, and encouragement. Thank you for the priceless gift of time and space and for your enduring kindness and good nature. To Nina, Nico, Alan, and Tali, who have all heard me talk about this book for years, thank you for your wholehearted support and patience as I closeted myself up in my office and hammered my way through each draft. I love you all.